THUNDERCLAP

THUNDERCLAP

JACK SHERIDAN

CUTTING EDGE

ISBN-13: 978-1-957868-90-5

Published by
Cutting Edge Books
PO Box 8212
Calabasas, CA 91372
www.cuttingedgebooks.com

CHAPTER ONE

THE BUNKHOUSE was peculiarly still after the rest of them had cleared out. Britt Callum stood alone in the aisle between the bed rows and looked around curiously. He'd never been in the place alone, without the other guys there too, not in all the months since he'd checked in here. It made him feel damned funny, staying behind like this while all the others were out on the place doing their everyday work.

He moved slowly, going down the length of the wide room to the screen door. Outside the place was gray and flat in the predawn light. There was no sign of Jakers, the foreman, yet. He yawned and scratched the back of his skull, wondering how the hell much longer he'd have to hang around just waiting. Jakers was a pretty good joe, offering like he did to give him a lift down to the highway, but he wished the bastard would show up so they could get started. If he was going to pull out, he wanted to get going. Irritably he turned from the screen and wandered down the empty room to the bed where the battered old suitcase was.

It was only when he reached out to take hold of the handle to set the case on the floor that he was suddenly aware again of the tight soreness of the knuckles of his right hand. Frowning, he rubbed them hard with the left palm, trying to dull the throbbing. The sonofabitch must have had a jaw of iron! He stretched himself on the cot and turned his head slightly so he could see the guy's cot. He could see the hollow trough where they had dumped the bastard after the blow-up last night. Britt flexed his fingers carefully. Christ, it's a wonder he hadn't killed the guy.

Sudden self-recrimination came like blinding steam and he twisted his head sharply, turning his face the other way, closing his eyes. Why'd he have to act like a horse's ass every time, gettin' sore, takin' a swing every time some crumby jerk got out of line? Swiftly the other times like last night came flaming to him. The guy in Topeka that time. The night in the bar in San Diego. Memphis, New Orleans, that time on the South Side when he'd broken that bum's nose and had to beat it quick before the cops came. Oh, Jesus, he'd left a trail to be proud of!

He licked his lips carefully, holding his eyes shut tight, trying to rid himself of the deep cancer of self-dislike. Funny thing, most times he didn't really have nothin' really against most of them, either. The bastard last night, he didn't feel anything about him one way or the other, except he'd been like the rest. He'd been shootin' off his mouth loud, makin' them cracks, ridin' him. He'd warned the sonofabitch but he kept on anyway, gettin' the others laughin', makin' fun, gettin' personal-like. So he'd let him have it, the dumb fool. It was the other guys, sobered now, who had picked the louse off the floor and tossed him on his cot. They kept ribbing Britt most of the night after that, only now they were kidding on the square, he knew. One-Punch Callum, they kept calling him. He could have taken that O.K.—after all, it was true, he reckoned. It was that look in the guy's eyes when he had come to that made Britt decide the time had come to pull out of here, too. If he stayed on now after last night somebody was gonna get hurt bad, he felt it. The next time—well, he didn't want nothin' like that happenin'. It was a helluva lot smarter to clear out now, this morning, and try to keep out of more trouble. He worked his mouth in irritation. If he could learn to keep cool, to keep his lousy big fists from flyin' around, he'd be a damn sight better off!

The sound of the opening door at the far end of the bunkhouse brought his eyes open. Jakers came to the cot and stood looking down on the big heavy frame regretfully.

"Still reckon as how you'll beat it?"

Britt nodded silently.

Jakers moved his shoulders slightly. "Ain't no need to take off 'count of what happened last night. Ain't the first time somebody got clipped in a bunkhouse."

Britt swung his legs off the bed and stood up, hitching his Levis snug. He towered over the older man. "It's better this way," he said doggedly.

The foreman eyed him thoughtfully. "You're sure one helluva big bruiser," he grunted. "Gonna miss you round here. Can always use strong young bucks like you on a ranch this big."

"It's better this way."

There was a momentary silence between them.

"Mebbe so."

Jakers straightened and went back to the screen door. He hesitated, his hand on the crossbar, and scowled out into the yard. He turned and peered up into the face of the man behind him. "Best take it easy with that there punch of yours, kid," he grunted. "Ain't no way on God's earth a guy can get out of payin' for a killin', once it's been done."

Britt flushed and stared at the floor, shuffling his feet uncomfortably. Jakers blinked and pursed his lips; suddenly he shucked the intimacy of the moment. "Let's get rollin'," he growled. "Hell's fire, I shot a lot of good workin' time already on you and your goddamn troubles."

His luck held good. He caught a ride a few minutes after Jakers had gone whipping off. He got another ride on the outskirts of Tulsa and that one took him all the way through to Oklahoma City. He stood in the gusty chill of the prairie alongside the highway strip for a half hour or so and then he got another lift. That one took him right on into Amarillo. Once there, he had to make up his mind where he was headed. He could turn north, toward Denver, if he wanted, or he could stay right on 66 and head on west, maybe New Mexico or Arizona. California, even. Or, he could turn south and see what he could find down Texas way.

He was not sure just what it was he wanted, or where he wanted to go, or what he wanted to do. All he knew for sure was he was short on money, shy on food.

The guy with the seamed weather-beaten face hunched over his beer in the bar gave him the steer. He said he had just come up from Childress, that there was plenty of work down that way. He was surprised Britt was wondering if he could find anything. Why, hell, there was always a spot for a big guy on the ranches. There was a tinge of wistful admiration in his voice. His eyes catalogued the hard set of the thick rounded shoulders. Britt was eying the beer bottle thoughtfully. He was not too crazy for Texas. But the state was big, the country isolated, the kind of country he knew and wanted. He had no real preference. He killed the beer and shoved back off the stool. He stooped down and found the handle of the battered suitcase. "Much obliged," he said.

The trucker brought his rig to a slowing, hissing stop and motioned him up into the cab. As Britt stowed his case under his legs the driver noted he was darker than most folks around north Texas. But that meant nothing. The country men, the farmers, the oil men were all seared by sun and wind. A pale complexion would have been unusual. The trucker nursed the rig into slow movement. Only when the outfit had gained its cruising speed did he glance at Britt again.

"Where you headed for, boy?"

Britt frowned. "Down the road a piece, I guess. No special place."

The man eyed him covertly. "Just on the road, or you lookin' for work?"

"Lookin' for work."

The trucker's gaze shifted carefully. He took stock of the big hard thigh in the tight Levis. "Don't reckon as how no old boy built like you is gonna have much trouble findin' himself somethin' to do 'round these here parts."

"Sure hope you're right."

Conversation lapsed. The wind had come to a gale. It came screaming from behind them, on an angle, from the north. Every now and then a wayward gust exploded against the broad side of the vehicle and the trailer section swayed, straining. The sky had spoiled to muddy darkness and the swift-running wind curried the fields, skimming off the topsoil, whipping the sand into tawny racing fog banks.

Britt could feel the jerking tug of the trailer and peered apprehensively at the driver. The man's hands were large and heavy, and the thick fingers were hooked on the rungs of the steering wheel. His khaki shirt sleeves were turned back midway between elbows and wrists and the forearms were hairy and grown hard in the demands of the job. He became aware of Britt's eyes on him and he turned his head slightly but did not take his attention from the road.

"Bastard wind's tryin' almighty hard to heave us right off'n the road!" He laughed.

Britt looked away. The man sent his gaze over and marked the profile silhouetted against the paling daylight. His eyes shifted and he squinted at the ominous sky. "Blowin' up a real norther, looks like," he shouted. "Could be we get some rain outta all this."

Britt watched the fields, veiled by the thin, streaking smoke lines of the streaming dust. The man's voice came rasping over the roar of the engine.

"Sure as hell need rain round these here parts. No rain and the goddamn farmers ain't gonna have no farms left."

The rig thundered on. Most of the time they were alone on the highway, solitary in the midst of the empty flatness. Now and then there was a scattering of buildings in a crook of the road, a filling station, a store, a house or two, then there was nothing but the stark open country, divided only by the black line of the narrow, two-laned highway. Occasionally they moved out into the oncoming traffic lane, skirting past a creeping car or loaded farm truck, blasting at the sluggish offender with the splitting air horn; occasionally some sleek heavy machine would come streaking up from behind them and go racing on ahead, leaving them dawdling snail-paced in its wake. The country was large and lonely and lousy.

Britt sensed the driver was looking at him again. He turned and grinned for the first time.

"Was just thinkin' you ain't from round these here parts," the man ventured.

"No," Britt said. "I ain't,"

They rumbled on through Childress. The wind howled. Off to the east they could see a great massing bank of formless dust. In a matter of minutes the scourge would overtake them, blanketing the town, cutting visibility down to a few meager yards, powdering the buildings and streets, sifting into eyes and ears, gritting in teeth. There was no point in getting out here. Besides, what was the difference? One place was as good as another.

At Vernon the driver pulled into the weighing station and got out to make a few routine checks. Britt lit a cigarette and slumped against the leather seat, listening to the vague sounds of tapping from the rear of the vehicle. It was getting late. His knuckles still hurt. He rubbed them and tried to put the remembrance from him. He twisted and peered at the skies. The wind had increased its velocity; dust silted the sky, undefined and everywhere. The sun had a dirty look, hanging low above the unbroken line of the horizon in the west. There was a damp penetrating chill in the air. Britt shivered and pulled the zipper of his leather jacket high. Lousy Texas climate—one day hot as hell, the next day cold enough to freeze the brass monkey. He took an irritable drag on the cigarette and ground the butt under his heel on the metal floor.

The trucker climbed up behind the wheel and spoke over the grind of the starter. "Damn couplin's gone bad," he raged. "Bolt's sheared, I reckon. Don't know if I can make it to Fort Worth or not." He made sure the engine had caught, raced it a moment, then very cautiously eased the rig into movement. He glanced at Britt with a rueful grin. "Ain't gonna hurt nothin' to try!"

The coupling held, with the trucker governing his speed. They moved steadily, carefully. At Electra they drew over to the roadside and the driver went back to have another look at the joint. When he returned he said nothing, but there was a sharp crease between his brows. They resumed the trip but the speed was slower. They were not more than a few miles beyond Iowa Park when the connection gave up entirely. There was a single sharp jerk, a peculiar swerving sensation, a sickening shift to their weighted movement.

"Goddamn, that's it!" The driver worked swiftly; he brought their speed down to a mere crawl and took the rig over on the crunching gravel of the wide shoulder. He switched off the ignition and swung in his place with a broad grin. "Well, old boy, reckon this here's the end of the line."

Britt grimaced and began to untangle his long legs. "O.K. Sure do thank you for the lift." He hesitated. "What about that coupling? Want some help?"

"Naw, hell!" The driver eased back and stretched his legs, yawning. "Ain't nothin' to do. I'll get a call through to the big boss and he'll send out the crew. Happens all the time. I gotta set some flares out so no damn fool rams me and then I'll just set here and sweat it out until the crew comes." He shrugged.

As Britt made preparations to leave, the driver hunched forward, peering through the bug-spattered windshield. The sun had just about gone and the lights of the town ahead were beginning to sparkle, bright even through the gathering dust and night.

"That there's Wichita Falls down yonder." He waved his hand comprehensively. "Ain't a bad spot. Might run across somethin' to do round here. Lots of oil and cattle. Some farmin' on the side, too—mostly wheat."

Britt cleared his throat, parched dry with the silt. "Well, thanks again for the lift."

"Forget it, son. I ain't supposed to be pickin' up nobody, accordin' to the rules. But hell, it gets kinda lonesome pushin' this bastard all over the state by yourself. Kinda nice havin' somebody just settin' there in the corner." His words were oddly wistful; he colored faintly with the realization of his confession. "So O.K.—glad to help out," he blurted.

Britt shoved open the heavy metal door and dropped to the ground. The swift raping wind caught him solidly in the small of the back and he staggered, almost falling. The butts of his palms smote the truck side and the driver grinned.

"Best watch your step, big boy. This goddamn Wichita wind'll blow you clean to Big D before you know it."

Britt smiled. He pulled the suitcase from the floor and slammed the door. He waved briefly as he moved out toward the truck front. The driver searched his pockets for a smoke, not taking his eyes from the back of the big fellow already starting to hike down the side of the road, headed for the distant cluster of the sprawled town.

Britt plodded on. The wind came from behind him, which helped. The dust threaded from the fields, hugging the earth ankle-high, streaming across the pavement like thin wisps of tannish smoke. All around the countryside the lights came blinking; the lamps of the town gathered in the distance, while here on the outskirts the lights of the dwellings and roadside cafés and tourist courts were scattered. Off to the left Britt recognized oil-refinery lights. Beyond that, half concealed by a swelling rise of hill, he saw the airport and some kind of big army installation. He was too close to town to bother flagging down another ride, so he hoofed it.

As he neared the town he suddenly realized he had had nothing to eat since early that morning. He picked out one of the shabbier-looking places, figuring it might be cheaper. There was a thin-faced raw-boned girl, blonde, behind the counter, and when she came forward and spoke her voice was the sharp razor-edged north-Texas twang. Britt ordered a hamburger and a cup of coffee. He was her only customer.

He eyed her curiously as she fried the meat. Her shoulder blades were spare and the faint hump of her back brought them edging sharp under the creased, ill-fitting uniform. While he ate she retreated to the rear of the place and watched him. There was something about the cut of his strong white teeth when he bit into the soft sandwich. She realized with a start that he had glanced up now, was looking at her, smiling. Her expression gathered instantly and hardened and she drew her narrow shoulders tight. "You know some good place to stay round here—cheap?" he was asking.

There was sudden cold suspicion in her eyes. She was used to all kinds of approaches in this racket. All the time they kept making passes, hints, propositions. Those black eyes of his were soft and alive on her. She shook her head faintly and cleared her throat. "No, I don't."

Britt took another bite. He glanced down the length of her stringy figure. "Guess it won't be too hard findin' somethin'," he said through his chewing.

She felt that sinking in her. She had not missed that casual sliding look of his. She was used to that, too. She knew that curious look and the short dismissal that always followed—unless the guy was blind drunk or just not too particular. She came edging forward now, sure of her safety, and looked down on the gloss of his curly hair. "There's a place," she offered lamely. "Some of the guys bunk there. Down by the station. Ain't much—kind of a dump, I reckon, only they say it's clean, and it's cheap." He had smiled again and she could not stem the funny little hopeful rise that came in her. "It's called the Grand," she supplemented. "Only I reckon it ain't."

"Sounds O.K. by me. Just so's it's got a bed."

She was quiet as he got to his feet. He dug down in the pocket of his tight Levis and fished out some coins. His legs were straight and strong and her attention came guiltily to his tanned face. The money brought the warmth of his body to her palm. She made no move as he got his suitcase and went from her. In a moment he was gone. Only then did she permit herself a full, deep breath. She turned slowly and faced the cash register. Suddenly, almost savagely, she jabbed the key and flung the coins into their proper slots. She slammed the drawer shut and wheeled sharply, peering to the highway. This was one of them hard times, them times when you wondered if you ought to let nature take its course. Gees, you didn't run across somethin' like that every day in the week.

Britt lay spread-eagled on the lumpy bed. Outside the wind was fitful. Everything in the narrow, pinched little room was dust-coated. He sneezed with sudden violence and wiped his nose on his forearm. The damned dirt got into everything. He swung his legs off the bed and sat up, feeling the coolness of the naked floor against the soles of his bare feet. He scratched his belly and peered curiously around the room. It was penny-sized, a cell. The old dresser, nicked and scarred, was shoved hard against the wall, and over in the corner a chair with one leg shorter than the others suffered the weight of the jacket and his T shirt.

He crossed the room to the sole window and raised the ripped shade a trifle. The opening looked out into an unbroken expanse of grimy brick. With a grunt Britt yanked the shade down and turned away. He wandered back to the bed and flung himself across, bunching the pillow into a compact ball under his head. He stared up at the yellow ceiling, at the blotched brownish stains. Idly he brought his hand up over the slack muscles of his belly; his fingers rose and found the ridging nib of his breast point. There was a sudden swift restlessness in him as he thought back to that girl in the joint. She had been all bones; he could recall clearly the twin knobby prominences at the base of her throat. She had been as flat as a board, too. She had also been interested. Britt moved his palm slowly over the hairs on his chest. He closed his eyes and tried hard to think back to the last time he had been with a woman. A long time back. It wasn't good for a man to go to long. Thinking brought the old hunger to his loins. He opened his eyes abruptly. He swung from the bed hurriedly and, straightening his jeans, ran his fingers through matted curls. He crossed the room and leaned forward to inspect himself in the smeared mirror. There was a warping in the glass that distorted his reflection, making him look misshapen and swollen.

He went over and put on the T shirt. The neckline was soiled with the grime of the road, but it would have to do until he got somewhere where he could wash up. He ran his tongue around inside his mouth. There was a dirty, dry taste. He felt for the rest of his money. He'd paid for the night's lodging in advance and there wasn't much dough left. He ought not to spend any more until he'd found some work. But the dust was choking in his throat, and his thirst became more intense with the thinking. Sitting on the bed he quickly put on his shoes and socks. He took the jacket from the chair and in a moment he had switched off the single light and closed the door swiftly behind him.

The Red Club on Ohio street was just another beer joint. The customer came off the street into a narrow, cluttered room. There was the bar along the left, some tables on the right, and the rear of the place was jammed with the telephone booth, the pin-ball machine, the juke box, and several doors. One of these led to the pool room in back, and over it was a sign warning minors to keep out "by police orders."

The mirror running the length of the bar was plastered with liquor advertisements, with placards heralding civic events long since come and forgotten; one or two ancient calendars boasted the dreamy pictures of the sleek, long-limbed, impossible females of the age.

The bar itself was actually L-shaped, the stem running the length of the room from street door to back, the shorter portion from bar to wall in front of the twin toilet doors. There were no stools; the patrons stood, their feet raised to the brass footrail. Midway from front to back was set the wide-mouthed, narrow-throated, full-bodied, much-dented spittoon.

As Britt entered the place he glanced around. There were perhaps a dozen customers, all men except two. The women were nondescript types, somewhere in their late thirties, perhaps early forties. Both were laughing, talking with male companions. The men in the room ranged in sizes and types. Some were obviously farm men, their khaki clothing soiled, well worn, their boots muddied and scuffed. Two young soldiers from the nearby base were talking together, standing apart from the others, their blue uniforms neat and clean. Everyone was quiet, minding his own business.

Britt moved down the bar length until he came to an empty place. As he waited for service his attention was drawn to the mirror, to the sudden awareness in the eyes of one of the women at the end of the room. She went on talking to her escort but her eyes were speaking to him. For a long moment he returned her frank stare. Then he moistened his lips and turned his head. Her companion had looked up, had caught the interplay. There was no use getting fouled up in another jam. In a moment he had his beer. He raised his glass and drank deeply, feverishly.

CHAPTER TWO

THE whole place knew when the little guy came in. He was a runt, not much more than five feet or so. Everything the little guy had was cut in miniature, but what he had was solid. Under a crew cut of sandy hair his head was bullet-shaped, set squarely on a short, thick neck that fused into small, thick shoulders. His body was wiry, the chest muscles corded and hard, ridging on the T shirt. He wore Levis, faded down to light blue, banded tight on his hips, skin-tight over short, hard thighs. The figure of a naked dancing girl was lividly tattooed on the smooth hairless tan of his forearm. He strutted and there was open cockiness and arrogance in every movement of his body.

Britt Callum took another sip of beer and held it in his mouth for a moment. He did not take his eyes from the newcomer. The little squirt had marched up to the couple now and was talking loudly with the woman, ignoring her escort. As he talked his arm went around her waist and his stubby fingers reached for her breast. She grinned down at him. Her companion apparently missed the act. The little guy left them now and came down along the bar, nodding, pausing every so often to slap someone on the back, swaggering all the way.

He came to a half space next to Britt and forced himself in. Britt, shoved aside hard, flushed. The little guy paid no attention to him. He had begun to pound on the bar with his fist, yelling for service.

Britt edged away from the touch of him and watched the performance in the mirror ahead with narrowing eyes. He knew this type. He wondered suddenly why all the little punks in the world always tried to make up for the fact that they'd been born runts by yelling and swaggering, by acting like prize sonsofbitches, pushing the bigger people around every chance they got.

The little guy got what he wanted. He downed the beer immediately and started banging on the counter again. There was more beer. The bartender said nothing as he served him. No one seemed to pay much attention to the little guy. When he had had his third beer he suddenly went off, leaving the glass to mark his place. He went back and disappeared into the toilet.

Suddenly the man on Britt's right spoke up. "There's one snotty little bastard, that Rigger Kates," he said.

Britt looked into the quiet eyes of an older man. "Yeah. I can see what you mean."

The man glanced at the toilet door contemptuously. "He's a mean one, too, when he gets a load on." He looked up at Britt. His lips were touched with scorn. "Likes to scrap all the time, that one. He was featherweight champ or some goddamn thing like that in school once. Reckon Rigger Kates never got over bein' it."

"He looks like he could be a fighter. He's got the build."

"The build! Oh, Jesus!" The man's brows arched. "That little body is his one pride and joy. God knows there ain't a helluva lot of it, but you can be mighty sure he takes right good care of every inch, believe you me. That Rigger's mighty damn careful of them muscles of his."

"Rigger ... " Britt frowned. "That some oil name?"

"Hell, no. Cripes, that there Rigger wouldn't know the top side of a drill from the ass end." The man paused and squinted in thought. "Don't know how he come by that name, come to think. Just always been Rigger, as far as I recall. Naw, Rigger Kates ain't no oil man. Hell, he ain't nothin' but a poor grubbin' dirt farmer, same as me. He's got a place maybe ten, fifteen miles out. Naw, hell, that there Kates boy just gets by, same's the rest of us."

The toilet door opened and Rigger came out. He brushed his lips along the tattooed forearm. He came up to the bar, his fingers working briefly on the tightly bunched fly of his snug Levis. As he pushed into the open place next to Britt he hitched his pants and reached for his glass. Three were several more beers in rapid succession. It was only now that Britt noticed the pint bottle of whisky in the rear pocket of the trousers.

Rigger caught the glance at his behind. He stared up into Britt's face with sudden swift belligerence but slowly the animosity began to fade back and he grinned. "Ain't nothin' like a couple of shots with beer to chase 'em." He tapped the flask significantly.

Britt nodded. "Yeah, sure."

Rigger Kates eyed him shrewdly. Britt stood stiffly as the little hard eyes went from his face carefully over his body, missing nothing. When Rigger Kates finally looked at Britt's face again there was a shiny gleam of envy in him. "Jesus H. Christ! You're sure one big bastard!" he breathed.

Britt relaxed a trifle and flushed. "Just grew up, I guess," he faltered uncomfortably.

Rigger darkened instantly and his lips thinned. "Size ain't always everything," he snapped.

Britt reached over cautiously for his glass. "I didn't mean it that way," he said quietly.

Rigger's look was suspicious and the grin came back very slowly. "Aw, what the hell," he crowed. He saw Britt's glass was empty. "How's about havin' a beer on me?" Without waiting for the answer he began to thump the bar again. "Hey, you, Charlie!" he bawled. "Get your big, fat rump in the saddle! Couple of beers down here, on the double!"

The bartender came up quickly. Scowling, he put his hand over Rigger's fist and stilled the racket. "Lookee, Rigger boy. How's about takin' it kinda easy, huh? You'll get your beer right off. Just cool down, see? And let's watch the talk." His eyes slipped to the woman at the other end of the bar. She was watching them and the smirk was broad on her face. It was only now that Britt realized the other woman had left the place. "Remember, boy, we got a dame in the place," the bartender was saying.

Rigger's face was surly and dark. "Go take a jump!" He jerked his hand free and peered down the bar at her. "I gotta watch my talk cause there's some dame around," he chanted. "Who the hell you mean—Ruby there?" He threw back his head and laughed coarsely. "Hey, Charlie," he yelled after the retreating bartender. "That goddamn Ruby could teach you a couple of new things!"

The smirk had tightened on her face and, shooting a quick glance at her companion, she moved as if she were going to step away from the bar. Britt saw the man catch her arm and hold her in place. Rigger turned his back on them and looked up at Britt expectantly, his hand back on the bulging hip pocket. "How's about a shot?"

Britt almost said no. But he knew what that would start with this guy, so he said yes.

Rigger led the way into the toilet. It was a little two-by-four hole lit by a dim light. The bowl was filthy and obscenities were scribbled and drawn on every inch of the broken, yellowed wall. Rigger sat down on the commode and unscrewed the cap of the bottle. "Here." He held up the flask. "Take a good shot."

Britt did. The raw liquor went down, burning, searing, harsh. He handed the bottle back to Rigger and rubbed his belly. The friendly glow began to spread, to fire his insides. He wiped his mouth on the back of his hand. Rigger drank, paused, and drank again. When he finished there was only a short nip left. He started to pass the bottle up to Britt, hesitated, and suddenly upended the flask, draining the last of the stuff. He got to his feet with an effort and flipped the bottle over into the corner of the place. It smashed. Rigger giggled.

They went back into the barroom together. The woman at the other end of the room glanced up and saw them. Her laugh came high and thin over the steady hum of conversation. "Oh, my God!" she shrilled. "What you two boys been doin' together in the can all this time?" The men along the bar stopped their talk and smirked at each other, careful to keep their faces away from Rigger's burning eyes.

He stood in front of Britt, his little legs braced, his hands on his hips, and scowled at her. "You shut your goddamn mouth, Ruby!" he bellowed. "One of these here days somebody's gonna knock them teeth of yours down your throat!"

"Well, well," she flounced her long hair over her shoulders. "Lookee who's talkin'! Listen to half-pint tryin' to make noises like a big man!"

His face was purple. "I'm warnin' ya, Ruby."

She sneered contemptuously and made some further derisive remark to her escort and they both laughed. She peered at Rigger. "Hey, little boy! Tell me, is you half-pint all over?" Her laugh was brittle in the room.

Rigger stood rooted in the center of the floor. His color was thick and the little eyes were chill and cruel, but he let the gibe pass. In a moment he moved into his place. He glanced at Britt, who had said nothing, was concentrating hard on the half-filled beer glass. "That crumby bitch's askin' for her lumps," Rigger snorted.

Britt grunted. Rigger found his beer. He peered down again at her. All the time she was busy talking and laughing with the other guy, paying no more attention to him, Rigger kept staring at her. At long last her eyes slid from the face of the man at her side and she looked full at Rigger. For a moment their eyes locked and then she began to laugh harshly. She held up her right hand and curled all the fingers back except the little one and this she wriggled at him slowly, unmistakably. Rigger's breath caught and when Britt glanced down he saw the hard pound of the blood in the puffed vein in the little guy's neck. Rigger Kates shoved himself from the bar and his small rounded buttocks jutted as he stalked down the length of the hushing room. Britt held his glass tightly and waited.

When Rigger got to where the man and the woman stood he reached out quickly and grabbed her by the fleshy part of the arm and pulled her around sharply, so that she faced him, her eyes going full and wide with fear. With almost studied deliberation Rigger brought his right arm up and slapped her hard across the mouth. The crack sang through the room. An uneven whimpering moan came from her hurt lips. Rigger turned away and started back to his place.

Before he had taken more than two or three steps the man was after him. He caught at Rigger's shoulder, jerking him around, and his fist caught Rigger flush on the mouth. The little guy staggered and his legs buckled, almost dropping him. His training paid off and he recovered swiftly. The men at the bar shifted quickly, scattering out of the way. The guy and Rigger had the floor to themselves. Rigger tried to grin through bruised lips. He moved carefully, feinted for the opening. When he struck he hit hard, with sure skill. There was a brief exchange of blows in a silence broken only by the sound of flesh against flesh. The bartender was riveted behind his barrier, his eyes angry and excited. The woman was in the far corner, close to the street door, and stood holding the back of her hand against her hurt mouth, her eyes stretched wide in fascinated horror. The man rocked Rigger with a smashing left to the side of the head. Suddenly Rigger's size and his favored art won out. He moved quickly and his fist found the pit of the man's belly. There was the whoosh of impact and the big man doubled, grabbing at his middle. Rigger's fist struck again, arcing, and there was a single sharp crack as knuckles found the man's jaw. He slipped to the floor with a faint sigh. He twitched once, rolled over, and lay quite still, blood trickling from the corner of his mouth.

Rigger straightened jerkily. He held himself erect, swaying, and his eyes left the mounded figure at his feet and found the woman cowering in the dark corner. He wiped the sweat from his face. "O.K., Ruby," he said gruffly. "Get the lousy bastard out of here. See if you can put him back together."

Rigger came back to Britt's side. He glanced up triumphantly. He made no comment, just grinned. Britt kept still. The fight had brought everything back so clearly, almost as if he himself had been mixed up in it. His T shirt was splotched with sweat marks.

Rigger reached out to pick up his beer. But something had happened. He scowled and tried to close his fingers on the glass but they refused to respond. His hand had already begun to swell and sharp pain shot along his forearm. Rigger's eyes widened instantly. He looked wildly at Britt and his voice came choked and pitched with sharp terror. "I can't move my damn fingers, big boy! I done somethin' to my hand!"

Britt reached over and took hold of the wrist. The puffiness was coming fast. He had seen this happen once before. The little guy sure as hell had busted his hand. He glanced down at Rigger's ashen face. He was hanging on grimly, waiting like a frightened kid for some verdict. "Looks like you done gone and busted your mitt on that guy's kisser, pal," he said quietly.

Rigger's lips began to tremble. The little guy looked ready to pass out. He managed to hold on. The truth sank in slowly and he wet his lips. "But I can't!" he wailed suddenly. "I gotta have my hands—I gotta use 'em all the time!"

Britt shook his head slowly. "You ain't gonna be usin' this one for a while, bud. You gotta go somewhere and get it fixed up right off, else you ain't gonna be usin' it ever."

Rigger grabbed at the bar edge and clung tightly with his good left hand. He shut his eyes and swayed slightly, his face gone sickly pale. When he looked at Britt his eyes were bright with tortured fright. "I ain't feelin' so good," he whispered hoarsely.

Britt managed to get him into the toilet, where Rigger heaved until there was nothing more to bring up. When they came out finally the man on the floor had been taken away and Ruby was gone. Britt and Rigger pushed out to the sidewalk. The excitement, the mixing of beer and whisky, the shock and the sickness all added up. Rigger was hopelessly stewed. Britt cursed, holding the little guy up as best he could, trying to think of what to do next. He could see the soft lights of the police station down the block. He hesitated. It was a strange town to him. There was no other place to go.

He half dragged Rigger into the place. The cops took one look at the busted hand and one at Rigger Kates. They knew him. They paid little attention to Britt. Before long he was waiting at the clinic for Rigger to come from the emergency room. When he did come he was still tight as a tick but the hand had been fixed up. Britt took him in tow again. What now? There was no choice; he had to drag him to the room at the Grand for the rest of the night. It was late. They'd both wind up in the cooler if the cops found them staggering all over the streets.

He had to pay fifty cents extra for Rigger. There was some money in Rigger's pockets and he paid the night clerk out of that. Once inside the room he let go of Rigger. The little guy folded up on the bed. Britt stripped him down and shoved him across the bed, over next to the wall. Rigger's breath was thick with stale alcohol. Minutes later Britt turned off the lights and crawled under the sheet. The wind outside sucked and blew at the tattered drawn shade. Rigger moaned something unintelligible and belched. Before Britt could bring himself to turn the little guy over so he would breathe the other way, he fell into exhausted sleep.

When Britt opened his eyes the next morning they came to focus on the naked body of Rigger Kates. The little guy was standing in front of the mirror, probing his body with care. Britt lay still, watching him.

The little guy was wholly absorbed, leaning forward, tracing the tips of his fingers along his bruised lips. He straightened. The body was as strong and hard naked as it had been clothed. He suddenly became aware of the watchful eyes of the man on the bed and turned and looked down at Britt with a rueful grin.

"Reckon I kinda screwed things up last night."

Britt stirred. He stretched lazily under the thin sheet, then brought himself up on his elbow. "Yeah, kinda."

Rigger turned and scowled at the mirror. "It was all that lousy bitch's fault—that goddamn Ruby." He ground his teeth. "One of these here days I'm gonna ... "

His words trailed off as Britt came from the bed and, standing behind Rigger, drew himself straight. The little guy turned and fed his eyes on the bigness of the body. Britt smiled down on him. "You feelin' kinda rough this mornin'?"

"Feel like I been headfirst through a thrasher!"

Britt went over to the chair and separated their clothing. He tossed Rigger's things to the bed. "Can you get 'em on O.K.?"

"Yeah, sure. Only maybe the shoes."

Britt dressed and came over to help Rigger with the shoes and socks.

Rigger smirked self-consciously, sitting on the edge of the bed. "Like a goddamn baby!"

"I had to take some of your dough to pay for the room—your share. I'm busted."

"Sure." Rigger tubbed the tight skin of his forehead. "Christ! I don't remember nothin' after sappin' that louse." He came from the bed. Almost immediately he dropped back and stretched out with a groan, pulling the pillow under his head. "Let's wait a minute," he begged. "Jesus, I feel like I was gonna die."

"You won't." Britt grinned.

There was a long silence. Rigger hunched himself a little on the pillow mound so that his head was raised. He got a better look at Britt, leaning idly against the dresser. "Say," Rigger said. "How come you done all this for me? Hell, you don't know me from Adam."

Britt shrugged. "Somebody sure as hell had to do somethin'. Boy, you was out on your feet."

They were silent. Rigger shifted slightly; his hand had begun to throb. "Where you headed for now?" he asked finally.

Britt frowned. "Get me some coffee first. Then I gotta start tryin' to line up some work—if I'm gonna keep on eatin' regular."

Rigger grunted and sat up experimentally. "Reckon some coffee'd help."

They left the room and went down the street to a grubby hole-in-the-wall café and had a couple of doughnuts and some coffee.

"Say, big boy, I been doin' some thinkin'." Rigger looked suddenly a little brighter. "Why the hell don't you come on home with me?"

"Home with you?"

"Yeah. Can't pay much, but sure as hell I'm gonna have to get somebody to do chores. I ain't gonna be able to do much with this busted flipper. There's a room in the barn and you'll eat. My wife cooks O.K."

Britt eyed him in surprise. Somehow he had not thought of Rigger Kates as being married. "You got a wife?"

"Yeah, sure." Rigger seemed equally surprised that Britt should ask. He shrugged. "Been hog-tied over four years. Name's Marcy."

"Kids?"

"Cripes, no!"

Britt wondered. Rigger's offer sounded O.K. All his cash was gone and he had to eat and sleep somewhere. There was Rigger, of course. He seemed like an O.K. joe, no better, no worse than the rest. He had a helluva temper, but Britt figured he could watch it, not let anything get under his skin. Christ, he could go on dodging everybody in the world if he didn't trust himself. At any rate, he could take care of himself, in case. It was worth a try. If it didn't work—well, he'd get the hell out like before, that's all.

"Well…" Britt looked at Rigger speculatively. "I gotta go someplace—might as well go with you."

"That's the old pepper!" Rigger struggled to his feet. "We're gonna get along like a house afire, you and me," he bubbled. "Say, big boy," he said as they started down the street, "you ever try any this here weight-liftin'? Say it's goddamn good for the muscles."

Rigger couldn't drive, not with that smashed hand of his. Britt took over. The machine was a late model Ford pickup, fiery red and fast. They went east from town, crossing the railroad tracks, going out past the ball park and the Negro section. In a matter of minutes they were in the flat greenless country. They rode along silently. Britt had no idea how far they had come from town or in what direction when Rigger suddenly touched his arm and waved his splinted bandage feebly. "There she is."

Britt eased his foot on the accelerator and looked off to the right. From what he could see—and he could see most of the place at one glance—it wasn't much. The land was tilled, flat sparse acres. There were a few nondescript battered buildings, their paint long since scoured away by the emery dusts of the region.

"We got mostly wheat," Rigger offered.

The house was tilted a little, settled in age, set upon the crest of a rise. Between the rear of the house and the bulking silhouette of the big barn the banners of a small wash flapped spasmodically.

The road up to the house was a mere tracing of hard-packed worn wheel tracks, rutted and severe. Britt guided the machine carefully toward a cleared area in front of the house. At the beginning of the planked steps to the screened porch he cut the engine and the two men sat quietly. Britt could see a man working in the far field. He rode a small tractor, plowing painstakingly, and around him the spuming dust curtained.

"That there's Newt, my bud," Rigger said shortly. When Britt glanced down at him he saw that Rigger's eyes on the far-off figure were strangely cold and antagonistic. Suddenly the little guy grinned. "Well, this here's home. Let's go!"

He swung his body, fumbling to open the door with the good hand, and dropped to the ground. Britt came around the nose of the truck to the little guy's side. He shaded his eyes and peered around. The land was open, flat, and unprotected. The only vegetation nearby was a few puny iris plants, their full plumage almost garish at the side of the house, and a single mesquite tree, feathery green with springtime newness, rearing between the house and the paved road to town.

Rigger had already gone ahead, mounting the few steps to the porch door. In a moment he had disappeared inside the house.

Britt waited at the foot of the steps. He heard the sounds of the woman's voice filtering out into the rising heat. "I know you're back. I heard you comin'." The statement was flat, toneless, stripped of concern or interest. Rigger's words came only as an indistinguishable murmur. Coherency was lost and only the dim hum of the conversation somewhere at the back of the house came through. Britt moved ahead to the edge of the frame building, where he could get another look at the man in the field. He was working methodically, guiding his machine back and forth. The Diesel smoke tailed, an uneven shoestring, across the acreage. The sound of footsteps on the porch snagged Britt's attention. Rigger remained behind the screens, grinning down. His wife stood framed in the inner doorway, just behind the little guy, and she was not smiling. Britt came to the foot of the steps and blinked up at them. Rigger made an offhand gesture, jerking his thumb over his left shoulder.

"This here's Marcy, I was tellin' you about."

"Howdy, ma'am."

She pushed forward suddenly, forcing her way to Rigger's side, and stood looking down through the close mesh of the screen at him, and it was plain she was angry about something. The fires stood high in her eyes and her head was held uncompromisingly rigid. She was staring down the length of her small nose at him. He swallowed and shot a quick look at Rigger, wondering just what the hell had been said inside. He wondered if she had got the damn-fool notion it was his fault what happened last night, that it was on account of him that Rigger got his hand all smashed up. Britt straightened and traded her look for look. He saw the flames diminish a little.

"You might as well come inside out of that hot sun," she said coolly.

He brushed past her, suddenly aware of the clean woman scent of her, past Rigger, and moved off to one side where he could get a good look at the two of them together. He dismissed Rigger and gave his full attention to the wife, to Marcy Kates.

Seeing her free of the obscuring shadow of the screens, he was startled. She was nothin' but a kid! Hell, she could pass easy for some damn high-school girl. She stood at Rigger's side, a little taller than he. Her hair was brownish with a faint threaded streak of gold and she wore it loose and fluffy. Her brows were arched gently and the eyes were large and clear and very blue. Her face was without fullness and the lips were right and parted slightly. She knew he was giving her the onceover. She held her ground, letting him. There was a tiny little defensive lift to her chin. The tiny movement pressed her shoulders back and tilted her small, round, firm breasts. Her waist had been made for the grip of a pair of hungry hands. There was a sleek flare to her hips, tapering down into good thighs. Her legs were right, and now, when she spoke, breaking into his absorbed perusal, her voice was cool and faintly husky.

"Rigger's been sayin' as how you done him—how you done us—a right good turn last night."

"It wasn't nothin'."

"I reckon as how we're much obliged."

His lips parted in a light smile. "It wasn't nothin'."

Rigger was ignoring them. He was busy with his injured hand. Britt and Marcy eyed each other steadily and a tightness came into his throat. She had not missed a trick on him, either.

Suddenly she raised her hand and fluffed the ends of her hair. Her fingers were long and careful. She turned her face a little, averting her eyes, and he saw the slow color creep high in her cheeks.

"Rigger's been sayin' as how you was gonna stick around a while," she murmured.

"Yeah, if it's O.K. with you."

She glanced at him in quick surprise. "This here's Rigger's place," she said simply.

"Then I guess I'm stayin'."

She crossed in front of Rigger and at the door she turned and glanced at him soberly. "It's—it's gonna be right nice, havin' you 'round, helpin' out," she said formally.

Rigger looked up and grinned. "Sure as hell is."

Like Rigger Kates had said, Marcy cooked O.K. The three of them, Rigger and Marcy and Britt, were well into the noonday meal when the man from the distant field came into the kitchen. He hesitated momentarily as he saw the stranger at the table. Without a word he crossed over and took the remaining chair. He sat between Marcy and Rigger, across the table from Britt.

"Okra again," he muttered as she set his plate before him. "Like eatin' goddamn greasy rubber tires."

"It don't hurt you none to eat some once in a while. Me and Rigger likes it," she snapped.

They were all silent for long minutes, the heat of the little outburst cooling slowly. Then Marcy cleared her throat and her tone came cool and normal. "Newt?" She waited until he had looked up from his food. "This here's Britt Callum." She smiled at Britt. "This here's Newt Kates, Rigger's brother."

Newt's eyes left her face and brushed over Britt. He grunted and nodded slightly.

"Glad to know you," Britt said.

Newt Kates had gone back to his meal. Britt stole a glance at Rigger. The little guy had paid no attention to his brother's entrance; his whole concentration was on the laborious task of eating with his unwieldy left hand. Marcy was sitting stiffly erect, hands in her lap, her eyes on the crest of her brother-in-law's bent head. Britt found his fork and started to eat once more.

Throughout the meal Britt snatched little appraising looks at the man across the table from him. Newt Kates was older than Rigger, perhaps as much as ten, fifteen years. He was a bigger man and his face was lined, leather-like, the nose sharp, inclined to a hook. His hair was sandy, like Rigger's, but thinning. Once he sensed Britt's curiosity and raised his head. His eyes were the kind one saw so often in Texas men, small, hard, gimlet eyes, guarded against any expression of friendship, sometimes cold with animosity. His mouth was his predominant feature. The lips were very thin, pinched tight at the corners, their color long since bleached out by distaste and dissatisfaction. When he looked at Britt his manner was cold, impersonal.

They finished the meal in silence. It was only after the last morsel had been mopped from the plates and cigarettes had been lit that the older man stirred and showed some hint of curiosity.

"You don't belong round these here parts," he commented flatly.

Britt raised his brows. "That's right," he admitted quietly.

"Where you from?"

"No special place. Just been knockin' around."

"Where?"

Britt flashed a quick look at Marcy. She was sitting forward, her elbows on the edge of the table, the smoke from her cigarette curling up, fogging lazily in her hair. Her eyes were closed and her face was empty, as if she were paying no attention, but he knew she was listening closely.

"Started out from New Mexico a long time back. Been all over since. Just headed in from the east."

Rigger coughed. He made no attempt to share the talk. He lolled in his chair, his free hand shoved down, the palm flat against his belly inside the band of the jeans, the cigarette limp in the corner of his slack mouth, and watched Britt sleepily.

"Didn't reckon as how you was Texan," Newt grunted. The statement came from him both an accusation and an abrupt dismissal.

Britt flushed. There was plenty about this Newt Kates he was beginning to dislike. There was some kind of meanness, a kind of chip-on-the-shoulder attitude in the man. It had come into the room with him, had shared a place at the table, had perched alert in their midst.

"You couldn't be no Texan," Newt amplified suddenly. "Skin's too damned dark."

Rigger's eyes widened. He came forward and peered at Britt curiously as if he had never noticed this before. "He's sure as hell right, big boy," he grunted. "you could almost pass for a Mexican."

Britt looked Newt squarely in the eye, then glanced at Rigger. Finally his eyes came to Marcy, sitting back a little now, her intent eyes half closed on him. He answered Newt. "My old lady was Italian," he said abruptly. "They all got dark skins."

"Eyetalian, eh?" Newt took the information and nursed it. "Ain't many foreigners round these here parts. Most folks round here is Texan."

Britt closed his eyes and mouth in annoyance. In a moment he glanced through the screen door beyond Newt's head. He knew this type. There had been plenty of them in the Army. Thought the goddamn state was the only place in the world, that no place else existed. If you were from Texas, O.K. If you weren't, to hell with you. He could see the hard-packed, bald ground outside, dead. Texas! Britt could almost taste his irritation. They could give the whole damn place back to Mexico, for all he cared.

Rigger got to his feet. Marcy had fixed him a makeshift sling out of remnants; he now carried the wounded member gently, protectively, as if the thing were a child. "Come on, big boy, I'll show you round the place." He paused behind his brother, staring down on the sunburned scalp. "You fixin' to get that field done soon?"

Newt Kates looked at Marcy and Britt saw the little derisive flicker come in his eyes. "Reckon so."

"You best be gettin' off your can, then."

Newt stabbed at the cracks of his teeth with a fragment of matchstick. He scowled but said nothing.

"Hear?"

Newt threw the bit of wood on the tabletop and swung in his chair, staring up at his brother with bright sudden anger. "I'm a-fixin' to, I said." He cooled quickly and shifted back to his original position and his eyes found Marcy once more. "I'm gonna set a spell yet," he declared stubbornly.

Rigger tightened his lips and shrugged. He crossed to the back screen door.

Marcy turned her head slightly, watching Britt as he crossed the room, and she smiled faintly. "It's gonna be right nice havin' you around, Britt Callum," she said lightly. "I got a feelin' things is gonna work out just fine."

He nodded, warmed by her quick, direct friendliness. Rigger, his good hand holding the screen door wide, waited patiently. As Britt started out after the little guy, he glanced back. Newt Kates was ignoring them. He had slumped back in his chair and was picking his teeth again with the match. His little pig eyes were even smaller, more intent. He was watching his sister-in-law.

CHAPTER THREE

L IFE on the Kates place slipped into the new pattern quickly and easily. Since Rigger's hand prevented him from doing much around the place, he showed Britt the setup, assigned him the chores he himself normally handled. He was pleased, relieved with the rapid, sure way Britt took over. He told Britt not to bother with Newt's work. Newt was a kind of law unto himself, Britt discovered quickly. The work he did was his alone; he never asked for assistance and never received any. Marcy fed the men, did the wash, broomed out the house occasionally; what else she could find to do with her time during the remnants of the day while the men worked outside was her problem.

The two bedrooms of the house were occupied, Marcy and Rigger in one and Newt in the other. Britt's quarters were in what had once passed for the toolroom in the big barn across the yard from the house. Marcy managed to create a comfortable if sparsely furnished little room. She had found a patched chair somewhere and there was a narrow, springless cot and a table that slanted precariously. Over the table she fixed a bit of broken mirror to the wall, using bent nails for brackets. One unshaded electric bulb hung naked, suspended from the ceiling on a single cord. The place was adequate; After all, Britt only slept here.

Once Britt Callum had taken firm grip on the routine, Rigger relaxed into lazy recuperation. He spent most of his time cushioned in the wicker rocker on the warped front porch, his booted feet crossed on the railing up before him, his head lolling against the chair back, his eyes closed. Rigger did not read or do anything with his time. He just sat there hour after hour and dozed in the ripening spring warmth.

Rigger raised his lids with an effort. A scowl of annoyance darkened his face and he hunched his body up in the chair to peer over the points of his toes to try to see what the hell was happening out front. His mouth pulled at the corners and he let himself slump down into the oversized wicker retreat. Nothing was happening despite the racket. Just Cora Winters trying to keep that damned old wreck of a Plymouth of hers on the tracks up to the house. He wondered what the hell she was comin' around for anyway, upsettin' everybody. Didn't she have no business of her own to tend? He shut his eyes and waited for the inevitable interruption.

Cora Winters shut off the engine and sat for a moment staring through the dirty windshield at the boards of the side of the house. The iris looked right pretty, she thought. The place itself looked lousy. You'd think Rigger Kates'd have the gumption to splash some paint on the place once in a while. She snorted loudly inside the car at the folly of thinking something like that where Rigger Kates was concerned. It was a wonder he hadn't got Marcy out here doin' it.

She felt blindly for the opened window at her side and reached down outside the car, groping for the door handle. She'd been after Fred Winters for God knows how long now to fix the inside latch. She wrenched the door open irritably and slid her feet to the ground. It was only when she had slammed the door hard to make it stick, when she had come around the end of the car to the front steps, that she glanced up and saw the twin boot soles propped on the railing. She paused for a split second, smoothing down the sleeveless cotton dress over her angular frame, running her hands back over her gray-streaked hair to the loose bun at the nape of her neck, and her expression tightened as she climbed the steps.

"Kinda early in the day for a siesta, ain't it?" Cora snapped acidly as she gained the porch level.

Rigger eyed her lazily from the cup of the chair. She was no pet of his by a long shot, this raw-boned, sharp-tongued neighbor from up the road. He got the creeps every time he tried to picture Fred Winters crawlin' into bed with her. But then, bald-headed, big-bellied Fred Winters wasn't no bull moose, either.

"Ain't if you know how to work the angles, Cora."

She said nothing to that, just stood looking down on him with that expression of disgust pinching the lines of her drawn face.

"Nobody told us you was reckonin' on retirin' so soon."

"Reckon you missed some gossip for once," Rigger retorted.

Her eyes narrowed at that. She wet her lips as if she were going to snap back, but she remained silent. Her eyes slipped down his chest to the cradled bandaged hand on the little round of his belly.

"Been scrappin' again?"

"Just a lil ole disagreement, that's all."

Her face lost some of its severity and clouded soberly. "Hurt it bad?"

He raised the ponderous weight carefully and displayed it for her. "Busted it clean," he said, not without pride.

The enormity of the injury against the constant press of chores around the place caused her to gasp. Now she knew why he was settin' around, doin' nothin', wastin' valuable spring time. Almost sadly she shook her head. "It ain't right," she pronounced grimly. "It ain't right to go round brawlin' like you do. One of these here days, Rigger Kates, you're gonna tangle up with somebody who's gonna kick the real stuffin' outta you, and then what's gonna happen?"

"Ain't never met up with him yet."

"Well, there's always a first time."

"Aw, go to hell."

Cora Winters straightened stiffly as if she had been struck. She ground her jaw and pushed past him to the open door of the hallway. There she turned and glanced at the back of the chair that concealed him from her. "Marcy around?"

"Yeah. Hell, she's always around."

Cora Winters' lips twitched. She went on down the hall to the kitchen doorway. Marcy stood at the sink, her back to her, her hands busy. Cora's face muscles slackened and her eyes warmed slightly. "Hi."

Marcy spun, grabbing at her apron with soapy hands. "Cora!" She smiled broadly. "I didn't hear you come up." She peered past the older woman's shoulder down the hall length. Her eyes came to Cora Winters' face. "Rigger out there still? Didn't you speak to him?"

Cora Winters grunted as she pulled a chair from the table and sat down heavily. "Yeah, he's there. Be there till hell freezes over, from the looks of him." She raised her head slowly and eyed Marcy glumly. "Yeah, we spoke," she added. "I see he went and busted his hand this time."

Marcy's face flushed and she crossed to the sink. "They say Rigger done pretty well. The other guy was a mess."

"That's sure somethin' to be proud of."

Marcy moved her hands through the sudsy water. Cora Winters could see the pinking skin on the girl's neck and knew she'd jabbed too hard. She came to her feet and went over and put her hand on Marcy's shoulder.

"I'm sorry, kid. Sometimes I shoot off my mouth too much. It ain't no skin off'n my nose."

Marcy raised her head and looked out of the window. "I reckon as how you're right," Marcy admitted slowly. "I ain't so proud of it, not really. I reckon it wasn't no different from all the other times. He was drinkin' and that's that. Only—I'm glad it was only his hand that got busted."

"Sure. Sure you are." Cora Winters took her hand away. She went back to the chair and sat down and kept silent, watching Marcy's back as the girl cleaned up the sink. It was only after Marcy had wiped her hands, had taken off her apron and come to the chair opposite, that she finally spoke what she was thinking.

"Kind of a bad time for somethin' like this to happen, what with the spring plantin' and all comin' on, ain't it?"

Marcy shrugged. "Yeah, it ain't so good. Only it ain't as bad as it might have been."

"No?"

"No. You see, this time he brought somebody home with him to help work the place till his hand's better."

"Brought somebody home with him?"

"Yeah, this fella's gonna help out till Rigger's able."

"Well, don't that beat all! So that's why his nibs is settin' out on the porch like the King of England! Got himself a hired hand to do all the work. Pretty fancy, I'd say."

Marcy frowned at the sarcasm. "This fella, Cora—he ain't like a hired hand, exactly. You see, he's just kinda helpin' out in a pinch, friendly-like, you might say."

"Oh?"

"Course, we're gonna pay him somethin', it ain't like we could afford a real hired hand all the time."

"I see." Cora Winters didn't get the drift of the thing at all. There were a lot more questions she wanted to ask. She discarded all of them for the moment but one. Her voice took on a confidential note and she leaned forward slyly. "What's this here new fella like? One of Rigger's fast-drinkin' town cronies?"

Marcy's head tilted and she peered through the screen to the looming hulk of the barn. "He don't seem like one of them kind," she said slowly. "He's different from them others, somehow. He's right nice, seems like."

"Where'd Rigger meet anybody right nice?"

"He was there when Rigger got himself hurt. He took care of Rigger."

"He was wastin' his time."

Marcy swallowed hard. Sometimes Cora Winters said things that weren't right bein' said to the wife of the man she was sayin' them about. Sometimes she wondered what Cora Winters would do if she told her some of the things Rigger said about her Fred. Still, sometimes, too, Marcy had the feeling Cora didn't always mean the things she said the way they sounded.

Cora Winters was saying nothing more. A sharp look came into her eyes and the squared planes of her face seemed bolder than ever.

"What's the matter?" Marcy asked anxiously.

Cora brought her eyes from the back screen door to Marcy's face and nodded. "This here your hired fella comin' up now?"

Marcy twisted. Britt was almost at the back steps. In a second he had come up to the screen, had pulled it open and stepped into the room. He came to a full stop as he saw the two of them sitting like that, staring at him.

Marcy broke the freeze. Hastily, confused, she got to her feet and went to his side. Looking down at Cora Winters, she smiled. "This here's Britt Callum, Rigger's friend."

Cora Winters had missed nothing. She eyed the two of them, him standing like a giant in the room and her at his side, her head barely reaching his breast muscle.

Tardily Cora Winters brought her eyes to Britt Callum's face. "Howdy," she said.

Britt nodded and glanced down at Marcy.

"Cora Winters. She's our next-door neighbor up the road," Marcy explained hurriedly.

"Howdy, ma'am." Britt turned to Marcy. "Can I have the truck keys? They're on the dresser, Rigger says."

"Sure thing." Marcy went into the bedroom and returned almost immediately, handing him the chain with a smile.

Britt nodded slightly. "Sure glad to have met you, ma'am."

Marcy stayed where she was as he left. Some moments after the sounds of his steps on the earth had faded into nothingness she turned back to the table. Cora Winters had leaned forward and had one elbow on the table edge, supporting her chin. Her eyes were thoughtful, set on the bright rectangle of the screen.

"He's nice, ain't he?" Marcy ventured as she sat down.

"Yeah, seems right nice." Cora pulled her head back and clasped her work-worn hands on the table in front of her. "Funny a clean-cut guy like that would bother with Rigger."

Marcy flushed. "Rigger ain't so bad when he likes somebody."

Cora Winters glanced dubiously at the girl and then shot another look at the door. A rare open smile brightened Cora's face tentatively. "Shouldn't reckon Rigger Kates'd be restin' so easy with that one around," she murmured.

Marcy missed the point. "Rigger's right fond of that old boy. He gets a kick outta just bein' round him, seems like."

Cora Winters' smile lingered in traces. She straightened and pulled her hands to her lap. "Reckon he can't see nothin' but all them beautiful muscles," she snorted. She pushed her chair back and got to her feet. "I gotta git," she said brusquely.

"Aw, don't rush off."

"Headin' into town for some supplies. Need anythin'?"

"No, much obliged."

Cora Winters led the way down the hall with Marcy trailing. As the two women came out onto the porch Rigger stirred irritably and opened his eyes.

"Christ! You have to come banging out like a coupla overweight steers, wakin' people up!"

Cora Winters stopped at the head of the steps and looked down on him coldly. "Cussin' ain't no sign of a man, Rigger Kates!"

She went down to her car and Marcy stood at the head of the steps by Rigger's chair watching as Cora worked to start the old Plymouth. She staved as she was until the car had clattered and bounced its way down the ruts to the pavement, had turned and headed for town. Slowly she turned and looked down at Rigger.

He had already closed his eyes. She hesitated and cleared her throat. "Anythin' you want?" she asked tentatively.

He shifted abruptly but did not open his eyes. "Naw. G'wan away and let a guy get some sleep, can'tcha?"

Marcy's shoulders dropped a trifle and she sighed. Moving quietly, she went down the hall to the kitchen and her unfinished chores.

CHAPTER FOUR

I<small>T WAS</small> early evening about three weeks after Britt Callum had come to the Kates place. He had dragged his chair outside the door to the barn room and made it firm in the dirt. Supper was over and now he sat, chair tilted back against the wall, his long legs splayed out before him, thinking of nothing in particular, relaxed. He felt good. The long hours of hard physical routine, coupled with food and solid sleep, had brought him to rested satisfaction. As he sat there letting his gaze go drifting over the place, moving along the firm clean sweep of the unbroken horizon to the northwest, he felt good. The last incident in Oklahoma, he hadn't even thought of it for days now. Evening was the best time in Texas.

The back screen door slammed. He brought his head up and shaded his eyes against the glare of the setting sun. Marcy was picking her way along the side of the house, heading for the little clump of pathetic rosebushes that fought for survival. She had a kettle of water and, stooping, she carefully administered the ration to the roots of each bush.

Britt wondered suddenly, watching her, how she had ever taken up with Rigger Kates in the first place. Rigger was man enough and all that, but she didn't strike him as the kind that went much for the rough-and-tumble stuff.

She had straightened and was plucking off the dead leaves. He let his eyes taste her figure. She was as ripe as a summer apricot. That Rigger sure had himself something. The old unguarded tightness came banding his loins. She had glanced his way and he could see the slow parting of her lips and the coming of her smile. She glanced toward the house and then she came on across the yard. She moved fluidly, her legs solid and sure, and every step she took was marked in the cadence of her breasts. He came forward on the chair and drew his legs under him, sitting straight, his lips tight and dry.

"You know, you could scrape up a smile—just a little one!" She laughed as she came before him. "Settin' out here all by yourself, scowlin' as if the whole world was sot agin you!"

He grinned sheepishly and relaxed somewhat, shoving one leg back out. "I wasn't bein' sour," he mumbled. "The damn sun's too bright."

Marcy Kates looked down on him and forgot what she had been going to say. He got to his feet and motioned to the chair. "Have a seat and rest up a bit."

She came forward and dropped into the seat, leaning over to set the kettle on the ground at her side. Her eyes rose up along the inverted V of his legs, over the masked hardness of his belly, his chest, to his big shoulders, the dark face, and the eyes steady on her. "I didn't mean to come along and rout you outta your chair," she offered lamely.

"Good to have company." He came past her and sat down on the ground at her side, his back up against the barn side, his heels brought up close to his buttocks, knees high before his face.

"You'll get yourself all dirty there," she commented.

"Dirty all ready." He slapped at the jeans and the fine dust smoked around them. "Ain't no way to keep from gettin' dirty round a farm."

For a moment she said nothing, sitting above him, looking down on him. His hair was a mass of unruly curls and she had never seen a black so rich, so glossy. For the instant she wanted to reach out and touch him, to see if the hair could be as soft, as thick as it looked. "Yeah," she said suddenly, and looked away hastily. "I know what you mean. It's a lousy, dirty hole, this place!"

He glanced up in sharp surprise. Suddenly he realized she was not happy, that under the general good humor of her there was the hard chafing core of trouble. "You don't like it here very much?"

"Like it? Here?" She turned widening eyes on him. "God, I hate it! I hate every stinkin' inch of it!" she exploded. The silence was hard around them, thick, vacuous, final.

Britt stared at the angled outline of the old house. She made no attempt to speak further, to explain. He had come to that moment when maybe he could ask her some of the things that had occurred to him over and again these weeks.

"How'd you happen to come out here in the first place, Marcy? How the hell'd you and Rigger come to match up?"

Her answer was very slow in coming. He thought at first she was refusing him, but he saw she was working out the thought before she trusted herself to speak. Her eyes were fixed on the distant meeting of the earth and sky, and finally, without shifting her gaze, she responded.

"It's one of them long stories. They usually are. You see, I came from Arkansas, originally. My daddy worked in the oil fields some until there—there was an accident and he got killed." She paused for a moment. "After Daddy was gone, Mamma and I came here to Wichita because Mamma had been a nurse and there was a job at the state hospital. I wasn't much mor'n a kid then, still in school. There was just the two of us, Mamma and me, and things weren't so hot. Then, all of a sudden, Mamma died, and I was alone."

"That was a tough break."

She glanced down at him dispassionately. "It don't matter no more. I was only fifteen then. Well, I had to stop schoolin' and get me a job to live. There wasn't much I could do, so I wound up waitin' tables. Funny." There was a faint harsh ripple in her voice. "I never did nothin' else. I was always workin' some cheesy café or beer joint, somehow. After a couple of years of that stuff—well, that's when I met up with Rigger."

She hesitated a long moment, then picked up the strands of her story and went on. "Yeah. So I met Rigger Kates. He hung around the place I was workin' in and he was—well, he was like he is sometimes now—shootin' off his mouth all the time, actin' smart. Only, I don't know … " She glanced at him briefly. "He was kinda cute." She faltered now, as if she were trying to gauge his reaction. There was none and she sighed and looked away. "Rigger was pretty hot-blooded. He ain't changed none that way, I reckon you know. It ain't hard to tell him and Newt's brothers— they always got it on their minds, lookin' for it all the time. I ain't never been able to figure why Rigger wanted me. Maybe other women don't like little guys much or somethin'. Anyhow, Rigger right off started shinin' up to me, and when I didn't go fussin' at him, I reckon he got ideas. He kept tellin' me how he was crazy in love with me and all that stuff. I reckon as how he got me thinkin' silly like that, too, after a while."

She looked down now at her hands, spread in her lap, the fingers long and sensitive, kept examining them elaborately as she went on.

"I been over what happened so many times it ain't funny. Maybe it happened because I was just plumb sick and tired of bein' alone all the time. I don't know. I wasn't no kid. You don't stay bein' a kid workin' in joints like that."

She heard his faint half-sigh and turned and stared down at him. Her face was gaunt, chalked in the rising dusk. She looked away.

"I'd only done somethin' wrong once before I met Rigger. I went to bed with a guy I didn't even know what his right name was." She choked for a moment. "You ever crawl into bed with a stranger?" she demanded suddenly. "You ever do somethin' like that just so's you can feel 'em warm and close up next to you, just so's you know for a little while there's somebody else alive and breathin' besides yourself?" Her sudden burst failed and he heard the swift catch in her throat. "Well, that's what I done once before I met Rigger," she said low. "I don't even remember now what the guy even looked like." She turned to him and her words shrilled. "It was only I was gettin' scared, Britt. I didn't know where I was headin' alone all the time and thinkin' bad, tangled-up thoughts all day and night, mostly at night when I went to my room alone."

"I know," he said quietly.

"Do you, Britt? Do you, honest?" she implored.

"Yeah, sure. You bet I know."

She let seconds slip past. When she resumed there was a new strange calm in her. "You wanted to know how come Rigger and I wound up together. Well, like I said, I met him and he kept tryin' to make me and I wouldn't let him have none. That near drove him nuts. You know how it is. Rigger was used to gettin' his way most times, I reckon, like he is now. The more I held out, the more he was gonna get me." Her voice lifted and went off on a slant. "I don't know—like I say, he was kinda cute and all. He was pretty nice to me all the time those days."

Britt's head raised suddenly. "Those days," she had said. What about now?

"Rigger got himself plastered up one Saturday night and we was married." She turned abruptly and her defenses were high. "I reckoned I had to do it that way, don't you see? He might not have married me at all, and I might have—I don't know ... " She looked away hastily. "I reckon as how I might have given in sooner or later, feelin' all hollow like I did. I just had to have someone, someplace."

"So you came out here."

She nodded dumbly. Her eyes went roving over the flat spread of the place. "Yeah, that's the story." She raised her hands and placed both palms against the sides of her head, pushing, tilting her head back, feeling the softness of her hair, her eyes wide on the purpling sky. "Yeah, we came out here. That's been four years now. And we been here ever since. Me and Rigger and dear Brother Newt—one happy little family."

He could not shake the thought. "You said Rigger was nice to you—'those days.' "

She cut him swiftly, abruptly. "I was just sayin' somethin' to say. He's all right. We get along as good as most. I reckon it ain't none of my business what he's out doin' when he ain't here. He's a hot-blooded, hell-raisin' man. Besides, I ain't so particular no more, anyhow." She put her hand forward and caught the whole of the place in a single sweep. "Sure," she cried thickly, "I said I hate this place. I do. Only, it ain't on account of him. It's the place. I hate the place and the country with its damn wind all the time and the dust and the hot one day and cold the next and all the lousy scrawny bits of crops we get if we're lucky and nothin' to do but sleep and work and maybe you get to town once in a blue moon and most times you don't!"

She was on her feet suddenly and her laugh was brittle. "Get me! I sure been shootin' off my trap! That ought to learn you, Britt Callum. Don't go round askin' a woman personal questions next time." She went away, going out into the open space beyond the barn. Once free of the building shadows, she stopped and bent her head, scuffing at the yellow dirt with the toe of her shoe.

He remained where he was, his eyes on her, on the small little patch of her neck showing. There was nothing he could say. He took his eyes from her and glanced at the house. The night shadows were welling up around the place but they were not yet thick enough to black out. In the frame of the back door Newt Kates stood watching them. Britt wondered how long he had been like that, wondered if the sound of her voice had carried, how much of what she had been saying Newt Kates had heard.

He got to his feet and slapped at the dust thick on his trouser legs. The air was powdered with the stuff. He stepped ahead and coughed. He came up behind her. He did not touch her but spoke very softly. "Newt's been watchin'."

"Let him!" She raised her head swiftly but kept her eyes away from the house. "Let him watch! That's all he can do, anyhow—just butt in where he ain't wanted!" Her lips curled in a twist of contempt. "He can't do nothin' else nohow—just stand around watchin', listenin' all the time!"

She left him. She wheeled and went back to the chair and picked up the kettle. She hesitated for a moment, looking over to where he was, still facing the other way, his back to her, the bigness of him solid and dark against the blackening sky. She drew a deep breath and started toward the back door, where the coal of Newt Kate's cigarette gleamed.

At the doorstep she paused and raised each foot, looking back over her shoulder to the soles of her shoes for traces of mud or manure before she entered. Newt stared over the tip of his cigarette, looking eagerly down into the deep cleft between her breasts. He raised his eyes tardily to find her icy gaze on him. For a moment they stood face to face, the screen an almost invisible meshed barrier between them. A sly smirk gathered on Newt's lips.

"Looks like maybe you got yourself a playmate, eh?"

She snatched at the door handle, yanked the door wide, and pushed past him, her shoulder catching him, spinning him off balance. He grabbed at the doorframe to steady himself. Wheeling angrily, he saw her come to a stop at the open door to her bedroom. She turned and looked across the kitchen space at him.

"You poor spyin' no-good…" she ground pityingly and slammed the door in his face.

CHAPTER FIVE

T HE MOMENT Britt took his place at the breakfast table the next morning he caught the tension. Newt Kates raised his eyes and there was a chill hardness in them. Newt went back to his food immediately. Britt glanced at Rigger. The little guy's face was flushed and his eyes remained on his plate. Marcy met his gaze levelly. Imperceptibly there was a drawing of her brows. He knew she was warning him to remain quiet, to stay out of it. He remembered Newt standing in the doorway last night.

The meal drifted on in deathly silence. When their eating was done Marcy got up and began to clear the table. Rigger broke the freeze. "Newt, you ain't been makin' the time you ought on that there field. You been screwin' around out there."

Newt's face went darker. He shoved his chair back and the matchstick went deep into the pits of his teeth. He stared contemptuously at his brother and without removing the pick he spoke. "I reckon I know my chores," he spat.

"There's lots of things need doin' here. We can't be puttin' all our time on the stinkin' lousy field."

Newt's mouth was tight. His eyes were dull, smoky. Rigger eyed him coldly. He suddenly shifted and managed a kind of grin at Britt. "Goddamn straw boss, that's me!" he crowed. "Crack the lil ole whip—that's what I gotta keep doin'."

Newt chewed nervously on the bit of stick and watched his brother callously. "That's what you *think* you gotta be doin'," he amended nastily.

"Damn well gotta if anythin's gonna get done," Rigger said loftily. "If nobody rode herd 'round here the whole damn place'd fall in ruins."

"Goddamn lucky for you that hand of yours got busted up," Newt snarled. "Gives you more time to set around on your fat little rump all day makin' noises like you was a big shot."

Rigger smoldered. "Why, hell, man, I could do twicet the work you do in one day, even with this hand out of whack, and you know it!"

"You can sure shoot off your mouth twicet as loud in one day—that's for sure."

Marcy suddenly spun from the sink. "Oh, shut your yaps, the two of you! Yammer, yammer, yammer—I get so sick and tired heatin' the two of you mornin', noon, and night I could scream! You been jawin' ever since last night. Now shut up and get out of here. Go somewheres else, go tb work! I'm just plumb sick to death listenin' to the sounds of you!"

Rigger straightened instantly and his expression was angry. "Well, I'll be goddamned!" he muttered ominously. "Old cat's found herself a tongue!" He made his words hard. "Shut up, you," he commanded. "You out lookin' for another bust in the mouth?"

She stared down on him icily. She became slowly conscious that Britt was watching her with the rest. Splotches of color tipped her cheeks and she moved her hands nervously under the cover of her apron. "No" she said limply. "It's only I get so tired of fights all the time. Why don't you go out there and do some work, Newt? You know he's all touchy with that hand hurt and all. Why can't you just let him be for a while? Why do we have to go on all the time bawlin' like a bunch of calves with a bellyful of loco weed?"

Newt's eyes were beady. He had found Britt's intent gaze on her. For a long moment he studied the man across the table. Finally he got to his feet and flicked the used matchstick on the tabletop. Without a further word or glance at any of them he left the room. The sounds of his steps in the yard faded out and the place was still.

Rigger took his hot eyes from Marcy slowly. He touched his soiling bandage gingerly. His gaze when it came to Britt was cool. "We been like that since we was kids," he said. "Ain't never seemed to get along. Newt's a damn good worker when he puts his mind to it. He just ain't got no ambition. Him and me's been workin' together since we was sprouts. I reckon we been fightin' ever since I remember, too. Sometimes I get wonderin' why the hell Newt just don't up and clear out, get himself a place of his own. But don't seem like Newt's got no ambition. He don't give a good goddamn for nothin'."

Marcy had not returned to her chores. Her body was slumped against the sink edge and she watched Rigger dully. Her eyes shifted and she found Britt. His glance brushed her face and she lifted her chin a little.

Britt got to his feet and stretched. "I best get goin'," he said. "You want to come down to the barn and show how you want them wires strung?"

Rigger touched his hand carefully and nodded.

She watched them leave; her gaze followed as they went across the yard toward the barn. Rigger seemed even shorter than ever next to him. He went strutting along, his head held as high as he could get it. Even then it only reached the other's ribs. Britt Callum moved with oily grace, effortlessly for the size of him, and she could see the heavy muscles cording in the spread of his back, welted on the snug cloth of the thin cotton shirt. Only when they had disappeared into the maw of the barn did she bring her eyes down slowly to the grease-flecked water gone lukewarm in the pan.

That night after supper when he was in his little cubicle she came again. He was standing in front of the table combing his hair when the sense of her touched him and he turned. She was standing in the open doorway and her smile was faint. She carried the kettle, as she had the night before. "Hello," she said.

"Hi." He set the comb down and crossed to her. "Hi," he said again.

She looked up and the color came. She took her eyes away and her voice was low and hesitant. "I'd kinda like to talk for a minute or two."

He felt a kind of instant flash in him. Moving back into the room, he snagged the chair by its crossbar and brought it outside, setting it in the dust where it had been the other time. She nodded silently and sat down, holding the kettle in her lap. She waited until he had gone around her and made himself comfortable on the earth at her side.

"Sure glad you came by again," he said. "Gets kinda lonesome down here."

She was giving her whole attention to the mechanics of the kettle handle, raising, lowering it, as if the operation were newly discovered. Suddenly she straightened and glanced at the house. "I just been wantin' to say how right sorry I am I run off at the mouth last night," she said carefully. She moistened her lips. "I reckon as how I said lots of things didn't make much sense. I can remember sayin' them so's they was kinda ugly." In her confusion she shifted on the chair and the kettle fell to the earth with a sharp clank. But when Britt drew his legs in to get up and retrieve it she stayed him with a brief touch of her hand. "Let it go. It don't matter. I want to say somethin' more." She swallowed hard and kept her eyes on him. "I reckon as how you must've been thinkin' I was a sap, with nothin' better to do than sit around gripin' about my life and all. Well, things ain't as bad as they sounded." She was looking off over the stretch of the land. "It ain't all bad. I got me the house to live in and there's food on the table. I get along O.K. when I set my mind to it. Me and Rigger gets by as good as most folks, I reckon. I even get along with that Newt, most times."

He remembered Newt framed in the doorway last night. The breakfast table and the tension and ill will that shrouded the morning meal came back. Newt Kates must have blabbed about what she had been saying last night and there had been a row. As if she knew his thinking, she spoke again.

"We had a beef last night after I got inside." She heard his breath snag and looked down on him, smiling thinly. "No, it wasn't about what you and me was talkin' about out here. I don't think he heard nothin'. It was just a good old-fashioned family fight. Newt made some crack and Rigger took him up on it. Like Rigger said, it goes on all the time. I get so's most times I don't pay much mind to what they're squallin' about."

He felt the relief seeping through the tiny pinhole she had pricked in the hardening shell of his apprehension. He wanted no more of that Oklahoma business; not because of him and her, especially. He didn't want nobody gettin' wrong ideas, kickin' up a fuss. If somethin' like that ever happened, if somebody started gettin' smart, gettin' her in trouble over him, there was only one thing to do, just clear out.

She had gone on. "I blew off a lot last night. I mean, with you. Some of the things I said, I reckon I'm sorry now I said 'em. I spilled all over you about things happened to me a long time back." Her voice was husky. "I made some mistakes in them days—bad ones, I reckon. But that was them days and it don't do no good bawlin' over them now."

"Everyone makes mistakes sooner or later, Marcy," he said softly. "I got me a few scratched up on the board, too."

"You?" She turned and studied him closely for a long moment. "It's your eyes," she said as if to herself. "You got eyes so clean. I reckon as how you ain't never made mistakes that counted for much."

He smiled. "It ain't the mistakes you make, it's the thinkin' about 'em too much after they're done that's bad."

Her response came with a lift to her lips and her teeth shone bright and even. "Yeah. I ain't thought about it that way. Maybe you got somethin' there."

"Them mistakes you was talkin' about," he continued. "Who don't make mistakes now and then, Marcy? Who says reachin' out to a stranger like you done just to know you ain't alone for a minute somewheres along the way—who can say that's wrong? All most folks is lookin' for is a little peace, the touch of a warm hand, a little lovin,' a little closeness. If you done things along the way that maybe ain't panned out so right when all you're doin' is just tryin'—maybe there's folks call 'em mistakes, but they can't be so bad, Marcy. Nobody can tell me it's bad to go lookin' for a little lovin' in the world somewheres."

She had turned her head from him and was holding her lids tight against the press of her tears. In a while she raised her hand and wiped at the wetness before she looked down on him. He was hunched forward, his arms crossed on his knees, his chin hard on his strong forearms. She reached down and her fingertips touched his shoulder. "Thanks a lot, Britt."

He watched as she rose and stooped to pick up the kettle. She straightened and glanced at him and her smile was warm and gentle. She shook her head, flinging the rich brush of her hair away, and she went from him, walking straight toward the pile of the beat-up old house.

CHAPTER SIX

RIGGER had picked up a habit as the days wore on. He would manufacture some excuse to drop around to the little room in the barn during Britt's off time, to perch on the edge of the cot, his injured hand held up close to his belly, and talk. All the time his eyes would go probing over Britt's massive physique, lingering on the strong bare arms, on the rounded bulge of the biceps, enviously wide on the broad chest, marking the firm tough cords of the breast muscles, the hard, thick thighs, the long, firm legs. Of all the things in the world Rigger Kates might have desired most, Britt Callum's body was the prize.

Britt was aware of the little guy's fascination. At first the rapt close attention had bothered him, made him hotly self-conscious. But as the time wore on, as Rigger kept coming around to make his light talk that ill screened his absorption, Britt got used to it. He conceded to himself it must be hard on a guy to have all the equipment, the build and the strength of a man, yet to look always like nothing more than a kid.

Rigger's flowing talk covered everything. He talked crops and Texas and women. He had never got into the Army and the slight still rankled within him. He had wanted passionately to go, to fight and kill, to have reaped the years of buddy talk that were harvested in every barroom. But they had rejected him. His size was against him, for one thing. Actually, there was a perforated eardrum from a childhood illness, but Rigger ignored this defect as cause. In himself he held his loathsome size responsible.

He talked most about women. His conquests had been innumerable, varied, and uninterrupted since puberty. He regarded each with pride and cockiness and conceit. He'd had all kinds, he'd done it every way in the book, and some not yet listed. He boastfully described each variance in thorough and meticulous detail, assuming Britt's natural admiration, hopeful for possible envy as well. In all the talk he brought to the little room he never once mentioned the name of his wife, nor did he touch on any facet of their lives together these past four years. It was as if she did not exist within his world.

One night, along about eight o'clock or so, Newt Kates paid his first visit to the little room. Britt was on his cot, his hands clasped under his head, staring up at the beamed ceiling, dreaming along, when Newt entered. He did not knock. He simply walked in, unannounced, and stood in the doorway, looking down with those little beady eyes of his.

Britt stared. For a long moment the two men eyed each other. Britt shoved himself up on an elbow and made a vague gesture toward the lone chair. "Hi, Newt. Have a seat."

"I reckon as how I'll stand," Newt said bluntly. He moved over to the foot of the bed and took his place, leaning up against the wall, crossing his legs, shoving his hands deep in the pockets of his dirty khaki trousers.

Britt hunched himself up a little to see better, bunching the pillow behind his shoulders against the wall and folded his arms. He watched Newt carefully, wondering what had brought him to the room. They were not companionable, had never been since the first. There had been no trouble between them but each was frankly guarded in the presence of the other.

Newt pulled his hands from his pockets and unbuttoned the flap of his shirt pocket, drawing forth a pack of cigarettes. He did not offer Britt one; he made an elaborate ceremony of selecting one, replacing the. pack, digging into his trousers for a match. He scratched the head on the sole of his boot and lit up. He inhaled a deep draught and expelled the smoke through his nostrils without removing the cigarette from the corner of his mouth. His hands were in his pockets again.

"You got somethin' on your mind?" Britt asked quietly.

Kates was studying him closely. Now he turned his head and surveyed the room with heightening interest. "She's made this into a right cozy place," he observed.

Britt had caught the faint stress on the word "she." "Yeah, it's right comfortable."

Kates peered at him, the cigarette bobbing as he spoke. "Like it was in the Army—never had it so good, eh?"

"Yeah, guess so."

"You was in the Army?" Newt's query seemed tinted with doubt.

"Yeah." Britt's eyes narrowed. "Five years."

"Infantry?"

"Air Corps."

"One of the Wild Blue Yonder boys, eh?"

"Ground crew."

Newt's tone was faintly scornful. "Pretty soft snap you guys had." He hesitated and seemed to straighten. "I was Infantry."

"I know. Rigger told me."

There was the sudden wash of contempt on the older man's face. He smiled coldly. He took the cigarette from his lips and regarded the ash with exaggerated interest. "Funny thing how all you muscle boys fanned out when the real test came. Or got themselves into nice sweet spots."

The line of Britt's jaw hardened and held. He let it pass. There was no point in swallowing the bait. No sense letting Newt Kates needle him into getting sore.

Kates dropped the military talk. He flicked the ash from the cigarette to the floor casually and replaced the stub between his lips, rolling it with the tip of his tongue to the far corner of his mouth. "You was sayin' a few days back how you come out of New Mexico."

"That's right."

"Whereabouts?"

"Albuquerque."

Kates's eyes brightened. He took his cigarette from his lips and held it off to one side. His brows were held high. "That so? Know Albuquerque pretty well myself. Was stationed there a while. What part?"

"East side."

"East side." Kates screwed his face in thought. "Lemme see. Lots of Mexicans there, huh?"

"Some, yeah, and Indians."

Kates took a quick nervous puff on the cigarette and slid it to one side again. "You got some Indian in you?"

"I told you—I'm part Italian."

Kates nodded slowly, thoughtfully. "Yeah, sure you did. Clean forgot." He brightened synthetically and waved the cigarette in wide circles. "Sure, remember now, Eyetalian. Got to thinkin' you was so dark-like, might have some Indian in you. Lot of Indians around them parts. Indians, that is—and Mex boys."

The implication was obvious. Britt's lips were thin. "Yeah, lots."

Kates fell silent. He made no move to leave. He finished the cigarette, dropped the butt on the floor, and crushed the coal under the toe of his boot. He straightened and smiled quite broadly, his eyes squeezing into little slits. "I see you been gettin' along mighty good with Rigger's woman, Marcy," he said without warning.

Britt jackknifed his legs and came forward alertly, setting his arms on his knees, his eyes sharp on the dim figure beyond the bed. "Yeah, guess we get along all right."

"Yeah, I seen." Kates glanced away. He shoved his hands back into his pockets. He was silent for a long moment. Britt saw the fingers of Newt's right hand reaching forth under the thin khaki to scratch himself. It was a funny trick he had caught Newt doing, that scratching, scratching whenever her name came up. Now he scratched and looked at Britt and grinned. "Kind of a nice little piece, ain't she?" he said. "Wouldn't mind havin' some of that for myself."

The dirty taste muddied Britt's mouth. Kates was smirking down on him as if they were buddies or something. He felt the whipping urge come flooding into his muscles. For the instant he fought down the old-time drive to get up and kick the living daylights out of Newt Kates. That would mean nothing but the same old trouble as before. He closed his eyes and shut out the sight of Newt's leering face.

"Don't reckon you'd have much trouble gettin' that for yourself if you was a mind to," Kates suggested sleekly. "Looks to me as how she's pantin' to have somebody like you, boy."

Britt clamped his jaws. Kates went babbling on, his words unhurried, easy, quiet.

"Yessir, that's about as warm a little number as I ever did see." Kates took a short step toward the bed and his voice warmed in oily confidence. "You know, that there Rigger's a goddamn fool. Here he's got himself the nicest chunk in north Texas, and what's he out doin'? Spendin' his time chasin' any old broad. Why, that little punk's just plain hump-happy, that's all. He ain't got no taste. Hell, it's just a plain waste of time and dough with him, if you was to ask me."

Britt sprang from the bed. He stared at the man in the shadows and revulsion was open, stark in his face. He moved to the table under the mirror fragment and took up his cigarettes with trembling fingers. Behind him the voice droned on relentlessly.

"I don't know—maybe that little ole runt of a Rigger ain't much good to her nohow. Now, if *you* was to sink her—a big, whopping buck like you'd kind of make her squeal real happy-like, I'm thinkin'. I got a feelin' what our gal's been hankerin' for's the good ole man treatment. She looks like she could use plenty, that one. Looks to me like you're the ole boy who's got it all round here!"

Britt stared at his own face in utter disbelief. What was wrong with him? Why didn't he knock every damn tooth in Newt Kates's head down his rotten throat? God knows he wanted to, but something kept holding him back. Was it Marcy herself? Was he afraid of the mess that would follow? Was it because of what the foreman Jakers had said about payin' for a killin' once it was done? His eyes were wide and the darkness of his face had paled into a kind of sickly yellow. Beyond his shoulder he could make out the oval that was the face of Newt Kates as he leaned against the wall, taking his time, his smirk broad, his thin lips wormlike, barely moving, as he went on. He saw Newt straighten now, pull his hands from his pockets, and flay them out at hip level in a gesture of helplessness.

"Course," Newt was saying airily, "every man's to his own taste. Maybe you ain't after somethin' like that. Maybe you got ideas of your own. Some likes it one way, some likes it another. I reckon how a man does it's his own business."

Britt spun swiftly. His eyes burned hot and his body quivered under the harsh arrest imposed on his muscles. His words knifed keen-edged, blazing with the flames of fury. "Shut your goddamn stinkin' mouth, Kates!" he cried. "Shut that filthy yap of yours good and right off, see? Else you're gonna be talkin' yourself into somethin' ain't gonna be so healthy!"

Newt Kates stiffened. He eyed Britt Callum warily but he stood his ground. From the look of him there was no fear. The smirk had evaporated but the traces remained. His eyes had opened a little wider and they were hard and full of slow hate.

"I done said my piece," Newt Kates said slowly, clearly. "I got eyes in my head. I know some of what's been goin' on round here. You and that no-good, stuck-up bitch settin' out in the dark, night after night, talkin', gettin' real acquainted like." He snorted. He emerged from the shadows and stood by the open door. "You best be keepin' them muscles quiet, big boy. You might be needin' 'em before long. I been thinkin' as how Rigger ain't gonna be takin' it too kindly when he gets wind of you out whorin' after his woman, nohow." He backed a step be-for Britt's swaying step. "Oh, I ain't gonna tell him—don't be frettin'." The pall darkened his face. "I ain't doin' him no favors. I hate his guts, him and his 'do this, do that' stuff. What he gets he's got comin'. Only I'm tellin' you somethin'—he ain't so dumb, see? He's a right smart cookie. He's an onery cuss when he gets riled up. There's times he ain't been far from a killin', that boy. You remember that. He'll go on bein' your buddy till he takes a fancy to change. Then, big fella, all I'm sayin' to you is—you best be watchin' out!"

As suddenly as he had come, Newt Kates left. He simply turned heel and melted into the darkness outside. Britt stared heavily at the door, at the vacant black hole into the night. His body shook like a leaf and the sweat was beaded on his flesh. After long moments the tension began to lessen. He groped behind him and set his palms on the table edge. Gradually he slumped, letting the weight of his frame come to rest. Finally he steadied himself with one hand and brought the other up slowly to his forehead and down across his face hard. In all his life, in all the twenty-eight years of it, no matter the time, the place, or the reason, he could not remember having come so close to doing murder.

CHAPTER SEVEN

THE TWO MEN stood at the fence line that divided the fields. Rigger's hands were deep in his hip pockets and his right foot rested on the rung of fence railing. Britt leaned idly against the post at his side. Together they watched the churning clouds of dust milling in the wake of the slow-moving tractor in the distance.

"That ole boy's workin' himself into a stroke today," Rigger mused.

Britt glanced down curiously. Rigger might as well have spoken of the hired man. Britt wet his lips and cleared his throat. Then he decided against mentioning Newt Kates.

In the midst of the rising heat of spring he began to think of Marcy, of the talks they kept having in the evenings. There was that something intangible about her that bridged one meeting to the other. He carried the picture of her always now in the wallet of his mind. After that first impassioned outburst, when she had pulled the curtains aside from her life, touching so briefly on her days with Rigger, she never again mentioned their lives. When they talked now, they avoided the past and its people; they talked of the present and sometimes hesitantly of the veiled, unknown future.

Looking down now on the cropped, sandy head of Rigger Kates, Britt Callum knew for the first time the sharp, unmistakable irritation of envy. Here was this little sawed-off runt, the luckiest guy in the world, and he didn't have enough of God's good sense to know when he was well off! He suddenly wanted to reach out, to take the hard small shoulders and shake him, to rattle the hell out of that capsule body until Rigger's teeth danced in his head, to try to knock some living sense into the bullet skull that was too thick. Why, with a woman like Marcy at his side, a man had the world by the short hairs. There was nothing, no one strong enough, big enough, that could begin to stop any bastard so lucky! And here he was now—Rigger Kates—at his side, his little-boy foot in its kid-sized cowboy boot, stuck up on the fence rail, his eyes squinting in the bright sun and God knows what cooking up in his fuzzy head for the nights to come, the hours in the crumby bars and flops of Wichita Falls.

"What the hell you got your face all screwed into a knot about?" Rigger was laughing at him. "You got some troubles, ole boy?" He hesitated and the knowing grin began to spread. "What you been needin's a lil ole trip to town, boy. You ain't been on a spree since you got here."

Britt flushed. He covered his thinking quickly with a responding grin. "Yeah, that's right."

"Sure thing. Reckon it's about time you and me took us a trip to town." Rigger spoke in a ludicrously professional way, as if he were the doctor prescribing the tonic trip, the purgative, the cure-all. "Yessir, I reckon it's high time my boy got his ashes hauled!"

When they checked into the Red Club that night it was as if they had turned back the clock to that first night. The same two soldiers were there, the same anonymous group of cowmen and farmers, the same two women, with different escorts this time. Rigger had picked up a whisky bottle on the way, and after a few shots and the beer chasers were down he was primed for action. He maneuvered and caught the eye of the woman who had seduced him into the broken hand. It was not long before she shed the guy with her and came over to join them.

"This here's my buddy Britt. This here's Ruby. She's an old friend." Rigger winked.

"Britt, eh?" She eyed him with open candor. Her appraisal began somewhere near his knees and came up slowly, thoroughly. She met his dark eyes and her teeth bared. "Jesus!" Ruby breathed. "There's a helluva lot of you, Britt boy!"

Over her head Britt saw the instant tiny scowl that came edging, darkening on Rigger's brow. He turned away abruptly, severing the contact, and found his beer.

Ruby stood nonplused for the moment. Then she grunted. She shrugged. "Suits the hell outta me," she muttered. She swung and brought her attention to Rigger. "How's my ole honey?" She reached out and tentatively touched the soiled bandage. "I sure was right sick about what happened last time, honey. I didn't mean nothin' like that to happen." She hesitated. "I been missin' you, man," she said softly. Then she laughed. "That ole boy you bopped ain't been doin' so well, hon." Her hand had come up gradually and rested easily, familiarly on his shoulder. "You sure do pack a wallop!"

Britt watched the idle play in the mirror. Rigger had drawn her close and Britt could see the good hand performing its chores accurately, deftly, and sharp, quick urgency come into her face. Suddenly Rigger held her from him. He grinned slyly and nodded toward Britt.

"How's about hustlin' up a dame for my boy here?"

She shot a disdainful look at Britt. "Somehow I kinda got the idea he wasn't havin' none."

"Yeah, yeah," Rigger snapped impatiently. "How's about it? Reckon you got one lined up?"

She eyed Rigger with faint surprise. "That ain't gonna be hard—not for him!" She nodded. "How's about Roseanne down yonder, honey? She ain't havin' such a good time with that old jerk hangin' onto her."

Britt let his eyes go along the mirror until they found her. She was late-thirtyish, blonde and tired. While he watched she glanced up and saw him. He could see the color come slow into her cheeks. Rigger had caught the interplay. He grinned.

"Go get her, baby." Rigger stung her behind with the flat of his palm. His firing eyes came to Britt as she left. "Boy, I mean, we're gonna have us a time!" he chortled.

They did.

They parked the pickup in the dark lee of the deserted pavil-ion on the blustery shore of Lake Wichita. Rigger and his Ruby stayed in the cab. It was not until Roseanne and Britt had gone some distance that they were able to lose the sounds of them.

Britt found a grassy clearing in the hollow near the irrigation ditch. He drew her down to him hungrily and his big hands went spreading, knowing, seeking. He took her harshly, explosively, and when he had done, he lost her.

They lay still in the grass, spent, side by side, saying noth-ing, feeling the sate of physical release and at the same time the troublesome denial of complete satisfaction. Britt suddenly wanted to say, "I'm sorry" to her—and yet, with some sadness, he knew she would never understand. She was accustomed to this halfhearted, empty result. She was calloused to ecstasy. It made no difference to her, he knew. He lay there alone within his shell, staring into the pricked cloth of the night sky, at the myriad lights shining through, and he knew suddenly why all this had added up to fruitless nothing, even after so long a fast. The emp-tiness was in him because all through the moments, from the first feeling seconds to that instant of lashing, straining comple-tion, Marcy had been in him, with him, around him, and not this one, at all. What had transpired here had been only the surface thing, counterfeit, the mere function performed from without, never from within. Marcy Kates had been with him all the way. Whatever she had done to him, whatever the knowing of her had brought to him, he did not know. She had drawn nevertheless her circle of full possession around him and no other could pen-etrate the ring. Suddenly he was here and he wanted to say, "I'm sorry" to the conquered, still form at his side, but he knew she would only be surprised and later troubled, that she would not be able to understand how a man who had taken her so violently, so hungrily, could in the next instant be sorry for the satisfaction that must be in him.

By the time they got back to the truck Rigger and Ruby were sitting in the dark, side by side, and the bottle had changed hands many times. They were both sloppy drunk. Britt drove back to town. He let the women off on a downtown corner and headed the truck for home. Rigger was fast asleep, his head lolling loosely against the back of the seat. He snored and smelled of cheap perfume and rotgut liquor. Britt eased back and watched the level shafts of the headlights reaching along the curving road.

When Britt came into the kitchen next morning only Marcy. was there. She was standing at the stove preparing the breakfast. As he entered she glanced only briefly at him, raising her arm to brush back a strand of hair from smoky eyes.

"Hi," he said quietly.

Her eyes seemed to spark slightly; she made no response. Her single glance had read his face. Britt was feeling curiously ashamed and a jab of resentment at her open condemnation prodded him. It was pretty clear Rigger had told her most of what had happened the night before. Probably he'd been bragging all over the place. As quickly and as unobtrusively as he could he crossed over to the table and took his place.

Marcy continued silently with her chores, saying nothing, working with a kind of fevered concentration, as if there were some inner compulsion driving her to bury herself from him in her job.

He sat straight in his chair, waiting for the food, his eyes anxious on her. He wanted suddenly, desperately, to reach out, to touch her, to renew the old contact with her. If he only could tell her how it had really been, then she would know and understand. In a moment she took the coffeepot from the burner and brought it to the table. Bending over, she poured the steaming liquid into his cup. Her glance slanted and met his eyes for a second.

"I reckon you can use some coffee right off this mornin'," she said coolly.

"Marcy, I—" His hand rose and hung arrested.

She straightened and looked at him, surprised. His face was contorted and the eyes were almost pleading. There was a faint softening in her.

"Reckon there ain't nothin' needs sayin'," she said quietly. "So you and Rigger went and had yourselves a time last night. O.K.,—that's good! I reckon you had fun." She had turned back to the stove. "That's O.K. Have all the fun you can get, I say. It's a damned short life, might as well enjoy yourself." She twisted her head and peered at him but her smile was artificial and quickly contrived.

He sipped at the hot coffee and stared into the muddy mix. The door to the bedroom opened and Rigger came into the room. He wore nothing except a pair of Levis, which he was working to button as he came to the table. He yawned loudly and scratched his belly. When he looked down at Britt there was a faint conspiratorial smirk. He glanced over at his wife, but she had her face averted, turned away from him. With a slight shrug Rigger dropped into his chair.

"Christ!" he muttered, rubbing puffed eyes. "Let's get some of that damn coffee over here pronto!"

She brought the pot over and poured a cupful. He ignored her and studied Britt curiously.

"You sure look O.K. this morning, big boy." He found his head and his fingers scraped on his scalp. "I'm all wore out."

Marcy did not join them for the meal. She remained in front of the stove, busying herself with the utensils. The eggs and bacon sizzled in the pan and their hiss grew loud, filling the whole of the room with the sounds and smell of hog fat burning. Britt and Rigger sat silent. As Marcy worked, Newt Kates came to the back door and let himself in. He made no greeting as he came to his place. He glanced once speculatively at Rigger, then over at Britt, and there was the shadow of scorn on his face.

Marcy ladled the food to their plates. She retreated to the sink and stood with her back to them, staring out of

the window, out over the reach of the place, her gaze somewhere far off in the neutral sweep of the land.

The breakfast passed without conversation. When they had finished, the men shoved back and smoked. Marcy came and began to clear the dishes away. As she came abreast of Rigger he reached out suddenly and circled her waist, pulling her thigh hard against him. She jerked away abruptly and hurried on with her work. She had made no sound. Rigger grinned wryly at Britt and his eyebrows lifted in mock surprise. Newt Kates sat still, his eyes sharp, not missing anything. When she had pulled away like that he glanced at Britt and there was the thin trace of a meaningful smile. Color darkened Britt's face. He forced his attention to the little puddle left in his coffee cup.

Rigger got up and, reaching high above his head, he stretched, grunting. His ribs came pressing, ridging on the smooth skin. With an explosive sigh he dropped his arms and slumped. "Well," he said spiritlessly, "reckon that does it."

Britt pushed himself to his feet. "I'll be gettin' on with my work."

Only Newt made no effort to rise. He glanced from one to the other with idle interest, his face devoid of expression. He fished in his pocket and found a match, snapped the head from the stem, splitting it lengthwise with his thumbnail, and, using the sliver, began to work on his teeth. Britt had left the room, pushing out into the bright warm sunlight.

Marcy, her hands churning the dishwater, paused. She watched him through the window, tracing his course toward the room in the barn.

Rigger had stepped up behind her, watching over her shoulder. When Britt had gone from view he turned and glanced down at his brother. "There's one good ole boy," he said.

Newt snagged a stray morsel from between his teeth and flicked the bacon blob from the tip of the stick across the room carelessly. "Reckon so," he said smoothly.

Rigger sat down. His eyes traveled lazily over the rounded hump of Marcy's back, bent over her work. There was a faint surge in him and he cleared his throat noisily. "You ain't griped about last night, are you?"

She stiffened slightly but did not take her hands from the sloppy water. "No," she murmured. "Makes no difference to me."

"That's the stuff. Don't get nobody nowheres gettin' sore about things they ain't concerned with."

Rigger pulled himself from the chair and came up close behind her. His left hand crept around to the front of her and his palm cupped the fullness of her breast. For a silent moment he nuzzled her tentatively under the ear. "Don't do no good at all," he repeated.

She stood very straight, making no effort to stop him. Her eyes were hard and she held them very fast on the rectangle of the little barn door. Suddenly, surprisingly, he left her and went back across the room to their bedroom door. He turned and glanced at her and there was the death of interest in his eyes. "I'm fixin' to take me a nap," he announced. The door closed behind him.

Marcy went over to the table. Her eyes brushed Newt's face. She kept them neutral and expressionless. He leaned back and watched her casually.

"Reckon Rigger and the big boy had themselves a time in town last night."

"Reckon so."

She leaned across the table, trying to reach Rigger's cup, her left hand flat on the oilcloth, supporting her weight. Newt came forward and put his right hand forth, covering her fingers. "That Rigger's a goddamn fool chasin' them whores all the time when he's got himself somethin' like you at home, Marcy."

She flushed and brought her head around, looking into his grim face. "That depends on how Rigger looks at it," she said.

"How come you stuck it out so long, kid? Why ain't you up and chucked the works before this? Dame like you'd have no trouble gettin' somebody else."

"I reckon I knowed what I was gettin' when I got him," she said quietly.

Newt suddenly began to stroke her hand. His fingers withdrew and he circled her wrist with his thumb and forefinger. "He'll up and kick you 'way the hell outta here one of these days," he prophesied gloomily. "He don't care for nothin', that one, and you know it. You know it, Marcy—same as me."

The ring around her wrist fell away and the pads of his fingers began to travel up and down her forearm slowly, probingly. Easily, yet positively, she took the cup and straightened, taking herself from his reach. "I reckon as how that's my worry, Newt," she said, looking down on him with steady eyes.

She had dismissed him and he knew it. He dropped back against the chair and rolled the matchstick to the far corner of his mouth. He watched silently as Marcy washed the last of the things. A noise from outside caught his attention. He twisted to see Britt Callum through the screen, piling some tools on the ground. He had pulled off his T shirt and the bright sun brought the deep tan of his big torso to richness. Newt glanced at Marcy. She was standing at the sink, and her eyes, too, were on Britt. Newt's gaze narrowed and slanted to the closed door to the bedroom. In the moment that followed he drew the matchstick from his lips and tossed it casually to the table and pulled out a cigarette. He lit it and got to his feet. He puffed rapidly a few times, making sure, and the cigarette found its usual place in the corner of his mouth. He crossed the little space between them. Leaning forward so that his lips were close by her ear, he gave his words to her. "You best be watchin' your step, girl, you and that guy. Rigger's gonna be raisin' all kinds of hell if he ever gets to sniffin' anything's up between the two of you. I'm tellin' you for your own good, hear?"

Marcy gave no indication if she had. Her gaze on Britt wavered and she closed her eyes. She heard the sounds of Newt Kates leaving the room, the slap of the screen door, the soft shuffle of his steps as he went down across the yard, skirting the area where Britt worked, going to the far end of the barn where the tractor was housed.

CHAPTER EIGHT

I
T WAS just a little after the noonday dinner several days later when Marcy came seeking him. He was in the little room, taking a few minutes' break, stretched out on the cot, cigarette in his lips, when she came to the door and tapped lightly. He raised himself and called her in. She stopped on the threshold and her smile set the bubbles on the rise in him.

"I didn't mean to bother you," she apologized.

"Just takin' a break."

She made no attempt to come into the room. "Rigger said I'd probably find you here."

He lowered himself to the pillow. "I'm gettin' real lazy." He grinned.

"Rigger said it was all right if you'd drive me to town this afternoon. There's things I need, food, stuff like that. Rigger can't manage yet with his hand."

Britt brightened. "Sure thing. I'll haul you to town. When do you want to go?"

"Right off, if it's O.K. with you. I'd like to have me the afternoon."

He swung off the bed and, coming up before the mirror, surveyed himself critically. The shirt was soiled and the Levis almost khaki-colored with the ingrained dust. "Gotta make myself purty first." He grinned. "I ain't so used to totin' ladies around. Gotta look good."

She giggled self-consciously. "I ain't so particular. Reckon I'm kinda used to dirt by now."

There was the keen edge of anticipation in him. "No." He glanced again at the mirror. "Can't be goin' off like this."

She turned and went outside. Once she had gone, he got the battered suitcase from under the bed. He had a brand-new pair of Levis and a couple of new T shirts he'd got in town the other night before he and Rigger had started their party. He stripped, tossing the dirty clothes off to the corner of the room. The new pants were stiff with the heavy dye, and as he pulled them on the legs felt boardlike and the copper rivets on the hip and rear pockets were cold dots on his flesh. The T shirt was snug and he tugged carefully, drawing it down over his chest. After he had carefully turned up the ends of the trousers an inch or so for cuffs, he put on his shoes and inspected himself. He looked pretty sharp. He ran his comb through his hair once or twice. The curls were stubborn and they plopped forward to their original position immediately. He was ready for a lady.

She wore a light summery dress and no hat. Her rich brushed hair was sleek and soft, full on her shoulders. As he brought the truck around the front of the house Rigger took his feet from the porch railing and leaned forward in his rocker, grinning down at him.

"Bet she'll wind up makin' you sit through one of them goddamn movie pitchers, boy. She's plumb nuts about them fool things."

She put her fingers on Britt's wrist and he stopped the truck. She craned out of the window and her question to Rigger was almost plaintive. "Could I—could we go to a movie?"

Rigger waved his hand expansively. "Go the hell where-ever you want," he said affably. "Place here ain't about to blow away. Have fun, Britt."

She took her touch away and the truck rolled forward, lurching along the rutted road to the highway. When the wheels had found the smooth paved surface they both settled back against the leather seat and sighed. It was so spontaneous an action, so unanticipated, they looked at each other and laughed.

She stretched her legs out lazily and closed her eyes. "Oh!" she breathed. "Gees, it's good to get off the place. It's been such a long time since I been anywhere."

He said nothing, just smiled at her radiant face. Her spirits were soaring and her mood touched him and there was in him a lighthearted airy feeling, new and strange and wonderful. Just this being with her, this sharing a little part of her happiness, was enough.

She was quiet, listening to the spinning song of rubber on pavement, letting her gaze go drifting over the rolling plain, seeing all the new freshness of the budding springtime as if she were seeing all this for the first time. The land was green and eager and full of promise. There was no need to say anything. He knew the things she saw, the thoughts she was thinking. He looked out over the countryside and saw birthing life even here in the hard-packed earth, the coming fertility struggling to assert itself in the tawny resistant crust that lay still and reluctant and Texas in the breathless day. Maytime was coming swiftly and the heat was quickening. As they rode steadily toward the distant looming cragline of the town, the cab of the truck grew close and thick with the hint of incipient summer.

The road turned sharp left, and as they came rounding the curve, the tires screaming their hysterical protest, she reached out suddenly and seized his arm. Britt cut their speed to an instant crawl. Her eyes were wide and shining on the field beyond the road. There, in solitary, brazen beauty, was a full-flowing sea of bluebonnets, nodding, bowing gracefully, caressed by the gentle faint breeze just come.

"Oh, stop a minute, Britt, please!"

The truck came to a halt on the roadside. Already she had her door open. She dropped lightly to the ground and went running into the open, splashing through the full blooms. He saw her kneel among them and all the rush of his warmth and hunger and need came flooding through him.

She rose, waving to him. Her head was high and even from here he could see the soft delicate arching of her throat, naked and creamy in the sunlight. He left the truck and made his way to her. She was laughing as he stumbled near her.

"You clumsy thing!" She held one of the flowers as she came to meet him. She raised the bloom high for his inspection? "Isn't that the most darlin' thing you ever did see?"

He took the flower from her and examined it gravely as if he had never seen a bluebonnet before. He gave the bloom back to her and stood watching as she stooped to gather a few into a slim blue-and-white bouquet. When she had all she wanted she straightened and he knew she was ready. Together they picked their way back to the truck. After they had resumed the trip she was very still in her corner of the cab. She held her few flowers carefully and there was in her eyes the soft shadow of the faraway dream.

She did her shopping while Britt leaned up against the drugstore wall, watching the people marching to and fro. There were others lolling near him, soldiers from the field, bored and lonely, cowmen come to town with their women for the day, now abandoned to unfamiliar devices, roughnecks and oil promoters clustered in sober discussion of common interests. Finally she came across the street, her arms full, the smile bright on her face. He took the bundles and they found the truck and stowed the purchases in the back.

"Where to now?"

She seemed to simmer in the warm pan of her enjoyment. "Oh, I don't care much. Let's—let's just drive around a while and look. Do you mind?"

He minded nothing, so long as she was there at his side. They drove out Tenth, out past the churches, out along the tree-lined streets, rolling slowly past the big beautiful inaccessible homes with their spread lawns, their carefully coaxed flower beds rampant in the declining April with iris and tulips and the first of the roses. They kept on, wandering out through the country-club district, where the homes were even grander, the flowers if possible even more beautiful. Suddenly they were far out of town, standing on the untidy wooden porch of the old pavilion, letting the breeze from Lake Wichita come blowing on them warm and strong and friendly.

She turned and sparkled at him. "Oh, Britt! It's all so grand! I've never had such a day, not ever!"

It was his idea to go get a beer after the movie that night. As they entered the place, Britt saw the woman Roseanne at the far end of the bar. While he and Marcy waited for service she looked up and saw him. He was sure she was going to leave her companion and come down the length of the place to him. Her eyes shifted rapidly and he knew she had seen Marcy with him, had put two and two together. There was tiny lift to her brows but she made no open sign. She stayed away. He smiled faintly and glanced down at Marcy.

She had not missed the byplay. Her eyes were clouded, and even though she knew he was looking down on her she kept her eyes on the mirror ahead and the reflection of that other woman. Slowly she brought her gaze to him and her expression was careful. "Friend of yours?"

"Met her once," he murmured.

Even though he certainly never made any bones about his past with her, had told her about some of the other women, even, she felt a kind of irritation in her that surprised and irked her. Not once in the past four years with Rigger Kates had she ever felt this way. And what had Britt's love life to do with her, anyway? She flushed and averted her eyes, fastening her sight on the glass of beer before her.

They talked about little inconsequential things. Finally the glasses stood foam-flecked and empty. She straightened.

"Well," she said reluctantly, "I reckon as how we best be headin' for home." She looked at him with a faint glimmer of hope, as if she were wishing he could think of something that might prolong the day, put off the unwanted hour of return. But he nodded slowly as his eyes found the fly-specked clock face on the wall.

"It's gettin' late," he agreed.

In weary surrender she took her purse from the bar and shoved it under her arm. She led the way out to the sidewalk. She went up the walk ahead of him, her head bent against the rising wind. He was close behind. He boosted her to the cab seat and went around to his side.

"Ready, set?" He grinned from the wheel.

"Go," she murmured, very low.

The place was dark when they came up the rutted path and edged the truck around the house to its place in the barn. When he had closed the doors, bolted them, and come out into the open windy yard, they stood sheltered from the blow by the jutting edge of the building. She was ahead of him a few steps, looking up the slow rise to the angled slant of the house. She was intent, as if she were reacquainting herself with the place, as if she had been gone a long, long time and now were not sure what changes might have been made in her absence. She turned and found him in the dark behind her.

"Britt, I want you to know I had a real nice time," she said softly. "I don't rightly know when I had me such a real nice time as I done today. Thanks."

He was smiling. She could see the whites of his teeth bright in the gloom. He came forward suddenly and his arms reached for her but she stepped back quickly and stayed him with her spread hand instantly. "Don't, Britt!" she whispered hoarsely. "Don't. It's no good that way. It'll only make trouble. It ain't right." She touched his arm briefly and went toward the house.

Britt heard the final click of the back door. There was no movement other than the uncertain wind as it muttered under the eaves of the barn roof. He let his body slump against the planked wall and lit a cigarette. In the darkness he felt the acute lonely emptiness in him. Now, in the full complete realization of what she had come to mean to him, there was in him the truth of her fears just uttered. She was right. There would only be trouble. Now that the thing had happened, he did not know what to do. He knew only that what had come to pass was right for him, for him and for her, and because it was so right, then it must be a good thing. Nothing could change or undo or alter the now promised pattern of their lives. There, the coal of his cigarette fanned to brilliance by the encouraging breeze, his face stroked by the fitful wind fingers, thinking of her, of himself, he thought, too, of Rigger Kates, who was her husband.

CHAPTER NINE

T HE IMMEDIATE days were difficult. The first May days arrived uniformly hot and the winds returned spasmodically. As the wheat crop grew close to harvest, the drift of dust was lessened; the plague of the thick, blinding, choking storms became more infrequent. On the place things went well. Rigger's hand was mending quickly. He still wore the cast, now dirtied and thick with grime. He did as little as he could, and if he were forced to the effort at all, he chose always to work with Britt.

Newt Kates stayed always on the rim of the circle. He made no attempt to come within, to be a part of the everyday group. He stood off to one side, watching them with those little hard eyes, masking his thoughts from them. He did not ignore them, but at the same time he did not enter into their association.

One afternoon Britt was busy working alone in the barn. Rigger had wanted some junk cleared out, old machine parts that had accumulated over the years. Britt worked as he generally did these hot days, stripped to the waist, and, as he grunted, struggling with the heavy rusted equipment, the smooth, bronzed spread of his back glistened with the oily wash of his sweat. He gave a rusted shaft a heave and came rearing, wiping the wet from his forehead on the back of his forearm. As he brought the arn down, his eyes came on Newt Kates, propped in the jamb of the door, eying him with interest.

"Looks like you done got yourself a chore." Newt's voice was slow, quiet, almost cordial.

Britt shrugged. "Yeah. Rigger was sayin as how he wanted this crap outta the way. It's one helluva job for a hot day, that's for sure."

Newt found his cigarette and fiddled with it until it was lit. The smoke plumed around his head, went drifting over his shoulder. "From the looks of you, you been used to doin' heavy work, I'd say."

Britt found a clear space on the pile of junk. He wiped his hands down the sides of his Levis and sat down. "I done a share in my time, I guess," he said.

Newt turned and flicked the butt far out into the yard. When he brought his attention back to Britt he saw he had left his place and was standing in the center of the floor. Newt's eyes slipped down the length of his figure, pausing momentarily on the bunching of the tight jeans. When he lifted his gaze he saw Britt's face coming to quick flame. Newt grinned broadly and made a vague gesture. "You been gettin' any lately?" he asked silkily.

"How do you mean?"

"Humping. You been gettin' any?"

Britt stared incredulously. His ears were playing tricks.

Newt shrugged. "If I had some of that muscle you're packin' around, I'd make damn sure it got exercised. No good lettin' it go to pot. Like to shrink up to nothin' if you don't use it ever so often."

Britt's face burned and he wheeled and turned his back on Newt. The crunch of the other man's step on the crust of the earthen floor brought him around sharply. Newt had come up close to him and his eyes were bright with curious intensity. He beckoned with a quick, short nod. "C'mere, big boy. Got somethin' to show you."

Britt responded automatically despite himself. Newt was busily unbuttoning the flap of his shirt pocket and now he drew out a little package. Quickly, fumblingly, he took the paper wrapping from whatever it was and thrust the thing into Britt's hand.

"Go on," he urged. "Go on, kid, take yourself a look-see." He retreated a single step and stood, his color high, watching closely as Britt looked down.

What Newt Kates had handed him was a collection of old picture postcards. They were thumbed and well worn from constant handling. They were not just ordinary scenic postal cards. Each photo was scratched and smudged and each dealt with the same subject. Some of them pictured nude women posed alone, but posed so that nothing was left to the imagination. Most of them showed naked men and women caught by the candid camera in all manner of erotic stances. In spite of the swift rise of embarrassment and revulsion that came, Britt was swept along by natural curiosity. A thickness came wedging in his throat as he went through the entire collection rapidly. Without comment he handed them back to Newt and stood uncertain, waiting guardedly. Newt wrapped the protective paper around his prize carefully. He stood there, holding the packet in his hand. His eyes when they rose to Britt's face were button-shiny and there was an odd slick on his lips.

"Pretty hot stuff, eh?" Newt gloated. He paused, waiting for agreement that never came. "I got 'em overseas. Get most anything overseas, anything you want. Ain't like it is here. You gotta be too damn careful here." He edged up to Britt and eyed him slyly. His grin seemed to ooze on his face. He nudged Britt. "Kinda gets you athinkin', don't it, big boy? Gets you kinda hot maybe, huh?"

Britt forced a swallow down a throat gone dry. He wanted to say something, to tell Newt Kates to get his slimy tail the hell out of there. Newt had begun to circle him slowly, studying him openly, speculatively, his grin hooked into place.

"Yeah, big guy like you oughtn't to go wastin' what he's got, I say. Get what you can, boy, while the gettin's good. If I had what you got—Christ! I'd be gettin' some all the time."

He was in front of Britt and his grin tapered to a smirk. His voice dipped and became suddenly wheedling, pleading, intense, almost intimate. "Bet you could tell about some pretty hot times you had, if you was a mind to. Whyn't you tell me about some, kid? Tell me about some of them broads you laid. Go on, go on, it's O.K.—I like hearin'. Don't you leave out nothin', either. I like hearin' stuff like that."

Newt put out his hand and his fingers touched Britt lightly on the thigh. Instantly the whole mass of disgust and horror burst through the yielding dam of Britt's control. It spumed forth and went spreading hot and white through him and his sight went blind in the glaring shine of Newt Kates's sweaty face. Savagely Britt struck out and caught Newt high on the cheekbone with his hard fist. He hit only the one time, furiously. Newt Kates spun away as if he had been jerked back by an unseen hand. He seemed to take off, to go flying through space, and the crack of his head against the barn wall was the sound of a rubber ball slammed against a backdrop. There was a splattering whisper in the stillness as the postcards rained down, scattering out over the floor.

Britt stood rooted. He raised his hand jerkily and stared at his knuckles, those same knuckles. There were no marks, no hurt, no bruises. He flexed his fingers carefully, testing. He felt as if he had hardly tapped the guy. Yet Newt Kates was far across the room, piled in a heap against the wall, staring at him stupidly.

Britt felt sick. Once again he had lost his temper, had smacked some character without remembering the other times. He went slowly across to Newt. The anger and revulsion had been dissipated in the single blow. Anxiety came nibbling at him. He had hoped things would not come to this. But Newt had kept it up, kept it up, had driven him too far. If only Newt had stayed away from him, none of this would have happened.

"You all right?"

Newt lowered his probing fingers from the throbbing cheekbone and stared up at Britt fearfully. He sat still, his hands now on each side of him, the fingers deep in the soft dirt floor, and the bleak look shaded and darkened and hate came seeding in his eyes. "You keep away from me!" Kates shrilled suddenly. "Don't you touch me! So help me, don't you hit me again!"

Britt backed off but he did not take his eyes from the collapsed figure. He retreated to the middle of the floor and stopped. The older man raised himself stiffly and got to his shaky feet. His lips worked nervously. He began to pick up the bits of scattered pasteboard. When he had got all of them he counted them through to make sure, then slipped them into his pocket and buttoned down the flap. He went past Britt, ignoring him, went out into the sunlight of the yard and disappeared.

Britt Callum stood confused, motionless. He listened. There was no sound. The world was as still as death. He sighed heavily and moved to the doorway and peered out across the fields. Far off in the distance he could see him making his way down along the lanes between the rows of new corn. Newt Kates was headed for his wheat field. Britt raised his hand and tugged at his lower lip thoughtfully.

Both Rigger and his brother were absent from the supper table that night. Marcy set the last of the dishes out and slipped into her place.

Britt smiled. "Just the two of us tonight?"

She shrugged. "Yeah. Rigger went off to town with a buddy of his, and he ain't come back. You know what that means." There was a tiny pause. She glanced at the closed door to Newt's room. "He's in there—in bed." She smiled. "He got a nasty bang on his face this afternoon." She looked at Britt and a faint giggle escaped her lips. "Boy, he's a mess!"

Britt's jaw tightened. "How—how'd he come to do it!"

She raised her brows and her left shoulder jogged. "I don't know. Says he slipped and fell in the field somewhere. Hit his face on a post. His cheek's all puffed up. That eye's gonna be as black as the ace of spades by mornin'."

Britt freed his breath carefully. He picked up his fork and speared a cut of meat from the platter. "He's a funny cuss," he murmured, and started to eat.

She eyed him gravely. "Yeah," she agreed. "You can say that again."

He glanced at her curiously. "What makes him—"

She cut him short with a sharp wave of her knife. Her head shook as she gestured to the closed door. "Lots of things," she said crisply. She raised her fingers, touching her hairline. Little beads of perspiration were bright under the kitchen light. "You know, it's sure gettin' hotter," she remarked.

"Will be from now on, I guess."

She settled herself with a grunt, shoving her chair back from the table to make leg room. "This here's the time I hate," she said slowly. "The heat! I don't know what's worse—the hot or the cold. One way or the other, it's a trial for fair." She paused, toying with a spare spoon. "It's a lot worse in Arkansas, though," she mused. "I can remember when we was there, in Smackover. We lived in an awful dump, house built right out over the swamp. We had everything, snakes and bugs and flies and mosquitoes, everything, and when it rained—it rained, brother! We was always afraid we was gonna be washed right out. Mamma just hated it. So did I. But Daddy, he never said. He was a hard-workin' man. He didn't never much care where we lived or how, just so's there'd be some work to do, work he liked."

"I never been in Arkansas."

"It ain't so much."

There was an easy pause between them. She took a proffered cigarette and they stretched back in their chairs and watched the bluish plumes wafting ceilingward.

"It's funny," she said suddenly. "You know, Rigger ain't never been nowheres." The thought rooted in her and expanded. "You'd think he'd get to wonderin' what it's like somewheres else. Gees, a man can go anywheres he wants, when he wants to. It ain't so easy for a woman. If I was a man I'd go and do everything. Why, I'd want to!"

Britt's eyes crinkled. "Reckon you would, Marcy." He regarded the ash intently. "There's lots of guys just plain satisfied with what they got, I reckon. They just ain't got no drive to get up and go. There's the other kinds, too, me. I guess I'm kinda like that song—old wild goose's brother, that's me."

"You *ain't* like that!" she said with hot vehemence. "I can tell! Them wild-goose fellas ain't nothin' but tramps, drifters. They ain't never in a spot long enough to leave a mark. It's like they was kinda sick or somethin'—they just can't stop, can't even settle down. They gotta keep on goin', goin', goin'. All the time they keep on movin', only they ain't really goin' nowheres. Sure, you knocked around, but you ain't like one of them, Britt. When the right time comes, then you'll hole up and stay put, you'll stick."

"I wonder."

She leaned forward and her eyes were grave on him. "I know! You take to the place here natural. You got roots that take quick hold. When you're out there workin', it's like the place here was a part of you. Why, you belong to the place already more'n Rigger or Newt does!"

He looked over her head to the bright blue of the sky framed by the window over the sink. "I guess I got a kind of feelin' for the earth in my hands," he said slowly. "There's somethin' livin' and real in the dirt. When I'm workin' I can feel it and hear it and there's a good warm feelin' that everythin's gonna be O.K., no matter what."

"Your folks was farmin' folks, wasn't they?"

"My mother came from Italy when she was a kid. They had a place there, her folks. But she came to America and never did get on a farm. She died when I was a kid."

"Your father?"

He hesitated. "He drifted here an' there. Wound up runnin' a gas station in New Mexico. He died a couple of years after my mother. Drank himself to death." Britt wet his lips. "I been on the road ever since I was twelve."

Marcy was silent for a long time. Then she said, "Britt, you ought to get a place of your own to work. My daddy always said life was hell unless a man was doin' somethin' he wanted to do for himself. When a man's got the job he likes he's bound to be satisfied. It's no matter about the money he makes or nothin' else, just so's the guy's doin' what he wants."

"Your daddy sounds like he was a smart man."

"Yeah—and a damn poor one."

"He didn't have the dough, maybe, but you said he was doin' what he wanted to do."

She apologized with a look. "I know." She nodded. "I can remember how Mamma's eyes used to get kinda soft watchin' him goin' off to work. She'd turn from the window and she'd be sayin' all hard-boiled-like, 'The old fool's gonna spend the rest of his days all covered with that damned oil, workin' like a slave, and in the end we'll all wind up in the poorhouse.' And then she couldn't keep from smilin' and she'd say, 'But bless his old heart, Marcy, he's doin' what he wants, and so long's we got us enough to eat and a roof to keep the rain from us and we get by, I reckon as how everything'll turn out all right.' "

"They must have been happy together."

Her eyes went soft. "I used to wonder as I got older how people could live so long together, whether they still loved each other or whether everything had just become a habit, that they just got used to each other, you know." She smiled slowly. "I remember once comin' across the two of them standin' out on the bridge that was over the swamp. It was along about sundown when the gold was splashed over everything, and one look at them and you knew the answers sure as shootin'. It was kinda like lookin' at one person, only there was two of them, of course. They didn't even have to say nothin' to each other—they just stood there and even their thinkin' was the same." Her voice trailed away. "I don't reckon as how Mamma could have gone on livin' too long after Daddy went. Somehow, after he died, most of Mamma was gone, too, and what was left behind wasn't enough to hold her here."

He sat watching her profile and the cigarette burned almost to nothingness in his fingers. He leaned forward suddenly and snuffed the bit in the saucer and he spoke very low. "You been lucky, Marcy, bein' part of somethin' like that. You got all good memories to fill you up inside."

She glanced at him and her eyes were warm and bright. "I know," she said quietly. A cloud passed close and the shadows darkened. "It's what I wanted out of all this." Her gaze had left him, went drifting around the room. "I wanted my life to be like that—only it ain't panned out the same, I reckon. Maybe it was me who loused up the deal somehow in the beginning somewheres. I don't know."

He felt helpless. His hand moved vaguely. "Marriage, I guess, is like horse racin'—a gamble. Sometimes you win, sometimes you don't. Sometimes it works out like with your ma and pa— lots of times it turns out like you said, like a habit, more. It ain't nobody's fault, it's just the way it works out in the end." She snorted and her eyes fired. "It must've been my fault!" she cried. "If I hadn't been such a damn fool, I could've gone on waitin' and held out. I didn't have to jump at the first chance without even thinkin' it out proper. No, first chance I get I run into the corral like a mare with a bee-stung behind!"

He said nothing. She looked at him steadily for moments and then she sighed. "Well, what's done's done," she said heavily. "It's my life and it'll work out somehow, I reckon, no matter what." She turned her head slightly. "I reckon it's time to clean up again," she said wearily.

He got to his feet and crossed to the door and stood there, gazing out over the shadowing back yard. She turned and watched him, wondering if he were going to say something more. But he made no comment. He went on outside and left her alone.

Newt refused to eat with them the following morning. She fixed a tray and took it to him. When she emerged from his room and closed the door she grinned at Britt. "His puss looks worse than ever," she reported jubilantly. "Boy, he sure picked himself up a shiner!"

Britt could not share her grin. His glance was anxious on the closed door. As she came to the table he took his eyes away and stared down into the thick black coffee. He could almost feel the smoldering hate in Newt Kates. He wished he'd come out of that room, come sit with them at the table so they could work out the problem in the open, so he could look into the other man's eyes and keep track of the thinking in him.

Britt ate his meal in troubled silence. She watched him curiously, wondering what was on his mind, why he remained so aloof, so distant this morning. She tried to think back over what they had been talking about the night before, wondering if she had said anything, done anything that could have gone amiss. There was nothing. Their talk had been general, so far as she could remember.

He nodded briefly and left as soon as he had finished. Glancing down at her unfinished meal, she shrugged. Her appetite had failed. Wearily, not rising, she began to gather the plates, scraping the remains into one dish, reaching over the table to bring them all in front of her.

She was stacking the plates when Rigger brought the pickup around the corner of the house. The engine raced and when she turned her head to peer through the screen all she could see at first was the billowing cloud of dust that came swamping the machine, swirling, striving to settle. She saw Rigger slide from the driver's seat and land easily on the ground. He slammed the car door and his arm raised in quick salute to Britt out there. He turned and glanced at the home, took a deep breath, and came to the door.

Marcy brought her eyes to the stack of dishes before her. She heard the door open behind her, smelled the sweat of him as he passed her. He moved around the table and dropped into Britt's chair. He scratched his unshaven chin and yawned. "What's for breakfast?"

"Same's always."

She got to her feet and turned up the stove fires under the remnants of the meal. "How'd it feel driving again?"

"O.K."

"Hand hurt any?"

"Stiff, that's all."

He watched her curiously as she worked. She wore a thin cotton dress and her feet were bare on the cool linoleum. He wet his lips. "Miss me?"

She glanced at him obliquely. "What do you think?"

"Smart talk this mornin', eh?" he scowled.

She made no reply. Rigger picked up his fork and began to trace little designs on the oilcloth. She brought the food over and set the plate down before him.

"Newt's gone and hurt himself," she said flatly.

Rigger stared up at her. "Bad?"

"No. He slipped and fell on a post. Got himself a shiner."

Rigger grinned. "Blacked an eye, eh?"

In spite of herself she could not withhold the smile. "It's a beaut!" she conceded.

Rigger glanced at the closed door. "He in there?"

"Yeah. Won't come out."

"Shy type." Rigger chuckled. Then he shrugged disinterestedly. "He'll get over it." He tasted his coffee and set the cup down with a clank. "It's cloudin' up fast. Looks like we might get some rain."

He ate rapidly, and when he sipped the coffee he made sucking noises. Standing behind him, she looked down on the smooth back of his neck, at the fine blond hairs there. As if he felt her gaze, he turned and glanced up at her. "I got that stuff you wanted," he said shortly. "It's out in the truck if you want it." He paused and frowned as she moved out into the center of the room. "Why the hell don't you sit?" She shook her head and he scowled. The sound of his eating resumed. He finished finally and shoved back from the table, stretching his legs. "Had me a lousy time in town last night," he grumbled. "Too damn muggy. Must be the storm brewin'."

She had not asked him for an accounting. She did not care. His eyes were clear and his skin was free of the sickly pallor that usually came in the wake of his prolonged excesses. She came behind him to pick up the plate. As she leaned over to reach for the dish he seized her suddenly and pulled her forward. His injured hand slipped behind her and pinned her close to him. With his free hand he reached up and shoved his fingers down inside her dress, seeking her breasts. She wrenched sharply, trying to free herself, but his hold was fast.

"No!" she cried. "No! Rigger, please!"

His fingers had found the nipple and the slow insistent chafing of his touch worked the wheels of her senses to movement against her desperate attempt at denial.

"No—please!"

He grinned and licked his lips. "Why not? Ain't nothin' so wrong with a man and his woman havin' themselves some fun, is there?"

Her quickening breath throttled her to silence. His grin wavered. "Is there?" he demanded. His fingers dug into the soft breast and she winced with pain.

"Please, Rigger—you're hurtin' me!" she whimpered.

"Now, that's a helluva lot better," he murmured. She had slumped suddenly, making no sound, abandoning her efforts to pull away from him. He toyed with her, found the buttons of her dress, and bared her all the way, putting his bearded face against her, rubbing the rough stubble of his beard against her body.

Her breath rasped. Frantically she fought against the rising responding tide within her. With all her heart she wanted suddenly to repel him, but he knew the levers of her control too well. She fought to hold the monitoring face of Britt Callum in her consciousness without realizing she was doing so. She felt the dress slipping from her shoulders and his hands on her and the vision warped and dissolved into slow nothingness. When Rigger rose sharply, upsetting the chair on the kitchen floor, she shut her burning eyes tight and yielded to the inviolable terms of the contract with the man whose driving touch possessed her.

The clouds hung low, muddied, slow-moving. There was little wind and the muggy, dank feeling persisted. Britt stood flanked by the slender green stalks of the new corn and pulled the T shirt free from the tight band of the Levis. He drew the thin covering high on his chest and stood patting the sticky flat of his hard belly. He drew the shirt down and sighed, returning to his labors. Slowly he went along the row, breaking the hard-packed earth at the base of each plant. Later on he would retrace the course with the watering can, feeding them the needed moisture. Sounds vague and formless came floating through the weighted stillness. He straightened and shaded his eyes. Rigger was over by the barn, waving his bandaged hand, motioning for him to come in from the field. He grunted and glanced irritably along the unfinished row. He had hoped to get the job done in case the rain did come. He swung the hoe over his shoulder and started back along the cleared aisle.

Rigger was balanced on an old sawhorse in the shade of the barn. He was swinging his short legs lazily as Britt came up. The grin was spread all over the little guy's map. "Hiya, big boy! How the hell 're ya doin'?"

Britt set the hoe against the barn and squatted down in the shade. "What's on your mind?"

"Nothin'," Rigger said blandly. "Just felt like bullin' a spell." He caught the faint scowl. "Why, what's up?"

"I was hopin' to get that job done."

"Aw, hell." Rigger dismissed the cornfield with a desultory wave. "Forget it. You can do it tomorrow or the next day. You take workin' too damn serious."

Britt said nothing. He sighed and eased himself from the squatting position and sat up against the wall, crossing his long legs in front of him. He passed his hand over his forehead and brought the palm away glistening. "It's sure gettin' damn hot," he complained.

Rigger measured the thick skies. "Clabberin' up for a shower, looks like."

"We can use it."

"Yeah."

Britt glanced up at him curiously. "You have yourself a time in town last night?"

"Nah—rotten. I was pooped. Too hot."

"Happens sometimes."

They slumped into familiar silence. Britt put his fingers at the back of his neck and rubbed, yawning. "That corn's goin' pretty good."

"Needs water, from the looks of it."

"I'll get some there, if the rain don't do the job." Rigger's eyes drifted slowly over the place. They came to a lingering pause on the distant wheat field. "Sure hope this blow don't get at that wheat," he muttered. "Ain't long now till harvest." His gaze lingered on the spread. "Newt ain't workin' today," he added.

"Yeah, I know."

"Fell and got himself a shiner. She says it's a corker."

Britt picked up a bit of twig and began snapping it carefully, breaking the stick into tiny segments. "Newt's a funny guy," he said slowly, carefully.

"Ain't nothin' so *funny* 'bout him, I can see."

"I didn't mean it that way. I mean he's kinda different, somehow."

"He's one mean sonofabitch!" Rigger said sharply. "He just ain't worth the shootin'. I sure wish to hell he'd pack up and dear out."

"Why don't he?"

"Who knows?" Rigger shrugged. His tone was weary. "My daddy owned this here place and another one down yonder a piece. He died just before the car came on and the other place was Newt's, see? I was here and he was there. Well, along comes the war and Newt got himself drafted. So he sold his place and we put in together here. I wasn't married then and it looked like we could both work this place O.K. With him gone I could still keep the place goin'." There was a pause. "They wouldn't take me. They took Newt." He grunted. "He was sure sore. He didn't want to go nohow. That ole boy sure tried all kinds of ways to get out, but they took him anyway."

"That's funny."

"What?"

"You sayin' he tried to beat it. He talks Army a lot now. I figured he liked it."

"The hell he did!"

Distant rolls of thunder sounded far off. Both men turned their heads slightly, listening. Rigger glanced down. "She's acomin', boy."

Britt saw the faraway lightning flashes. In a moment Rigger's words recaptured his attention.

"The war done hurt Newt bad. Oh, he's always been a sorehead, goin' off into them black sulks of his, fussin' all the time, wantin' everything his way. Only, when he came back from overseas, somehow he was worse. He's downright mean all the time."

The wind had begun. It came from all directions, gusting, fingering the things of the earth rudely. Overhead the clouds began to bank; they turned inky black and ominous, evil, with curious whorls and rounded, like a field of dark beehives, turned upside down.

Rigger hesitated again. He motioned to the dark scalloped mass and his face was sober. "Gonna be a good one when it breaks." They watched the gathering sky silently. Rigger glanced at Britt and then up to the house. He could see Marcy's head through the kitchen window and the sudden remembered feel of her naked against him brought the sweat quick along his brow. He hurried on about Newt.

"I ain't never knowed much about what did happen over yonder," he said. "Newt ain't talked much about it. He got himself a dose of clap or somethin' a couple of times. The second or third round finished him. Know what I mean?" He glanced down at Britt to make sure. "Some Eyetalian broad fixed him good. Women ain't no damn good to him no more, see? He ain't nothin' now but a goddamn shell. His head's still bustin' with ideas, only it don't do him no good, see?"

Britt wet his lips. "So that's it!" His eyes squinted. "The poor damn bastard!" he said. "The poor damn bastard."

"Funny thing," Rigger mused. "Every time me and Marcy has us some fun, he's always meaner afterward." He straightened and looked at Britt. "Once, when we was first hitched, he tried somethin' with Marcy. Caught her in the barn and tried. Course, it wasn't no use. Nothin' happened—nothin' could. Sure scared hell outta her. We had one big bust-up then, batted each other all over the yard here. I damn near killed him. I wanted to. I would have, I reckon, only Marcy conked me with a shovel." He grinned ruefully. "Knocked me colder'n a witch." He sobered. "I reckon it was bettern' coppin' life in the pen, at that." Rigger slid to his feet and hitched his jeans tight. "He don't bother her so much now, far as I know. She ain't said much and I ain't had no time to pay much attention. I ain't worried. He'd just fool around, anyway. It ain't as if he could do anything, after all." Rigger stretched lazily and scanned the sky. Thunder rolled intermittently and off to the west they could see the blue-white lightning shafts come jabbing earthward in increasing frequency. "She's acomin', big boy, and she's acomin' fast!"

Britt scrambled to his feet. "I best get them tools inside."

Rigger watched him go, swinging toward the lanes of corn, stooping now and then, gathering the scattered pieces of equipment. Rigger was tired; he turned and made his way to the house.

Marcy had been watching them talking out there. Rigger was doing most of the chatter. She wondered suddenly with a sharp stab if he were telling Britt about what they'd been doing a little while back. He was pretty free with his mouth. She had not cared so much before. Before there was only Newt, and every time it happened Newt knew anyhow. But with Britt it was different.

Rigger stepped inside but did not glance at her. "Storm's comin' fast," he growled. "Best get that window down."

She closed the pane. Cautiously she opened the door to Newt's room. He was on top of the bed in his shorts. When he looked at her his face was twisted and ugly, made more evil-looking by the livid blue-black of his eye.

"I gotta shut the window," she offered. "There's a storm comin'."

His eyes shifted slightly as she crossed the room to tug the frame into place. When she straightened and glanced over at him stretched out like that sympathy welled in her. "You feelin' any better?"

"If I am, it ain't your fault," he muttered. "A body can't get no rest round this dump. Not with you and that damn fool squallin' and gruntin' like a pair of hound dogs in heat."

She stiffened and her face flushed deep. "You got a dirty filthy mouth, Newt Kates!" she rasped. "All you ever got to do is make dirty nasty pictures in your wicked brain! I ain't never heard tell even of a man so rotten as you!"

"Hey." He was nodding at her, trying to entice her closer to the bedside.

She stayed where she was. "What do you want now?"

"Tell me somethin', that's all. Hey. You like it better with the big guy, with that Britt fella? He's better'n Rigger any day, eh?"

Her lips were bloodless against the harsh barrier of her teeth. "God, how I hate you, Newt!" she spat. "I wish—I wish you'd busted your ugly head wide open, that's what I wish!"

Newt arched his body on the bed and bounced suggestively, grinning at her. Everything in her strained for action. She wanted to reach down and slap his face as hard as she could; she wanted to get her nails into him, to claw his eyes, his nose, those nasty lips into bleeding ribbons. The moment dissolved. She was used to him and his ways by now. She marched stiff-legged to the door and went out, slamming the panel as hard as she could in her wake, taking her pleasure from the explosion that came blasting in her eardrums.

The storm broke swiftly. There was a brilliant splitting in the sky, a swift-running jag of violence, and the darkness came rushing in and closed down the world. The thunderclap split sharp, paused for a moment, then came crashing down on the house, trembling its foundations, rattling every movable piece. The crack went rolling, swelling, echoing over the flat outside without destination or definition. The wind came from nowhere and was a gale. It howled over the fields, smiting against the house, pushing, shoving, pulling at the scarred timbers as if its sole purpose was to level, to destroy and obliterate any standing thing before it. The rain began without preamble. It came hammering at the frame, beating on the earth savagely, and muddy streams came cascading from the roof of the house and barn, splattering, flooding out over the resistant pack of the ground.

Marcy trembled and turned her back to the window over the sink. "I hate these things!" she cried. "I just can't stand 'em!"

Rigger scowled. "Stop actin' like a goddamn fool!" he shouted.

Britt wanted to go across the room and take her into his arms, to shelter her, to comfort her.

They winced as another brilliant flash illuminated the room. They waited for the thunderclap. After an endless delay it came, the ripping, tearing sound of boards pulled loose, the hesitation, the crash leaden and heavy on the house, on their ears. The wind grew wilder. Rigger got up and went through the house to the screened front porch. He stood, his legs apart, staring at the lone tree between the house and the highway. Its limbs flayed and whipped, a mad silhouette against the raving sky. The sun hung low in the west, setting, and the sky between the storm and the earth was a band of blue and red and pink and yellow. Off to the east the angry mottled clouds had turned to an odd greenish color. The door slammed shut and he glanced back at Britt, coming up behind him.

Rigger made a wry face. "I don't like the looks of them clouds." He indicated the eastern bank. "They got hail in 'em." He hesitated. "Get the wheat."

Britt stared. The color was unusual. Everything was unreal, the greenish sky, that band of brilliance ahead, and the wind, immense, tearing at him, clutching. He went past Rigger as if he were being drawn forth. He pushed open the screen door and stepped down into the front yard, out into the maelstrom. The wind came rushing at him, striking him, pummeling. He braced his legs and stood solid, letting the warm wet wind arms fling themselves about him, holding him. Rigger had followed him into the yard and stood uneasily nearby. Off in the distance flashes jabbed at the naked earth and now and then there was a chain reaction, one jagged bolt leading to another until it seemed within seconds that the whole roof of heaven was split asunder, revealing for the instant the awesome brightness of the world beyond the world. Lightning struck the earth close by and Rigger started violently. Britt laughed. Rigger's face was ashen, his eyes wide, struck with his fear.

"I'm gettin' the hell inside!" he yelled.

Britt watched him go curiously. It was the only time he had ever seen Rigger turn tail. Every man had a sneaking unholy fear in him of something. With Rigger he knew now it was for the thing he could not touch, couldn't fight with his bare fists.

After a moment Britt returned to the wind. He threw his head back and let the force batter him full-faced, surrendering himself to the assaulting raping passion of the thing. His hair was tousled, buffeted, and when he parted his lips the wind became a brush, cleaning his teeth, swabbing his throat. Another bolt jammed earthward nearby. He started. Maybe he ought to take cover, too. There's no percentage actin' like a damn fool. He turned and went up the steps to the porch. Rigger was over in the doorway to the hall. Silently they watched the storm spend itself. The green clouds had moved farther eastward, away. The wheat would be safe this time. The skies seemed to lighten gradually. The rains stopped as quickly as they had begun and over toward the west there was a little blue, purpling slowly in the end of the day.

"It's most done," Rigger said. He peered out to the crush of the yard, already drying. "Hell, not enough to make much difference," he remarked disappointedly.

They waited a few short minutes. The winds failed swiftly. Rigger glanced at him and grinned. "Well, you gotta admit, when we have 'em in Texas, we have 'em!" He was standing spraddle-legged, grabbing at the crotch of his Levis, tugging them down. "Tight sonsofbitches!" he grunted. As they turned and started for the kitchen, he chuckled.

"Don't matter they grow short or tall in Texas, Britt, so long's you're a good middle man."

Rigger squinted, then laughed loudly.

Marcy went into the bedroom and shut the door, blocking the sights and sounds of them from her. The storm had left her nervous and edgy, and Newt, once again at the table with them, saying nothing, just feeding his ugly face, irritated her. She let herself slump against the door and closed her eyes. She felt tired all over, washed out. There were little furrings along the network of her nerves and little tappers seemed to be working along the sensitive track of her spine. She put up her hand and pushed the hair from her sticky forehead. When she opened her eyes her sight was on the disordered bed. She stayed as she was for a long moment, staring at the twisted sheets, at the summer blanket half on, half off, dragging on the floor. The bunched pillow was humped in the troughed center like a battered pylon. Wearily she moved. She skirted the end of the bed and went to the dresser.

The surface was untidy with his things and hers. She moved her hands among them, separating them, setting hers on one side, his on the other. She stared at the curling-edged snapshots of her mother and father stuck in the cracks between the mirror and the frame and sudden salt stung her eyes. There was in her a momentary instant hunger for them. Hastily, defensively, she backed away.

She went across the room and sat down on the side of the unkempt bed and peered around. Here Rigger Kates had brought her that first morning so long back. Little had changed with her coming, little had altered in the four years. Here on this bed he had taken her that first time, here every time since—how many times? There was a smear on the pillowcase; she reached down absently and touched the mark with her fingernail, but it was hard and crusted and dry. She wet her lips. Her life with Rigger was symbolized in that mark. She was surprised how little else she could remember their sharing in their time together. She sat limp, sending her gaze across the room, through the windows to the now placid dullness outside. There was utter stillness in the wake of the storm, as if life itself had been snatched up and carried off in the tight arms of the fury. Dimly her ears picked up the sounds of talking in the other room, Rigger's voice hurried, the tone high-pitched and strident, Britt's low, fluted, soft, lazy-warm. She closed her eyes, working to shut away the higher tone, to hold onto the gentle flow of the other. In her mind's eye she could see him at the table, sprawled easily, the T shirt tight, hugging his chest, his thumbs hooked, his big hands hung from the belt loops of his Levis, his eyes liquid and deep, steady and sure, smiling.

Marcy Kates suddenly opened her eyes and stared at herself in disbelief in the mirror beyond the end of the bed, and her breath died in her throat. "I'm in love with him!" she whispered aloud.

The sound of her alien words, the very realization, stunned her. She glanced hastily, guiltily around the room, and she went to meet herself. Setting her palms on the edge of the dresser-top, she bent forward. In her face there was color she had never seen before. Her eyes were bright and clear, their flame fanned to high brilliance by the quick sharp wind of truth. She drew herself straight and tried to fight down the rising tide of surety that came swamping her.

"It's true!" she murmured. "I'm in love with Britt Callum!"

The woman before her wore an intent, eager face. She stared deep into the eyes and read the naked confirmation. There was growing in her now the tree of exultation, fierce-rooted with certainty, flowering with the bud of peaking excitement, and she breathed deeply of the sweet perfume of its blossoming. And, as she looked upon its massing strength, she saw coming too, the swift-reaching thing, twining around the trunk, reaching along the budding limbs, this mistletoe, this delicate, sapping parasite that fed hungrily; and as it grew and embraced the mother tree with its choking desperation, there came from the growth thin garlands of black flowers and she knew the vine by the name of fear.

CHAPTER TEN

I N THE DAYS that followed the storm Marcy Kates fought desperately to crush down this new, terrifying restlessness that had come to her. She was frightened, guilty in the possession of her incredible knowledge. She tried to keep the traces from her manner, from her eyes, her face. As she moved about her duties around the house, in the long hours when they were outside, she waged a ceaseless battle, striving to put away from her the crowding thoughts of him. She frantically tried to rationalize her sense of failure to Rigger, to oust the trespasser emotion, to reaffirm the solid truth of her status.

Mealtimes were difficult. She thought she could not hold her clamps firm when the three men were grouped around the table, their eyes waiting, expectant on her. She kept herself busy, her face from them. She denied the firing source of his eyes; she avoided Rigger's always derisive gaze; she was ever alert to the possible discovery in Newt's shrewd, speculative stare. Only when they had finished their eating, when they went off and left her alone with her chores, dared she allow herself to relax a little.

In the silent sanctuary of the bedroom she could let herself go. The tears came at times; she gave vent to them, encouraged them, praying their fierce flow might bring an easing to the awful tension in her. She knew somehow things could not go on like this. These sessions did little good. Mercifully through all this Rigger let her alone. She knew instinctively that if he once tried to touch her, to reach forth to take her as was his right, she would crumble. Everything was massed, cored in her, fear, confusion, dread, happiness, sadness, love, and numbness.

Cora Winters was no fool. She took one look at Marcy as she came into the kitchen and knew something was up. "How's everythin' goin'?" she greeted.

Marcy had heard her footsteps in the hall but had not risen from her place at the table. She managed a shaky smile and waved to the opposite chair. "Good to see you, Cora." She hesitated. "Everythin's O.K."

Cora caught the infinite weariness in the girl's tone, the tremble in her hands now as she worked to light a cigarette. "You're lookin' kinda puny, girl. Been feelin' poorly?"

Marcy shook her head sharply. "No, no, I'm all right. It's just—well, I ain't been sleepin' so good. Change of seasons, maybe—what with summer comin' on and all."

"Summer ain't comin' on as fast as all that, child." Cora felt a stab of sympathy and reached over, putting her crusty palm on Marcy's hand on the oilcloth. The hand was feverishly hot. "What's botherin'?"

"Nothin'."

Cora took her hand away and shrugged. "If you don't want to talk—"

Marcy swallowed hard. This was no day for Cora Winters to come pokin' around. "Talkin' ain't gonna do no good," Marcy said quietly.

There was a noise on the front porch and Cora Winters glanced down the hallway with beading eyes. "That Rigger been up to somethin' more? Been actin' up?"

Marcy shook her head. "It ain't him. He's been O.K."

"Newt?"

Marcy turned her face. "Ain't nobody. Nobody but me."

Cora Winters frowned. The girl wasn't even makin' sense. She decided to change the subject and cast around in her mind for a new tack. "How's your hired fella doin' these days?" It was

the quick way that Marcy's face swung back, the peaking brightness in her eyes that gave the show away. Cora Winters caught
her breath and stared across the table at her neighbor. "It's him!"
she whispered incredulously. "Ain't it?"

Marcy did nothing; she had no need to do anything, to
answer, even. Cora Winters had been utterly unprepared for this.
She kept staring at the girl, working swiftly to rearrange the pattern of her thinking. There was a look of dull misery on the girl's
face that hurt. Cora Winters got up from her chair and moved
to the sink and stood there looking out over the flat carpet of
the brown earth. She stood remembering back, seeing Marcy
as a bride, trying so damn hard to make a home here, battling
from the very start for something too good to be true. She had
watched the slow decline into mockery of life with Rigger Kates.
The memory scenes kept changing swiftly but the face of Marcy
Kates remained constantly centered. She saw that face changing
slowly, the shadowing eyes, the thinning cheeks, the paling lips.
She had seen the life draining away, sucked by the ever demanding hunger of Rigger Kates and his selfishness. A gigantic wave of
anger against Rigger Kates came swamping in her. Cora Winters
shuddered and blinked her eyes.

"It ain't gonna come to nothin'," Marcy was saying thickly.

Cora Winters did not answer, did not turn from the sink.
She was thinking still of Rigger Kates, not in anger now, but
coldly, surely. She'd known the Kates boys for years. She knew
what made them tick. She knew, too, without a doubt, that Rigger
Kates would kill Britt Callum if he ever so much as got wind of
this. Cora Winters bit her lip. "You mustn't do nothin' foolish,"
she suddenly heard herself say.

"Nothin's gonna happen," Marcy said. "He's a nice guy. I
never met no one like him before. He ain't like the others."

"He's a man, ain't he?" Cora Winters wheeled at the sink and
her mouth was tight. "He's like the rest, don't you kid yourself.
You go doin' somethin' foolish and you'll be sorry!"

"I know what I'm doin'," Marcy said unconvincingly.

"I hope so." Cora came to the table and for a moment her fingertips touched Marcy's shoulder. "I ain't up on these things," Cora Winters said slowly. "I ain't never been in love with nobody, not even with Fred, not really. I don't know what to say." She took her fingertips away. Confused, she crossed the room to the hallway door and hesitated, then turned and looked back with muddied eyes. Marcy was still sitting there and she was smiling faintly.

"Thanks, Cora," Marcy said quietly. "Don't go worryin' 'bout me."

Cora Winters frowned and straightened. "I gotta get on back to the place," she said brusquely.

Marcy went down to the front of the house with her and stood beside the old Plymouth until Cora had the engine running and was ready. "Thanks for comin' by, Cora."

"That's all right, kid." Cora Winters reached up and touched the fingers on the window frame. "You take it easy, see?" She gulped, trying to think of something right to say. "Look, Marcy. If anything ever happens—well, you know—if there's anythin' me or Fred can do—well, you know where the place is. You just come arunnin', hear?"

Marcy smiled weakly. "Thanks, Cora. Ain't nothin' gonna happen, believe me." She took her fingers from the window and locked her hands together and looked out over the roll of the land. "I ain't a fool. It's just somethin' I reckon I got to go through."

"Everythin'll work out," Cora contributed laxly.

"Sure. Sure it will."

Cora raced the engine and put the car into slow movement. " 'By, now," she called with a short wave. Once the car had gained the pavement Cora Winters glanced back. Marcy Kates was standing where she had left her, watching her go. Cora Winters breathed freely for the first time. She felt better, a helluva lot better, away from that mess.

Marcy went up the few steps to the porch. The sound of the car had faded out. It was very still around the place, no sign of anyone. She felt a little better for having told an outsider, even Cora Winters. She went on down the hall to the kitchen. Only when her gaze went ahead of her, on through the back screen, and came to Rigger and Britt going side by side toward the fields, did she falter. She felt some of the confidence go seeping from her and the little hint of disquiet come back. Hastily she reset her control, clamping her hold tight. Somehow, some way, things would work out right, she told herself. They had to.

CHAPTER ELEVEN

A ROUND three o'clock that following Saturday afternoon the three of them climbed into the truck and started for town. Rigger's hand was fit now and it was he who drove this time, with Marcy wedged down between the men and Britt mashed into the corner, holding himself small so she would not be crushed. It was hot and muggy and the vapor shimmered mercurially on the distant flats. There was only a trace of breeze; the sky was cobalt and clear.

"It's a scorcher," Rigger grunted.

Britt sighed. "Sure is."

"I'm right glad we're gettin' into town at last," she said.

Britt was silent. He was sharply conscious of the close feel of her thigh against his; awkwardly he tried to relocate his legs so that the pressure would be lessened.

She turned her head and smiled up at him. "Crowdin' you?" She shifted, trying to make room, but they were packed tight together.

"Naw, it's O.K." He chuckled. "I figured I was crowdin' you."

She flushed. The big hardness of him was against her; she could not escape the warmth of him.

Rigger was sitting forward on the edge of the seat, his forearms laid on the round of the steering wheel, his fingers curved, hooked on the rungs. He glanced at them with a grin. "Ain't much better'n a pack of goddamn sardines."

Marcy surrendered herself to the closeness and tried to relax. She closed her eyes. Britt sneaked little glances at her profile. Her long lashes dusted her cheeks and in slack repose her face was a little-girl face, clear and open and defenseless. He felt the thickness taking hold in his throat and coughed noisily.

"It's that bastard dust comin' up again." Rigger said. "Gets down there, boy!"

Britt peered past her to the man at the wheel and touched his lips with his tongue. "Yeah, it's sure lousy."

There was a long silence. Rigger drove hard. Each time the truck leaned for a curve their bodies weighted, packing tighter. Marcy opened her eyes. They were rounding the turn where the bluebonnets had been the other time. The merciless sun had seared the field to death brown already. She glanced at Britt. He was watching the road ahead, staring dully at the weaving black macadam strip. There was no sign in him that he had remembered too.

They put the truck in a parking lot for the day and grouped on the corner of Tenth and Ohio, working out the plan for the day. Rigger had said he was just going to bat around and see what was cooking. Marcy wanted to shop, to see all the things in the stores. Britt had no plan. He would just knock around, he said. They agreed to meet on the corner of Scott and Ninth, across from the Kemp Hotel, about seven for supper somewhere. They scattered.

Britt would have enjoyed going along with her. That was, of course, impossible. So he had nothing to do. He walked idly around the streets for a while, just watching the people, looking in the store windows. He found himself on Ohio Street finally. He went past the Red Club. His straying eye caught a glimpse of Rigger laughing and drinking beer with some men. He had no desire to get mixed up in that crowd today. Farther up the block he came to a small movie house. The ads were for some western film. He stood for a long moment undecided. There were more than a couple of hours before they were to meet for supper, and it was hot. He sighed and bought a ticket and went on inside.

The place was dark and cool and the picture was only so-so. Sitting over close to the wall, Britt tried to keep his attention on the flickering screen, but the effort was too much. He struggled to keep his eyes open but failed. When he woke his sight came to the pale bluish face of the clock on the wall by the screen. It was after eight!

He left the theatre hurriedly. It was dark outside and the neon signs up and down the street buzzed and twitched, reflected in oily, distorted patterns in the polish of parked autos. Britt hesitated. He supposed that by now they had given him up for missing, had had their supper, had started for home.

He moved now, slowly, down along the dirty front of the buildings, past the strung bars, down toward Eighth Street. The yellow block of light on the sidewalk before him came from the open door of the Red Club. His ears picked up the clatter of talk, the laughter. As he came abreast of the opening he saw Rigger, his head tossed back, laughing loudly at some sally. The woman Ruby was at his side, her arms draped across his shoulders loosely, and, from outside here, Britt could see they were both stewed to the gills. He frowned, wondering where Marcy could be. He had to know where she was. He stepped into the place and pushed across the floor toward Rigger Kates.

Rigger's head came forward and, as his laughter failed, the pull of his face muscles lessened and he saw the big fellow coming toward him. "Well, I'll be goddamned! Hiya, big boy!" he shouted gleefully. "Hey." He poked Ruby in the ribs with his elbow. "Lookee here. Here's good ole Britt."

"Hiya, Britt," she managed to say through rubber lips. Her mouth was slack and her eyes had begun to glaze a little. Her hand on Rigger's shoulder flapped a faint greeting.

Britt ignored her. He stepped up close to Rigger and he reached out and took a firm grasp on the small hard free shoulder. "Where's Marcy, Rigger?"

"Marcy? Marcy, Marcy—who the hell knows, who cares?" Rigger's shoulders heaved mightily and Ruby's arm fell away and her hand slapped against her thigh. She swayed slightly and fought to bring her arm once more around him.

Britt frowned. "Did she go home? Rigger, tell me—where is she?"

Rigger grinned mischievously. "Here she is!" He hugged Ruby close to him.

"I ain't kiddin', Rigger. I want to find Marcy."

Rigger suddenly scowled. He reached up and found Ruby's fingers and pulled the hand down on his collarbone, drawing the arm tight and firm against the back of his neck. "Don't know where the hell old Marcy went," he muttered. "Don't know, don't care." He laughed inanely at this and reaching back he slapped Ruby's thinly covered behind. The crack of his hand on flesh sent his laughter shrilling.

Britt's face went hard. His fingers tightened on Rigger's shoulder muscle like a clamp and the little guy curled and winced.

"Hey! Hey! Cut it out, boy! You're hurtin'." He twisted and jerked away. He reached up and rubbed the sore spot. For the moment sobriety came back to his eyes. Ugliness followed swiftly. His lips pushed forward angrily. "What the hell you tryin' to do, huh? I don't know where the hell she's gone. She ain't gone home—she can't. I got the keys right here. See?" He patted the pocket of his Levis. "She can't go home until I'm goddamn good and ready to go, see? Not unless she gets out and hoofs it."

Britt released him. He stepped back and bit his lip. Rigger was no use. He had to get out of here, to find her. She had to be around somewhere. He wheeled and went quickly from the place, leaving the sound of their laughter behind him.

He went up Eighth Street carefully until he came to the bank corner across from the hotel. There was a bus stop with a wooden bench set on the curbing. He glanced toward it. There was only one person sitting there, huddled up in the cool breeze that came down the broad street. He looked away, waiting for the light to change, but something brought his eyes back. It was Marcy, alone, looking forlorn, dejected, abandoned. Quickly he crossed over and slid onto the seat. His hands went out and covered hers and he looked down into her swift-rising startled gaze.

"Britt!"

"Marcy, how long you been here? Not ever since seven!"

She nodded. "Yeah, I been here." She said it quietly, letting the faint accusation underscore her tone.

He tightened his hold on her hands and looked away, at the darkened front of the Majestic Theatre, cold and closed for renovation. "I fell asleep in a lousy movie," he confessed sheepishly.

She stared at him for a second and then laughed. "Oh, Britt, you fool!"

"I'm awfully sorry, Marcy." He looked like a kid caught with his hand in the cookie jar.

"It's all right. I didn't mind waitin', honest. I knew you'd show up," she lied. "It was interestin', watchin' the cars and the people and all."

"We best get somethin' to eat."

"Yeah. I'm kinda hungry." She got to her feet and pulled him after her. "We gotta be gettin' for home soon."

They had their supper at the cafeteria down the block. Neither of them had mentioned Rigger or his absence. Afterward, as they came up to the truck, she suddenly pulled him to a halt. "We can't take the truck," she said. "Rigger's got the keys."

He remembered tardily and cursed softly. "You wait here," he said. "I know where he is. You wait for me. I'll get him."

He had taken a step away from her when she stopped him again. "He won't come," she said quietly. "He's bugeyed drunk, and he's with her—that woman."

His brows peaked. "How come you know?"

"I saw them together earlier. I went past that place."

"You stay, Marcy. I'll get him—or the keys."

She came after him, catching up, clutching his bare forearm with cold fingers, going along the sidewalk with him. "I'm not gonna stay behind!" she cried stubbornly. "You might not come back!"

He flushed at the implication, but she was smiling. "If you want—" He shrugged.

"I'm comin' along."

Together they crossed Eighth and went up to where the light lay like a toss rug in front of the place. Even before they reached the doorway they could hear the sounds of Rigger, loud and argumentative.

"He's awful loaded," she murmured.

"Yeah. Sure sounds like it."

As they entered they saw him. Rigger was attempting to put a coin in the juke box, unsteady on his feet, fumbling, trying to find the slot. There was a thump from inside the machine as the coin fell and the mechanism was set into motion. In a second or so the music came blaring forth, drowning out the human sounds in the place. Rigger turned and cocked his head, making sure of the tempo. He weaved across the floor and his arms went out and caught Ruby around her soft, bulging middle. "C'mon, baby. Let's you and me have us a hoedown!"

He half pranced, half dragged her around the little space the others cleared. Ruby was sodden. Her hair had become disarranged and her mouth was loose, the lips shiny with drool. Her head bobbled loosely and her chin found a weighted rest on Rigger's shoulder; this brought her body to a peculiar bend, so that her rump protruded, the thin skirt dented by the division of her fleshy buttocks.

Around and around they moved, shuffling and scraping. Rigger kept laughing without pause. He supported her body, kept her from collapsing, his arms tight around her, his face buried hard between the gelatinous mounds of her unfettered breasts. The men along the bar grinned. They watched the performance with sharp, appreciative eyes, yet careful, ready to black out their interest should Rigger lift his head and that funny, instant change come over him.

Marcy stood a little behind Britt and open revulsion was in her face. Though they stood apart, not even their glances shared, he knew the pattern of her thoughts, sensed the sickness in her. He stepped forward quickly and his hand caught Rigger's free shoulder. The little guy kept his face buried. Britt hooked his fingers, digging deep into the big cord near the neck. Rigger sucked his breath sharply and jerked his head back, twisting with the sudden, paralyzing pain. He peered up foggily.

"Rigger! Come on, pal, it's time to go. Come on, break it up, kid!"

Rigger wriggled his trunk violently and wrested himself from the clutch. "Lemme alone, can'tcha? I'm havin' me some fun. For chrissake, go 'way, beat it, get lost!" He buried his face deep in his partner and shook his head like a pup with a rag, making blustery noises through slack lips as he did so. The men along the bar laughed loudly. Britt flushed, becoming aware of them. His sweeping glance found Marcy, standing off to one side. Her face had gone ash pale; she looked tiny, frightened, ashamed. Britt touched Rigger gently this time.

"Come on, Rigger," he urged. "Let's get outta here, boy. It's time. It's gettin' late. Marcy's here, Rigger. She wants to get headin' for home."

Rigger paid no heed. He continued to push the heavy woman around the floor with Britt trailing them a step or so behind. She had not changed her position; her eyes were closed and Britt wondered if she had gone to sleep or passed out. Either way she managed to stay on her feet somehow; her legs moved in blind accord with Rigger's.

"Marcy's here, Rigger. She wants to get goin'."

The men at the bar peered down at her curiously and one or two pairs of eyes showed a kind of momentary embarrassment. In the majority there was a quick sparking, an anticipation.

Rigger drew his head from the woman now and stumbled to a halt. He squinted up at Britt, trying to focus his sight. "Who?" he croaked. "Who's here? Did you say old Marcy's here?"

Britt stepped up close to him and tried to keep his voice low. "Marcy's wantin' to go, Rigger. Come on, let's get outta this dump. Come on, you had enough, boy."

The music blasted to a final brassy chord. There was a long silence broken only by the clicks and whirrings of the machinery in the ornate box. Beyond Rigger's shoulder Britt could see the next recording sliding out from the cylindrical pile, the tone arm swinging easily into place, heard the soft hiss as the needle found the introductory groove on the disc. He frowned. If the music had stopped for good, he might have been able to do something with Rigger. Now it was too late. The tune was loud and strident, banishing further talk and reason.

Rigger did not resume the dance, however. He suddenly swung the woman in a half circle and shoved her away from him. She went staggering back, her control lost, her head raising, her lids fluttering open. There was a dim look of surprise in her clouded eyes. Two of the men at the bar grabbed, catching her under the armpits, holding her on her feet. Rigger stood alone in the center of the room, his eyes round as he tried to separate, to catalogue the people in the place.

"Marcy's here," he kept repeating. "Ole stuck-up Marcy's here!" He giggled vacantly and the audience along the bar shared his amusement. "Ole woman Marcy's here!" he informed them jauntily, nodding confirmation. "Ole cow Marcy's come down off her high horse. She's gonna have some fun like the white folks, Marcy is!"

He shuffled forward slowly, brushing past the reaching hook of Britt's fingers. His eyes had found her. She was at the far end of the bar, a little distance from the rest of them, just inside the front door, where Britt had left her. Rigger came weaving toward her and her eyes were wide and full of dread.

"Rigger!" She put out her hand as if she might by this slim measure halt him, keep him from her.

Rigger did not hesitate. He felt his way cautiously, putting one foot in front of the other, as if he were treading on brittle spring ice. Now he was directly in front of her and his smile was crooked. He suddenly bowed very low in mocking gallantry and lost his balance, toppling forward, his arms flying up in the effort to catch himself. His hands caught at her, seized her, and he clung fast for support. He brought his face up close to hers. She recoiled from the nauseous strength of his breath. Slowly he pulled himself straight and stood, shoulder high to her. He grinned. "C'mon, baby, let's you and me have us a dance, hey?"

She shook her head violently. Her humiliation was high and her eyes went darting along the row of avid faces strung along the bar. "No, no, no! Please, Rigger, please!"

His grin faded and that look came pushing into his eyes, dark and ugly. "I said let's us have a dance, see? You and me's gonna show these poor bastards somethin' real sharp."

She went on shaking her head, trying to keep her eyes away from them. She saw Britt suddenly and that look in his eyes and her look implored him to stay away, to keep out of the mess. He turned suddenly and set his back on them, staring down into the bowels of the music box, hearing the sounds of them above the dinning music.

Rigger's hands went over her slowly. She stared with horror into his bloodshot eyes, wondering if he could see her at all, and all the time those stubby-fingered hands went over her carefully, as if he were feeling his way. The palms slipped from her arms where he had seized her in his fall and came upon her body and stopped, each upon a breast. She pulled herself rigid and tore her eyes from the mocking sight of him; she bit her lips and felt the quick run of blood warm her mouth. She shut her eyes tight. His hands were moving again. They came up and on her skin his fingers were crusty and strong, seeking the column of her neck, circling tentatively. The pads of his fingers went spreading, sliding along the square of her shoulders. He let his touch go slipping down along her trembling bare arms until he had found her hands. Now his fingers locked on her wrists and he drew her forward. There was no resistance in her; she went with him dully, automatically. Rigger pulled her out into the open circle of the floor. The music had come crashing to a finish. Britt turned slowly and stared. Rigger had brought her around gradually as he had drawn her forth, and now she stood with her back to Britt, facing the open door. Rigger was beyond her, looking up, and his gaze slanted over her shoulder and he looked at Britt. He grinned without humor and Britt knew suddenly that his vision was quite clear, that he saw everything now. He took a step forward and the grin died instantly as Rigger's fingers tightened on Marcy's wrists. Britt stopped; he did not want to hurt her further, he dared not interfere. There was no telling what Rigger might do. Rigger agreed and the grin crept back.

There was a distant pumping sound and a slow waltz began to ooze from the juke box. Rigger released her wrists and her arms fell listlessly to her sides but she did not move. Her face was blank and she had not opened her eyes. Rigger stared at her and his face flushed darkly. "Dance!" he commanded hoarsely. "Start dancin', you!"

She remained motionless. Angered, he reached out and found the hollow between her right shoulder and breast and he shoved her hard. "Goddamnit! I said start dancin'!"

As if she were in some kind of hypnotic dream, cut off, set apart from all of them, she began to move in measured time to the music. She took her steps and, alone like that, she slowly circled the floor, dipping and swaying in strict cadence. As she went around Rigger pivoted on his high boot heel and the cocky grin on his face was broad. He glanced triumphantly to the battery of fascinated eyes on her. "Got her damn well trained, hey?" he crowed. "Get a load of the ole woman—dancin' like a goddamn trained bear! Ain't she a cutie?"

The sound of him brought Ruby alive. She straightened and belched loudly, smearing the spittle from her lips on the back of her hand. She came lurching from the corner of the bar, staggering out into the clearing, groping for Rigger, but he paid her no heed. She came up to him and fumbled with him, trying to pick up his arms, to put them around her. "Let's us dance some more, Rigger boy," she slurred. "Let's you and me show that one, baby." She fought to hold herself erect and her head wagged. The eyes were distorted and the very motion seemed to set the eyeballs to individual jiggling. "That one, she ain't so damn good!" Ruby judged loudly. "She ain't no goddamn good at all! What good's dancin' round all by yourself? What the hell's wrong with her, she ain't got no fella? for chrissake, why ain't she got no guy dancin' with her? Whatsa matter with her, anyway, huh?"

She kept trying for Rigger, trying to make him take hold of her, but he was held by the automaton that kept moving steadily around the room. Suddenly Ruby began running her palms over him. She had maneuvered herself behind him and she put both hands on his shoulders and slowly, grinning foolishly, she brought them down over the little body, over his chest, down over the hard little round of his belly. Her stubby fingers found the waistline of his Levis and tried to work her fingers down inside. Only now did he become suddenly aware of her and what she was doing. He scowled and wheeled and his voice was keen and ugly.

"Cut that out, you bitch! Can'tcha see I got somethin' better to do? For chrissake, go drop dead somewheres!"

He raised his hand, put the palm flat on her face, and shoved hard. She went swiftly, as if she had been flung back by the kick of a giant spring. Her feet pattered on the boards and there was a thumping shock as her legs buckled and she sat heavily on the floor. Her face was wide with surprise and shock. She heard the exploding laughter of the bar gallery and she peered up at them uncomprehendingly. "Gees," she whispered plaintively. "Whatsa matter with ever'body? That's what he goes for, some feelin' round like that."

Rigger had found Marcy again. He moved at last, stealthily, tracking her as she moved, and suddenly he caught up with her.

His hard little arms reached and he seized her as she came turning slowly. He pulled her close and hard against him. The music droned on and together they danced. Rigger held her tight in the vise of his arms and as the melody came tapering to a finish he bent her down, away from him, until it seemed her spine must snap. Holding her in this helpless position, he moved her body down between his legs and his lips found her mouth and he fastened himself upon her.

It was as if that contact of him brought the life stirring in her. She remained inert for a moment and then her head jerked and she fought to take her mouth from his. Her hands flew up and the long slender fingers curled into little balls and dug into the armored shell of his chest. He laughed and one hand slid back to cup her head. He struggled to hold her still. His lips slipped over the smoothness of her cheek as he fought to recapture her mouth. Suddenly she reached up and dug into his face with her nails, drawing the sharp blades down his flesh as hard as she could. Rigger gasped and grabbed at his stung face. She fell to the floor and scrambled away from him. Britt had come in swiftly and he caught her from the floor, pulling her to her feet, shoving her behind him. He faced Rigger and his eyes were murderously dark and angry.

She saw instantly and terror lashed her. "We've got to go, go, go, go." She tugged at him in growing hysteria. "Britt, Britt! Come on, please, please, let's go!"

Her insistence brought his attention to her. He saw the naked horror, the stark fear in her. He wanted nothing more than to take care of the little bastard now, to settle the score on the spot, but she looked as if she were going to blow her top. She suddenly moved and there was a tremendous surprising strength in her. She dragged him stumbling in her wake. They went across the deserted space, leaving Rigger cursing, dabbing at his face with his handkerchief, making no attempt to follow. She dragged Britt out into the blessed coolness of the dark street.

She released him and went off, striking out ahead of him. She did not turn south, toward the parking lot and the truck. She went north, the other way, up past the theatre where he had been, to the corner, and turned right and went down toward the railroad line. In the shadow of the warehouse beside the tracks he caught up with her. She stopped short as he stepped in front of her, blocking her. They faced each other, both fighting to bring their breathing down, to marshal some reason, striving to sponge the smear of the recent scene away.

"I feel like hell!" Britt muttered thickly. "All I did was stand there like a dope! I shoulda beat his lousy brains out!"

She could say nothing, keeping her burning eyes from him.

"Marcy!" He felt for her hand. "I was too scared to try anything. I was—I was afraid he might do somethin' to you."

Dimly she felt him reaching for her. She took his hand and the pressure was short and reassuring. She swallowed with difficulty. "It's O.K., Britt. Forget it."

He stood at her side now and remorse swept over him in a great wave. He stood looking off down the street and his eyes were dim with self-recrimination and concern. Impulsively she tightened her hold.

"It's O.K.—honest, Britt," she said again. "It wouldn't have done no good for you to get mixed up in it, see? It was just Rigger and me, nobody else."

He pulled away, unable to keep watching the tortuous changing play in her face any longer. The traffic light over the intersection behind them bounced crazily in the rising wind. "The little sonofabitch!" he ground suddenly. "I shoulda killed him!"

Her fingers were sudden steel and her nails bit into his flesh. She jerked him around sharply and her eyes were bright. "No!" she cried. "Don't ever say that! Don't you ever be thinkin' things like that, never!"

"But he—"

She shook her head. "It wouldn't do no good for nobody. Rigger's like he is, ain't nothin' ever gonna change that. This—this ain't the first time somethin' like this has happened, Britt," she admitted in a low voice. "This is just one more time, see? He can't help himself when there's people watchin' and he's been drinkin'. He likes to show off and he doesn't care how, sometimes."

"What's he gonna do? Go on doin' things like this any ole time he feels like it?" Britt stormed.

She stared at him and her lips paled. "There ain't no call to go shoutin', Britt," she said quietly.

He tried to read her face but all the answers seemed to escape him. "I don't see how you—"

"There's lots you don't see," she said huskily. "There's lots you don't know about things between Rigger and me. It wouldn't make nothin' better for you to know." She hesitated. "Rigger's my husband, and me, I'm his wife. We got our problems to work out, but they're ours. That's the way it is."

She walked away from him. She picked her way across the many-ribboned path of the tracks and started down the incline on the other side. He moved swiftly and caught her arm.

"Where you think you're goin'?"

The resolve in her was melting and weariness was taking over and her eyes were dull and apathetic. "I'm goin' home," she pronounced slowly. "I reckon as how it's time to git for home now."

"What happens when he gets home? He's gonna come home sooner or later."

She eyed him in faint surprise, then shrugged her shoulders. "Why not? It's where he lives, ain't it?" she said. "I reckon he'll be comin' home, sooner or later, like you say."

"He'll be meaner'n a bastard."

"Yes, I reckon so."

"He'll raise hell."

"That ain't nothin' new."

"What if he—" He was avoiding her eyes.

There was a tiny catch in her throat. "He won't," she said flatly. "He ain't got them kind of guts."

He reached out and touched her because he could not help himself. He saw the quick glittering spark of tears in her eyes. She drew her hand from his hold quickly.

"Oh, Britt! For God's sake, let's go home!" Her voice broke. "I just can't take no more tonight!"

The lash of her fatigue stung him. She slipped from his grasp and started again toward the shadowed fence of the ball park. "Wait!" He caught up with her. "What're you gonna do—walk?"

"Ain't no other way, is there?"

"You can't walk all that way. It's miles."

"Rigger's got the keys, remember?" She smiled thinly. "Somehow I got a feelin' he ain't gonna be ready to come home, not yet."

"I'll get them keys."

He had turned back but she stopped him. "You can't go back there!" she cried. "There'll be more trouble, worse trouble!"

His eyes were grim on her. "There won't be no trouble, and I'll get them keys."

She wanted to run after him, to throw herself in front of him, to hold him, but he had already gone from her, back along the way they had come. She sighed and brushed her hair from her forehead. Slowly she began to retrace her steps.

The moment Britt came into the place the stillness came rising like a swift fog from the floor, deadening, blotting out the hum of conversation. Rows of eyes swung to him instantly; as quickly they darted to the other end of the room, widening with fearful speculation on Rigger Kates, standing with Ruby at the far end of the bar.

Britt moistened his lips and went down past the unknown faces to where the couple stood. Rigger was ghastly pale and the long scratches were livid across his cheek. He was quite sober. As if his return to sobriety were contagious, Ruby was drawn and quiet at his side. He eyed Britt warily. Suddenly he looked away, shifting uncomfortably under the hard level look in Britt's eyes. "Hi," he murmured.

Britt was alert. "You comin' on home?"

"No," Rigger mumbled. "No, I ain't."

"I want them keys to the truck."

Though they were speaking very quietly, their voices seemed to fill the room. The multiple eyes were close on Rigger, watching for any possible move, waiting for his decision. Britt instinctively held himself rigid. His arms hung stonily at his sides and the fingers were half rolled into fists. A little nerve high on his cheek near the temple had begun to twitch.

Rigger drew a long wobbling breath and brought his head up slowly. "O.K.," he said simply.

The escaping breaths in the room behind Britt fanned his neck. Perspiration beaded at the roots of his hair. He did not relax. His fingers remained ready to form fists. "O.K.," he said evenly, "let's have 'em."

Rigger took a long look at him. For the moment it looked as if he might have changed his mind. He wet his lips and took his eyes away. He began to force his fingers down into the tight opening of his jeans pocket. He handed the key ring over meekly.

Britt glanced from Rigger's white face to the woman beyond. She was staring over Rigger's shoulder and he saw the print of fear stamped deep in her eyes. With a stab of surprise he realized Ruby had been sure he was going to whip Rigger. Her hand was tight on the little guy's shoulder and she had shifted so that her body was close against him, as if she were prepared to try to defend him. Britt stared. He had never for a moment figured things this way. Now he knew. On her side of the fence she was not just Rigger's fancy. She was in love with the little bastard! She was up to her neck in love, and it showed! Her eyes flamed with the heat of it.

Britt's fingers closed slowly over the sharp edge of the keys. He glanced down at Rigger, mute before him, gaze fixed to the bar edge. "Thanks," Britt said.

As he strode across the floor to the street door he could hear them shifting along the length of the bar, returning disappointedly to their talk and their drinks. He pushed out into the cool night and breathed deeply of the clean air. There had been no trouble. Not like he had expected.

The May night was lush and velvety and the warmth of the breeze close and intimate. They rode silently, slowly. Beyond the Negro section they emerged into open fields; behind them the city lights were bright, white-splashed in the night. There was nothing to say.

Now and again an automobile would come at them, its headlights blinding bright for an instant, then it brushed past them with a quick whisper, headed for town. After a long while she stirred restlessly in the far corner of the seat and her voice was very soft.

"Sometimes it—it seems like a long way," she murmured.

"Gettin' pooped?"

He wanted to reach out and touch her, comfort her. The affair had left its obvious mark. Anything more, any slight, meaningless thing might be too much.

"A little." She turned and gazed through the open window at her side. "It's such a lovely night," she said. She leaned forward, her face pressed into the breeze, her hair puffing. He could see the perfect tracing of her throat, soft, white, curved, lovely. The dull pounding in his neck, under his ears, made his head seem to rock with its beat. Hastily he took his eyes from her and held them rigidly to the pavement guide.

The wind had failed to spasmodic gusty breezes, tiny and tentative. It was as if the mother wind had chosen these sleeping hours to wean her pups, to give them her instruction.

Eventually the lights of the Kates place came into view, reeled in on invisible lines. They said nothing as the truck lights swung and picked up the ruts to the porch steps, found the way around the house to the barn. When he had bolted the doors and come along to the end of the barn he found she was waiting for him. Her fingers were cool on his wrist.

"Don't you worry 'bout Rigger's comin' home," she said quietly. "By the time he gets here he ain't gonna be feelin' too good. Like as not he'll be wore out."

"Marcy!" Britt's arms reached for her, but she stepped back and shook her head.

"No!" was all she said. She turned then and went quickly across the yard, pushed open the back screen, and went inside.

Britt blinked and rubbed his palms hard and his thighs. The palms were slippery with sudden, sleek sweat. Unsteadily he found the door to the little barn room and went inside. He lay on the cot for a long time, fully clothed, just staring up into the darkness, trying hard to put the picture of her out of his mind.

CHAPTER TWELVE

RIGGER did not come back that night. Marcy said nothing, made no sign one way or the other to him during breakfast. Later on, from the field where he was working, Britt saw her come outside and hang up a few pieces of wash on the line in the yard. She did not look his way. He stood tall in the sun, shielding his eyes, watching her. There was in him the sudden swift desire to talk to her but he held himself in check. His attention was drawn magnetically from her, beyond the barn, off to the farthest field. Newt Kates was there, and he too was standing erect, motionless. The sun colored the bright yellow of his straw work hat and he was standing very still and Britt knew Newt was watching him. Shifting guiltily, he bent forward and resumed his labors.

Rigger came back from town that afternoon. Marcy stopped her work, hearing the sudden screech of rubber on the highway pavement. She wiped her hands on her apron and went down the little hall to the porch. The car had come to a stop out front, partially hidden by the leafy fan of the tree in the yard. She caught a glimpse of Rigger as he stepped down to the shoulder, saw him nod and wave. There was a quick scuff as the heavy machine spurted forward, swung in a careening half circle, backed, then completed the turn and went speeding back to town. As Rigger came up the drive to the house she retreated hastily to the kitchen. Seconds later she heard the whine of the door, its spatting contact, and the sounds of him coming down the hall.

She busied herself at the sink so she would not have to look at him. He had come to the doorway, she knew. He went on into the bedroom and she could hear him moving around in there. Shortly he came back to the kitchen.

"Hey."

She steeled herself to purposeful silence.

He had come up behind her and she tensed her flesh for the expected contact but he did not touch her. "Where the hell's Britt?" he asked.

She shrugged and said nothing.

Rigger stared at the hard set of her back and his lips thinned out. "Goddamnit, I asked where Britt is!"

She still denied him words and stood motionless. He reached out and caught her shoulder, pulling her around abruptly. "What the hell's eatin' you? I asked you where's Britt!"

She stared down on him, at the crusted thin scratches on his cheek, and the disgust in her eyes was clear and hard. There was a funny little twitching in his cheek and she felt the licking of the cold tongue of fear. "He's—he's somewheres outside workin', I reckon," she gulped. "Where else would he be this time of day?"

His lips went tight with the thrust. He shoved her away, knocking her back against the hard edge of the sink. He paid no attention to her sharp gasp as the pain went charging through her. He crossed over to the back door and stood for a moment as if he were debating whether or not to go out in the hot sun. He went back to the bedroom, this time closing the door behind him. Marcy wet her lips and drew herself stiffly erect. Her hand found the bruised area of her back. She turned slowly and her fingers picked up the strands of her unfinished work.

Supper was tense. The four ate in mute silence, their faces drawn, their thinking mired in the bitter-thick sirup of strain. The kitchen was electric with apprehension. They ate overrapidly, avoiding any contact with each other, as if the merest meeting of eyes alone might be sufficient to spark the latent explosion.

Only Newt Kates seemed curiously relaxed, quite comfortable. He ate his meal slowly, chewing carefully, keeping his eyes occupied with them, peering from face to face, as if he were judging the potential of their feeling. There was in him the bright flame of anticipation, eager curiosity. They were at odds for some reason and Newt Kates was vastly pleased.

As soon as the meal was over Rigger got up and left the table. He went into the bedroom and closed the door. Without thinking, Marcy glanced at Britt. Their eyes met and held. When Britt looked away from her pale, worried face, he saw that Newt had missed nothing. He was almost smiling. Britt flushed. Marcy got to her feet and her face contorted with a sudden twinge from her hurt back. She began to remove the plates slowly. Newt cleared his throat.

"Must've been one helluva party y'all had last night in town," he observed dryly.

"It was O.K.," Britt said quietly.

"Sure must've been, from the looks of y'all."

The fragment of conversation died. Marcy worked doggedly at the sink. Britt busied himself, keeping his eyes away from the man opposite. Newt finally tossed his stick to the table and shoved his chair back. He left the room and went outside without further comment.

Britt turned and watched her. "Want some help?" he offered.

She shook her head without looking up. "There ain't so much," she said. "Besides, gives me somethin' to do."

He stayed until she had finished up the chores. She came back to the table and lowered herself carefully into the chair. There was a faint contraction of her lips.

"Somethin' the matter?"

"It's nothin'," she said. "I just whacked myself on a chair this afternoon, that's all."

There was an odd restraint on their words in the room. The barrier door stood monitor, holding their words, their thinking apart. Britt finally pushed to his feet. "Well," he said vaguely, "I guess I'll be movin' on."

He waited as if he were hoping she might ask him to stay longer. The only thing she did was to raise her head slightly, to summon the faintest response of a smile. "Sure," she said.

She listened to the falling pad of his steps in the yard. Her eyes came slowly to the closed door to the bedroom. Wearily she raised her hand and brushed the hair from her forehead. The night meal was done. In a couple of hours it would be time to go to bed. Tomorrow was not so far away. Perhaps things would look different then. She put her elbows on the table and covered her face with the long slender fingers, bringing synthetic darkness to her. Outside the wind had come up; there was the heavy tension of brewing storm in the air. She wished suddenly a cyclone or something would come and blow the whole goddamn works to kingdom come!

The storm failed to materialize. The epicenter divided itself in the north somewhere, and the piled jagged thunderheads sailed galleon-like off to the east and west of them, bearing away the rain and the cooling off and the threat of hail as well. The promised relief from the thickening heat had not come. It was humid and uncomfortable, even in the morning.

Breakfast was a repetition of the night before. No one spoke. Only when the meal had been accomplished and the start of the day was ripe was the silence dissolved.

"Want you should come down and take a look at that wheat," Newt said. "It's startin' to show up pretty good."

Rigger nodded glumly. " 'Bout time the goddamn stuff's showin', after all the time you been on it."

Britt and Marcy went on eating, saying nothing. The brothers got up and left them alone. Moments later Britt trailed the others to work and she was left alone. She sat back, rubbing the sore spot in her back. It felt better this morning. She sat and remembered. It was with relief that she had found Rigger fast asleep when she finally had gone to bed last night. She had slept badly, keeping herself on the wakeful edge, holding her body taut against the danger of touching him, even by accident. He had slept straight through the night without even turning once. She reckoned he must have been plumb wore out.

Bareheaded, stepping quickly, Rigger led the way. Newt lagged, his straw hat set firmly on his head, his pace heavy, unhurried. By the time he reached the truck Rigger was already up behind the steering wheel, waiting for him.

There were no words between them. The coming heat pressed on the earth, and even though all the windows and vents to the cab were open, there was little relief. The manufactured breeze was only a mixing of dust and heat. At the edge of the new wheat field they left the truck and went on ahead afoot.

Rigger walked on some distance, stopped, bent down, and touched a slender bright green shoot. Newt stayed behind, holding his counsel, watching his brother with sharpening eyes. Rigger moved along the side of the field, pausing now and then to check. Finally he straightened and peered out over the reaching spiked sea of green. He glanced back at his brother. "Comin' along pretty damn good," he called.

"Figgers to be a pretty good one this year," Newt judged, coming up.

"Gotta keep your eyes on that stuff when it's just gettin' goin'." Rigger spoke authoritatively, commandingly. "One slip and the whole works is shot to hell."

"I'm takin' care of my work!" Newt snapped. He raised his head and scanned the sky, rounded, blue. "Just so's it don't come any bad trouble," he murmured prayerfully.

"The rot," Rigger supplemented.

Newt's eyes came down to the little guy and there was a swift paling dread in him. "That's for sure," he breathed.

Rigger headed for the truck. Newt stole a last lingering look at his embryo field, and there was in his eyes a kind of prideful paternity as he gazed over the green carpet. Almost reluctantly he moved down the footpath and climbed up beside his brother in the cab.

Rigger worked the truck around, maneuvering skillfully, setting the wheels on the narrow tracks, heading back to the house. Recent rains had left a gummy mud base in the scooped-out trough along each side of the narrow road trail. Rigger raised his eyes and caught sight of Britt working on the distant fence line. "There's one hard-workin' bastard," he commented with a nod.

Newt moistened his lips. Even from here he could see the strength of the big body. His eyes narrowed.

Rigger grinned. "Sure was a right lucky day I ran across that ole boy."

Newt Kates twisted his head suddenly and eyed his brother with a trace of swift contempt. "That's what you think!" he hissed.

Rigger caught the words and frowned. He slowed the truck, bringing his eyes from the uneven wheel tracks. "Just what the hell do you mean by that crack?"

Newt smirked. "If you don't know, I reckon it ain't up to me to be tellin' you."

The truck ground to an instant stop, skidding off the path into the soft churned mire of the adjacent field. It came to rest on a crazy tilt, the front wheels on the plowed ground, the rear ones weighting into the grabbing mud of the trough.

"Just what the hell you got against that boy, anyhow?"

Newt kept his eyes from Rigger's hot face. He watched Britt working on the fence. His voice was careful, sure. He shrugged. "Nothin'. I ain't got nothin' against him."

"You sure as hell spend a lot of time makin' cracks."

Newt made no reply.

Rigger's face thickened. "Trouble with you, Newt, you keep stickin' your goddamn nose into things ain't none of your business." His words shrilled a little. "Trouble with you is you just don't like nobody."

Newt stared down at his crossed feet under the dashboard. He locked his jaws.

Rigger went plowing on. "Christ Almighty! It's been goin' on ever since you come back from the Army. You're forever kickin' up a squall over nothin' at all. Hell, man, I can't help it if you got yourself burned out overseas. Why the hell don't you cut it out, lay off. I'm gettin' good goddamn sick and fed up!"

Newt brought his head up swiftly. He stared at Rigger and there was the bright flaring hate in him. "What you gonna do about it?"

Rigger's lips thinned. "What am I gonna do? One of these here days I'm gonna kick you off the place, that's what I'm gonna do about it!"

Newt snorted. "You all the time shootin' off your yap plenty big for a lousy little punk!"

Rigger's grip tightened on the wheel. "Newt, I'm warnin' ya! You been askin' for it a helluva long time."

Newt jerked his head and the threat went glancing off the hard shell of his ear. His eyes picked out Britt Callum, marked the easy swing of the big hammer as it came to the fencepost time and again. In a moment he had brought his muddied eyes back to Rigger. He eyed him coldly. "You know somethin'?" he demanded suddenly. "You ain't so goddamn smart as you think, boy."

"I'm smart enough to know when I got a bellyful!"

Newt sniffed. There was a curt nod of his head toward the distant figure. "You best be watchin' your step, Rigger boy. One of these here days that ole buddy of yours out yonder's gonna maybe be workin' you over."

Rigger scowled and his eyes went flinty. "What the hell's Callum got to do with it?"

Newt smiled with chilled patience. "You poor stupid cluck!" he jibed. "You poor sawed-off dope! Why, you ain't got the sense to see what's before your own eyes!"

Rigger caught his breath. He came sideways from the wheel and his fingers hooked into Newt's shoulder. "Goddamn you, Newt! Say out what you mean!"

Newt did not flinch under the cutting hold. He smiled icily. "It's him, you hump-happy sonofabitch! Him and your own wife!"

Rigger stared at Newt, the meaning of the words seeping slowly into his understanding. His grip lessened and he took his hand away. His eyes went from Newt's flushed, triumphant face and moved sluggishly over the sweep of the field to Britt Callum. He stared in disbelief for a long moment but said nothing. Then, again, slowly, he turned and his gaze came back to Newt. "Him?" Rigger croaked. "Him and Marcy?" The picture of them swelled to immense proportions in his brain and burst, pricked by the needle of his instant rejection. He pulled himself erect. "You filthy-minded bastard! Why, you're plumb full of crap!"

Newt's face was hard. He worked his lips nervously. "It's true!" he shouted. "Every time you ain't around they're off somewheres together! Right from the first they been hangin' onto each other!"

"He's just a friendly kinda guy."

"Friendly kinda guy!" Newt gasped. "Oh, my Christ! That's a hot one!" His laugh was brittle. "Oh, Jesus! He's friendly!" Newt straightened. "Why, you goddamn peanut brain, why the hell do you think he's hangin' on here, now you're O.K.? What the hell do you have to do—catch 'em doin' it before you'll say it's so?" He grunted scornfully. "Well, you ain't gonna have such a damn long wait, bud. They been steamin' for each other a long time now! You just stick around, brother boy. They's a hay pile nearby got their names on it right now!"

Rigger could no longer hear the words. The blood had come thick and blocking in his ears. Newt went on talking, but no sound reached Rigger's ears. The heat was unbearable in the cab. Sweat oozed fast; his clothes were wet through, clinging to him.

Newt's ugly slash of a mouth went on opening and closing, the thin whitish lips rounding and contracting as the words formed, but Rigger could not separate the sounds into sense. He sent a long glance off to the far field. Newt was laughing now at something, laughing at him. Rigger lifted his hand and held the palm hard on his face, the fingertips firm on his eyeballs, the flat pressing the tip of his nose down harshly. "Get out," he cried suddenly, hoarsely. "Get out, Newt, get out!"

The older man stopped speaking. His lips curled. Rigger suddenly heard the voice again, as from afar. "You go to hell," Newt snarled.

Rigger began to tremble. The pressure of his hand on his face increased and the sweat coursed from his pores. "Get out, Newt! Get out while you can! So help me God, I'm gonna kill you now if you don't get the hell outta here!"

Newt clung to his place. He sneered. "Some more big-man talk, eh?"

Rigger's hand suddenly moved from his face and the fist was steel, held high and close above Newt's blanching face. Only his color and the sudden twitch of the nerve in the lid of his left eye betrayed his swift, paralyzing fear.

Rigger shook violently, his teeth chattering. With a tremendous effort he slowly recalled his arm. He jerked away and grabbed the door handle on his side. He stumbled down to the ground and ran blindly to the head of the truck, going ahead of the nose of the car, coming to a faltering stop, wavering in the assaulting sun, his back to the machine.

Newt Kates shivered, a chill gripping him in spite of the heat. He tried to bring his jagged breathing under control. His eyes were wide on the little hated figure up front. Sharp unbridled fear piled like a thunderhead in him. He had said too much this time. He knew what Rigger would do now. Rigger would do as he had so often threatened; he'd throw him off the place. There'd be no place for him any more. The sudden panic of being forced out mushroomed swiftly. He jerked his eyes from Rigger and averted his head, beating down the tide of nausea.

Slowly he began to stiffen. His head remained bent; his eyes narrowed slowly, working into mere slitted cracks. The accelerator pedal was a miniature springboard at his feet. Newt's head raised ponderously. He peered through the windshield. Rigger was still standing like that, his back to the truck. Newt's breath began to scrape, fighting through the shrinking gap of his throat. Gradually, noiselessly, he began to uncoil his legs.

He set his hands on the seat at his sides, and, using his arms as bracing supports, he began to shift his body. He hoisted himself carefully, swung his body over an inch or so, then lowered his weight to the seat. Each move brought him a little closer. The still running engine was almost silent. His eyes did not waver on the solid little figure ahead. Newt began to count. Three more moves could do it. Straining, he lifted himself again, very carefully, to avoid any sudden motion that might rock the carriage of the machine. Again. The steering wheel cracked against the metal of his belt buckle and he froze, his body held suspended above the seat on the scaffold of his arms. Rigger had not turned, had not heard. Once more. Newt raised himself with exacting care, not too high this time; he sucked in his breath, keeping his belly flat, the buckle away from the wheel. As he exhaled he smiled and his eyes widened and fired.

With the swift silent movement of a cat he pressed the clutch pedal down to the floor and eased the gear lever down to low position. There was no change in the murmuring tone of the running engine. Rigger still stood that way, unaware. Newt straightened slowly and moved his right leg. The corners of his mouth pulled tight. His breath snagged in his closing throat. His seeking right foot ached. In that instant he seized the wheel, let the clutch pedal fly free, and jammed his foot down hard on the accelerator. There was a sudden high roar from the engine and the sharp whirring whine of rubber biting into the earth.

Dimly Marcy heard the sounds of the truck returning to the yard. She paid no attention and went on with her work, making Newt's bed, trying to tidy things around the room. She kept her eyes averted, held away from the pornographic display plastered on his walls. The whine of the screen door opening and the scuff of a boot on the kitchen floor surprised her. She straightened and twisted to find the face of the alarm clock on the dresser. She relaxed. There was still an hour or so before she had to think about the noonday dinner. Puzzled, however, at their coming into the house this time of day, she stopped her work and went to the doorway.

Her arms flew up instantly to shield herself. Newt burst past her, bumping her to one side, as he entered. He did not speak, did not even look at her. His face was grimy and there was a smear of dried, caked blood on his forehead from a cut, a slanting accent mark over the right eye. His lips were puffed and she saw now that he limped. There was a long tear in his dirty khaki trousers. Movement at her side brought her startled eyes around. Rigger was in the doorway. He stood centered, his little legs braced, hands on hips, his chin pushed forward angrily, his eyes hard and cruel, marking Newt's every move. He, too, ignored her.

She looked again at Newt. He had found the suitcase he kept over in the corner. He brought it to the rumpled bed and opened it with shaking fingers. Crossing to the dresser, he began to empty the drawers, tossing clothing and personal articles indiscriminately toward the bed. He made no sound.

"Whatever—" She turned questioning eyes to Rigger.

"Shut your mouth!" he snapped. He did not take his eyes from his brother.

She swallowed and her face burned. She moved a little, edging from him. Fascinated, she watched Newt. Only once did he hesitate in his forced labor. He half-turned and looked at his brother. His face was pinched and tight with anger and his mouth worked constantly, convulsively, but he said nothing.

"Hurry up!" Rigger commanded. "Get the lead out."

Marcy's eyes widened as she sensed the danger in Rigger's rage. Fear corkscrewed in her, scoring the walls of her stomach, biting deep into her nerves. She was between them, a little off to one side, where Newt had shoved her. She was trapped in the cross-fire of their mutual hatred. Her body stiffened impercepti-bly. Her ears, acting like sensitized antennas, had picked up the sounds of hurried steps outside. She peered at Rigger. He had noticed nothing, kept his unblinking eyes on his brother. Newt had his back to them now, stuffing things into the case. She summoned her will and drove her legs to action. She crossed in front of Rigger and, pushing against him, wedged herself through the narrow exit between his body and the doorframe.

In the center of the kitchen she looked back. Rigger was unchanged. The sounds of the outside pounded closer. Hurriedly she crossed to the back door and ran down into the yard. Britt was hurrying across the clearing, his face troubled, his eyes intent on the house. She ran as fast as she could to him. She seized his big arms with all her strength. "You can't!" she cried. "Go back, Britt! You can't go into the house!"

He was breathing heavily and the sweat was oily on his face. His eyes were round with apprehension. "Let go, Marcy," he said. "There's gonna be trouble."

"There's already trouble. It won't do no good you gettin' mixed up in it. It won't do no good!"

He stared down at her, stopping his efforts to break away. He lifted his head and glanced at the angled house. His voice was steady. "I seen some of what happened," he said. "Rigger beat the livin' daylights out of him."

She still had her fingers tight on his arms. "Newt's leavin'. Rigger's puttin' him off the place."

Britt drew a sharp breath. "So?" he muttered. "Newt's finally leavin', eh?"

She nodded. "He's in there packin' now. Rigger's makin' him go. He's throwin' him off the place."

He shifted suddenly and her grip tightened. "There ain't nothin' you could do, Britt!" She shook him. "It ain't your fuss. It's them. Keep out of it, please."

Her desperation touched him and she was right. He had no business messing in the row. His body eased and her hold lessened gradually.

"You said you seen some of what happened?"

"I saw the truck stop over there between the fields. Rigger got out and went ahead a ways. I figured he was just lookin' around, so I went back to work. Then I could hear the truck churnin' and I looked up again. Looked like they was stuck in the mud."

"It's still mucky along the road," she murmured.

"Yeah. That's how I figured. Only I see Rigger turn and come runnin' back to the truck. He yanks the door open and drags Newt down and starts beatin' the hell outta him right off!"

"He don't look so good."

"It's a wonder Rigger didn't kill him, punchin' and kickin' that way. Newt went down a couple of times and the last time he didn't get up." Britt's tone shaded to faint wonder. "That little punk's sure strong as an ox! He picked Newt up like he was nothin' and chucked him in the cab. That was all I could see. Rigger had to work like a dog gettin' them wheels out of that mud. I watched them come to the house. I knew you was here. I didn't want nothin' to go wrong."

There was a tiny smile in her eyes.

Britt's mind was busy. "Funny," he mused, "them startin' a row over somethin' so little as gettin' the truck stuck in the mud."

There was a queer ominous stillness in the house after Newt and Rigger had gone. The door to Newt's abandoned room hung partially open. From her place at the table she could see the drawers of the dresser jutting crookedly out of place, the way he had gone off and left them, the walls and the mirror rim stripped bare of his treasured pin-ups. The silence was heavy, folded into the heat, oppressive. The afternoon dragged on. She was alone at last in the house, but there was no peace.

The trouble had come on Tuesday morning. Rigger had taken Newt and his things into town in the truck before lunchtime. He had not come back to the place Tuesday night. Wednesday passed and Rigger did not return. She followed the prescribed pattern of her routine. Britt worked hard outside, trying to take up the slack caused by the absence of the other two. At mealtimes they talked casually of general things. There was a kind of unspoken agreement between them to avoid anything personal, to keep away from even the usual friendly intimacy. The empty places at the table were hostile. In Rigger's disappearance there was the suggestion of uneasy threat, of a latent, brewing danger. As if he were actually sitting at the table, working around the place, ever present with them, they held conscious guard on their actions, their words, their thinking. The unused door to Newt's deserted room was an added reminder, watching, a gaunt, single, staring eye. Rigger did not come back Thursday or Friday.

It was Cora Winters who inadvertently broke the tension that Friday night. She brought her old Plymouth up in front of the house and left the car, moving curiously around the house, seeking someone out. As she came to the end of the building she saw the two of them sitting out by the open door to Britt's barn room, talking.

"Hi!" Marcy waved.

Cora Winters crossed the yard and came up before them. The evening was sultry and the sun, though gone, still made itself felt in the twilight. "Lordy, it's cookin' me!" Cora gasped and ran her fingers around the neckline of her thin dress.

Britt came to his feet.

"How's things, Britt Callum?" Cora demanded.

"Gettin' along," he said quietly.

Her eyes lingered a moment on his face, as if she were trying to read answers. "That's good," she said. Britt had moved off. "Where you headin'?" Cora called.

"Get you a chair from the kitchen."

She watched him swing across the yard and her attention came tardily to Marcy, sitting there, watching her quietly. "He's a nice guy," Cora conceded. She ran her sweaty palms against her hips. "Ain't the heat awful?" Marcy nodded. Cora eyed her curiously. "What's this I been hearin' 'bout Rigger and Newt havin' a fallin' out?"

"Yeah," Marcy admitted. "Happened Tuesday."

"How come?"

Marcy looked up at her levelly. "I don't know. Rigger never said."

Cora Winters was disappointed. She'd stopped by hoping to get some information. She sighed and scratched at her back. "Damn mosquitoes worse this year, seems like." Her mind swung. "Well, I knowed somethin' was wrong, seein' Newt downtown this mornin'. He ain't never been one to hang round town much."

"Did—did you see Rigger anywhere?"

Cora's brows lifted. "No. Ain't he here?"

"No."

Cora thought for a moment. "All odds he's probably shacked up with that woman of his again." Marcy flushed but Cora rode right on. "You sure drew a prize package in that one!" She caught the distress in Marcy's eyes and for a moment she felt an obscure wave of sympathy. "Don't you be gettin' all in a stew, honey. He'll be comin' back, don't you fret, draggin' his tail behind him." With that she dismissed the subject and turned as Britt came up with the extra chair. "Thanks, Britt. That's right nice of you."

Britt settled himself with his back to the barn wall again while Cora Winters made herself comfortable. "How's Fred doin' on the place?" Britt asked genially.

"Workin' himself to death, of course," Cora Winters said wearily. "Sometimes I don't know if all this workin's worth it."

"Wheat looks good."

Cora snorted. "Probably rain on it 'fore we're done."

Britt sneaked a glance at Marcy but she was sitting with her hands clasped in her lap loosely, her head back, eyes closed. She looked tired.

Cora Winters sensed his gaze and looked at Marcy. She, too, saw the deep cut of fatigue in the girl's face. There was a tiny frown in Cora's brow and she squinted as if she were trying to think something out, to make up her mind about something. Suddenly, in an action rapid for Cora Winters, she leaned over and put her tough hand on Marcy's. "Look, honey, I got a suggestion. Why don't the two of you go on into town tonight, go see a movie or somethin' like that? You're needin' to get off'n the place for a spell. Do you some good. You can't just go on stickin' round here, feelin' like you do. It'll get you sooner or later."

Marcy did not open her eyes. She shrugged dispiritedly. "Rigger took the truck," she said heavily.

Cora Winters frowned, bit her lip, and looked at Britt. "You take my car," she said to him. "Go on." She spoke hurriedly now as the idea took root. "You take the Plymouth, take her into town."

He nodded. "If Marcy wants."

Cora Winters was committed now. "Marcy, honey, give yourself a break. Go on in town, see a show, get some of this outta your system. Ain't gonna hurt nothin' at all. You'll feel better, believe me."

Marcy opened her eyes and peered at her neighbor uncertainly. "Well, I don't know."

"What you worried 'bout—the place here? Shucks, I'll hang round till you get back."

"No need," Britt said. "We'll drop you off home first." He looked at Marcy. "How's about it?"

Marcy was suddenly sick and tired of looking at nothing but the same four walls, fed up with the relentless tension of the past days, weary of the waiting for the sounds of Rigger's inevitable return, for the resumption of the conflict within her, her nerves were worn thin with the constant rub of apprehension. She turned her head and found Britt's eyes. "I'd kinda like to go, if it's all right with you."

CHAPTER THIRTEEN

T HE THICK furry heat of the night slapped them with padded fists as they came out of the air-conditioned theatre. It was still early in the evening and Marcy and Britt walked casually along Indiana Street. The film had been a light, entertaining musical and they felt relaxed. The breeze dusted the pavement idly.

"She's so pretty, "Marcy murmured.

"Who?"

"That Jane Powell."

"Yeah, she sure is," he agreed. "I like him, too."

"Who—Fred Astaire?"

"Yeah."

"He's a good dancer," she said soberly.

"I like that other guy—what's his name?—better."

"Gene Kelly?"

"Guess that's it."

"He's good, too," she conceded. "Only I like Joan Crawford best of all them movie stars. She always looks like a lady, and she can act good, too."

Their conversation dwindled. They idled along without purpose. When they had come to Seventh Street she touched his arm. "Let's walk on up by the courthouse, you want to?"

"O.K. with me."

The lawn in front of the big building looked cool and inviting. Britt turned away from her and sat down at the base of a tree. He grinned at her. "Come on over. The grass feels good." He patted the turf at his side.

She hesitated and then came over and sat down, facing him. He leaned back against the tree trunk and stretched luxuriously. "This here's the life," he grunted.

She eyed the ground around them suspiciously. "We'll get chiggers," she predicted.

As if her comment had brought the pesky little bugs, he reached down and scratched his ankle vigorously.

"You see?" She laughed. "You just wait until they start diggin' in round your middle. Sometimes they nearly set me crazy."

He groaned loudly. "What a lousy country!" he complained. "Texas, hah! Bugs all the time!"

They shared a smile. They sat in silence, watching the people and the cars going up and down Seventh Street, watching the activity around the bus terminal across the street.

"I'd sure like to be goin' somewheres," she murmured.

He brought his eyes to her. The sudden longing to get away was sharp in him and he knew what she meant. He said nothing.

The bus for El Paso came down the street and pulled into its berth alongside the building with spitting brakes. He watched the passengers beginning to line up at the door. She was watching not them but him. His chin was so firm; his dark soft eyes had caught the reflection of the multicolored lights from across the way and there was strength and comfort in his profile.

"What're you lookin' at?"

"You."

"See somethin' wrong?"

She shook her head with a smile.

Suddenly he drew his legs up under him and came forward on the spring of his muscles. He seized her hands in her lap. "How much longer can we go on like this, Marcy?" he demanded. "How the hell long do we have to go on makin' believe it don't mean nothin' at all?"

she held herself rigid from him, tugging vainly, trying to free herself of his hold. "Don't, Britt. You mustn't!" She shot a frantic glance toward the street. "Someone'll see us!"

"Let 'em!"

Her hands slipped from his grasp and went behind her; her fingers crooked, anchoring in the hard crust of the earth. Her arms were braced, supporting her bent back like that. His arms came around her and he took her close to him. Her face was tilted and their lips met, not harshly in the insistence of denied passion, not fiercely in the drive of tardy fulfillment, but softly, gently, come together because the time had run out. Unmindful of the lights, of the presence of people nearby, putting away the ever present threat of discovery, he held her to him and the tide of understanding and completeness came over them, swamping them in the swift flood of release. A tiny breeze came from the north and hesitated, surprised, reluctant to touch them, and, then, tossing all caution aside, gaily, puckishly it came running, buffeting, poking, swirling about them in happy laughing joyousness.

There were no words between them afterward. There was no need for talking about what had finally happened. The thing known to each of them for so long was shared now. The moment was come and the long days of knowing and keeping silent were done between them. The future stretched forth uncharted and full of doubt. The present, these little seconds alone, this was the only reality. They sat apart from each other, each staring at the bustling beehive of the terminal across the way, needing to say nothing, drawing peace and strength from each other's nearness.

The sound as she suddenly slapped her leg cracked his preoccupation. He glanced at her quickly.

"Mosquito this time!" She grinned ruefully.

He smiled faintly. A moment later he scratched his back hard. "Chigger?"

He grunted. "Feels like it."

She got to her feet and stood above him, her dress billowing gently in the breeze. "You best get off that grass," she observed. "We're gonna have to take us a bath in ammonia water as it is."

She pulled him to his feet and looked up into his eyes and saw the quickening impulse born. "No!" She moved away. "We mustn't! If someone should see us ... "

There was no need for her to finish the thought. As if she had sounded an alarm, he peered off to the street. There was no one close by. The people waiting for the bus to load were too far from them. She had already struck out for the sidewalk. He caught up with her on the corner and they waited for the light to change. As they crossed to the other side he felt as if he were walking back into yesterday.

They had left Cora Winters' old Plymouth parked near Tenth Street on Ohio, behind the theatre. They walked unhurriedly, slowly, looking casually at the displays in the stores, staring with fascinated eyes at the piled, unassorted treasures in the pawn-shop windows. The heat was heavy, the night humid. Britt's shirt stuck to his sweating back. He ran a testing tongue along his lips.

"How's about gettin' us a beer before we start back?"

She hesitated and he saw her eyes slant to the Red Club across the street and he knew she was remembering.

"We don't have to go to the same place every time," he offered.

"It don't matter," she murmured. "I reckon one place is as good as another."

He steered her down the sidewalk, his eyes busy. He was try-ing to pick out the right place, some joint not too crowded, some place that looked cool and comfortable. The Indian Head looked O.K. He glanced down at her for approval and she nodded. They went in and came up to the bar almost directly under the big whirring blades of the ceiling fan. Her hair seemed to lift, to go floating in the cross draft.

They chanced the second beer. There was little talk between them. They stood side by side, comfortable in their shared time,

taking as long as they liked, listening absently to the steady patter of the people in the room. She was making some little comment about one of the scenes in the movie they had seen earlier.
She was standing between him and the door, facing him, looking
down along the bar length as she spoke. It was over her shoulder
that he saw Rigger Kates and Ruby coming along the sidewalk
outside. He clamped his muscles, guarding himself against any
sign that she might be able to read or feel. What he so desperately
hoped was not to be. Rigger Kates and his woman came through
the front door into the place.

Rigger looked bad. His eyes were bloodshot, dark-circled,
and his skin was tainted with that sickly greenish pallor earned
with excesses. He entered first, trailed by Ruby, who moved sluggishly, as if she were near to exhaustion. Rigger came ahead,
walking toward them slowly. Britt held himself in harsh control;
he was praying Rigger would somehow fail to see them, would
go right on by.

It was Ruby who saw him first. She glanced up and caught
sight of him in Rigger's path. Her eyes shifted instantly and she
saw Marcy. There was a quick flash of distress in her face and he
saw her hand come up short, as if she had moved instinctively
to grab Rigger, to stop him. He was beyond her reach. Her eyes
found Britt in the instant before Rigger looked up. He saw a kind
of defeat darken her.

Rigger stopped dead in his tracks. He peered up dully,
frowning faintly. He looked first at Britt and then he shifted his
hardening eyes to Marcy.

She caught the instant alert in Britt the moment Rigger came
before them. There was in immediate stiffening in her and she
wheeled to come face to face with her husband. She sucked her
breath and trapped her lower lip under her teeth. Rigger stood
solid, his eyes darting quickly from Britt to her and back again.
Marcy felt the scream knotting in her throat. The quick hot lust
was bright in her husband's eyes.

"Rigger!" she cried, reaching out swiftly.

Ruby skirted past them hurriedly, unnoticed, and went down to the end of the room.

Rigger's face hardened. "You two been havin' yourselves some fun?"

"We just come in for a movie," she faltered.

"I bet!"

"It's true!" She began to twist her hands nervously. "It—it was all my idea, Rigger, honest. I—it was me who wanted to come."

"Sure," Rigger agreed nastily. "Person ought to do what he wants."

Britt was uneasy. There was a deadliness in Rigger's manner. His face was tight, expressionless, and the eyes had ceased their shifting, were steady, close on Marcy. She had her head bent and her hands kept washing themselves.

"You figure on comin' back to the place soon?" Britt ventured quietly. "Wheat's comin' right along."

Rigger's head twisted and he stared along the beam of the voice. "Shove the wheat where you can't eat it!" he snarled. "I'll be comin' back when I get plenty ready!" The mean little eyes were level and then they went down and found Marcy again. "You're gettin' pretty damn gay, steppin' out all of a sudden-like, ain'tcha?" he goaded. "Hell, I remember back when you ain't never been so all-fired hot to come runnin' to town."

She made a helpless little movement with her hands. "I been feelin' bad," she offered in a low, tiny voice. "I just got to thinkin' maybe a movie might make me feel kinda better."

"Yeah."

She raised her head sharply, defiantly. "I did!" she cried. "I reckoned as how it might take my thinkin' off things."

"What the hell kinda thinkin' you been tryin' to get shut of?"

She caught the slyness of his words, saw that funny look in his eyes. Her face flushed. "No kind," she whispered. "Only what with you and Newt fightin' like you done and all—well, I was kinda upset."

Rigger's sneer was broad. He glanced at Britt. His eyes found her again. "Couldn't be what Newt was tellin' me was right, maybe?"

The sickness balled on the floor of her stomach and she shifted and lowered her eyes. "I—I don't know what Newt's been tellin' you. He's crazy, anyhow."

"Maybe we been barkin' up the wrong tree all the time. Maybe Newt ain't so crazy."

Britt knew now what Newt had told him, what had caused the row. He felt the sweat skittering down along the hollow of his spine. "Wait up, Rigger." He took hold of Rigger's arm.

"Get your goddamn hands off'n me!" Rigger shouted. He twisted sharply, wrenching himself free. "You got nothin' to say to me, big boy!" His eyes narrowed. "I sure was a chump. I shoulda had better sense. Pickin' you outta the gutter like I done, givin' you a place to stay. Jesus, I must be gettin' soft. First thing outta the bag you start tomcattin' after the old lady." He heard Marcy's sudden gasp, brought his firing eyes to her dead giveaway face. His little body hunched and tightened and his head pushed forth from the cup of his shoulders. "You—you double-timin' bitch! So that no-good bastard's right, after all!" he croaked. "So maybe Newt's not so nuts, hey? You and this tramp's been hookin' together all the time!"

Britt's face weighted dark with blood; his temples throbbed under the bursting pressure. He reached down between them and seized Rigger's shoulder, jerking him off balance, snapping the hold of his eyes on her. The little guy's face contorted grotesquely. He raised his fist and brought it down with all his strength on the thick forearm high across his chest. Britt's breath whistled through clenched teeth as the pain shot along his arm. He stepped back against a stranger struggling to get out of the way behind him. Rigger was after him instantly. Before Britt was ready Rigger struck. The little hard-balled fist came crashing through the void and brought the shock of exploding night to Britt's brain. Only the unknown man behind him, unable to escape the staggering body, kept him from falling to the floor. His arms flailed out and his fingers found the edge of the bar, locking immediately, holding him. He shook his head sharply, trying to clear his eyes.

Rigger had raised his arm again. He swung back to face Marcy and his fingers stretched as the hand chopped down to catch her flat across the mouth. There was a single sharp cry from her: She had made no move to protect herself. There was the crack of the blow, the cry, and nothing more. She stood very still, her eyes wide with disbelief. Slowly she pulled herself straight and her lips tightened, underlining the surging pain in her eyes. Then, quietly, almost leisurely, she moved forward. She passed directly in front of him and did not look back. She went down the length of the room to the front door and went outside.

Britt's anger burst in his face. His words came spitting through stiff lips. "I'm gonna kill you, you no-good cowardly sonofabitch! I'll kill you, so help me!"

Rigger stared up at the man who came at him. He blinked once. It was as if his striking her had unhooked the framework of his co-ordination. Britt's blow was simple, direct, telling. Rigger's head snapped back on the stem of his neck and his knees buckled slowly. He wavered slightly, then toppled forward and slid along the floor, a dead weight. His right arm was hung over the scuffed brass rail, his left pushed straight before his body, the hand flat, the fingers hooked on the lip of the cuspidor, tipping the thing over, spewing its contents on him, over the floor. Britt stared down at the little guy at his feet. Rigger lay quite still. Britt brought himself straight and lifted his chin. He stepped over the body and started after Marcy.

Newt Kates sat alone at the table in the corner of the Indian Head and shook himself, licking his lips. He reached up and rubbed his right eye hard. He could hardly believe what he had just seen with his own eyes. He had been startled out of his wits when they had come in, the big fellow and Marcy, when they had gone past him not more than a few feet away, not seeing him. He had hunched down low, stroking the sleek side of the wet beer bottle, watching them covertly at the bar. When he had seen that funny look come over Callum's face, he knew instantly what was up. He did not even have to turn his head to see his brother enter. Rigger had gone right up to them before he stopped. The rest of it had been played out like a silent movie. He saw their lips move soundlessly; the sudden climax of blows had been noiseless to him. Surprise caught him; his excitement had come swiftly, he had wanted to climb right up on the table to try to get a better look.

Newt Kates drained the last of the beer from the bottle hurriedly and got to his feet. His insides were spinning around like wet clothes in a washing machine. There was a fullness in his head that threatened an ache. Some men had gathered quickly, screening Rigger's prostrate body from his sight. He stooped down, trying to peer through the spread arches of their legs. He could see the whitish soles of Rigger's boots, the bits of faded denim that were his Levis. As he tried to see more, someone grabbed Rigger by the armpits. The legs and the feet were drawn scuffling forward. The knot of men moved, going down along the bar toward the other end of the room. Newt straightened irritably and squinted. He could see Rigger's sandy head now and then, bobbing heavily from one side to the other in the midst of them. Carefully he moved, picking his way between the tables, following them. They had propped Rigger in a chair at the table where the woman was. They had accomplished their duty; now they disappeared, leaving him slumped over the table, his arms flat, his head turned cheek down on the surface, with the woman bending anxiously over him.

Newt found an empty table near them and sat down. He motioned silently for service and got another beer. He watched in curious fascination. Ruby had got a towel from somewhere and she was working feverishly, holding Rigger's head up from the table by the hair, wiping away the blood specks, sapping him with the damp end. Newt could see consciousness returning in the flicker of the lids. Rigger stirred fitfully and tried to turn his head away, to avoid her steady slapping. Eventually she managed to bring him awake. He slumped back in the chair, his eyes glazed and dull, while she went on with her ministrations, wiping away the scum of the emptied cuspidor from his arms and hands, trying to lessen the stain of the stuff from the T shirt. Newt was wholly absorbed. He drank occasionally from the bottle.

When he was sure Rigger had been restored to full consciousness, Newt Kates finished his beer. He pushed the bottle aside and got to his feet. He took a final look at the two of them and started back between the tables, headed for the door to the street. At the entrance he stopped and glanced back once more. Over the heads of the others, through the thick bluish haze of smoke in the place, he could see them. The woman Ruby was helping the little guy to his feet. They started toward him, she with her arm around his little waist, he uncertain, unsteady, trusting to her lead and support.

Newt Kates stepped down off the high curbstone and crossed the wide, cobbled street. On the opposite side he stopped. He glanced over to the front of the Indian Head. He moved a little to one side and propped himself against a parking meter. He watched curiously as Ruby struggled to hold open the door, to help Rigger out to the sidewalk. As they started down the walk, Newt gave himself a little shove away from the meter. He went down his side of the road, moving in the same direction as they did. His eyes were pinched and narrow, and, even though his lips worked in constant spasms, there was a faint smile of deep, confident satisfaction on his face.

CHAPTER FOURTEEN

H E TRIED to bring some measure of comfort to her once they were in the old Plymouth. He reached over and held her close to him. She made no resistance nor did she make any effort to accept him voluntarily. She simply sat there, gathered up against him, and her breathing was tattered, uneven, her palms hard against the breadth of his back. She no longer wept, but a kind of ceaseless uncontrollable sobbing went on somewhere deep inside her, racking her body under vicious recurrent tremors.

When he released her finally and put his hands on the steering wheel she slid away from him and drew herself into the far corner of the seat, huddled down, her eyes wide and empty, set sightless on the road.

There was no word spoken on the way home. When they came to the ruts of the road to the house Britt slowed the machine and looked over at her again. She had not changed her position, had made no sound of any kind. The place was shadowed, dark, ghostly in its aloneness. He hesitated and then swung the car abruptly onto the twin trail up to the house. He glanced at her with sharp concern. She was still over in the corner, small, rolled up into a little trembling ball, and her eyes were big and dark with hurt.

Britt brought the car around to the back of the house and stopped. He turned off the engine and the headlights and they sat still together, swallowed up in the stillness and the utter desolate blackness of the place. Automatically she came to slow life and felt for the door handle. Britt said nothing, made no move, just sat quietly watching her as she pushed the door open and stepped down. The door clicked but did not shut. She did not move to close it or to move away from the side of the machine. She straightened gradually and passed her hand down one side of her face, as if she were awakening from a dream. Britt stared at her. His hand found the outside handle of the driver's door and he got out of the car and went around to her. Standing in front of her, looking down on her, he reached forth slowly and touched her arm. There was no response in her. He quickened his pressure and slowly, gradually, she brought her head up and looked into his face with dreadful eyes.

"Oh, Marcy, Marcy, my darling!" he whispered hoarsely. "My darling, my darling!"

She stood frowning, uncomprehending, staring up at him almost as if he were some stranger, almost as if she were unsure of him as well. Then, suddenly, her whole reserve cracked and crumbled and she hurled herself to him. "Oh, my God!" she cried, and her arms went around him and she buried her face hard against the firm warm column of his neck. The great pulsing maleness of him came cloaking her and hiding her from all the outside and she clung tightly, hungrily, demandingly to him.

He worked to break the lock of her grasp and finally he pressed her away from him, looking down into her eyes to make sure, and then his lips came down and took hers and his arms went around her and gathered her into the tight circle of his protection. Easily, gently, he held her for a long moment, and then together they crossed the little space of the bleak yard to the shadowed rectangle that was the open door to the little room in the barn.

They lay very quiet afterward, side by side, and the stillness and the peace that was in them both seemed to have spilled out from them to fill the whole world. There was no sound anywhere. Even the fitful breezes of the earlier evening had failed to nothingness; there was no reminder of life beyond them.

Britt lay on his back, his eyes closed, breathing in long, deep draughts, holding her hand clasped loosely in his down between their thighs. She could not tell if he had fallen asleep or not. Rising on her elbow, she bent over him, trying to make out his features in the blackness. She brought her free hand to his chest and stroked him carefully, feeling her way to his neck, his chin, putting her fingertips to his parted lips lightly. He was awake; he reached up and took her hand and kissed the open palm gently.

She remained like that, bent over him, for a long time. She moved her free hand over him slowly, as if she were trying to familiarize herself with his body, to capture the outline of him in the memory pads of her fingers. At length she withdrew her other hand and pressed him away from her side. Britt swung from the cot and stood in the center of the little room, uncertain of her action and its reason. She came to her feet, saying nothing, and dressed swiftly. Britt pulled on his Levis and shirt, watching her closely. She came past him and went to the doorway and stood there looking out over the familiar flat of the place. He came up behind her and put his arms around her waist.

"What's the matter?"

She drew a long solid breath and turned and looked into his face searchingly. "We done somethin' awful wrong," she pronounced slowly. "I didn't want nothin' like this happenin'. We shouldn't have done it."

He tightened the loop of his arms and drew her up against him, putting his face down into the softness of her hair. "We'll go away," he said. "We'll go away, a long ways away, where there'll be just the two of us, like it's meant to be."

Marcy held herself firm, looking up over his wide shoulder into the darkness of the room. "Like it's meant to be," she whispered. "Oh, Britt, if it only could be like that!"

"It will be. It will be, Marcy." He held her by the shoulders and looked eagerly down into her troubled face. "You can get a divorce, and we'll get married. Ain't no reason why it can't be you and me together all the time."

Marcy felt the spiral start and then die away. Her mouth was sore and she remembered that look in the eyes of Rigger Kates. Inside her suddenly she felt black and hollowed out. She reached up and touched Britt Callum's cheek with her fingertips almost wonderingly, sadly. "There's all kinds of reasons for everything," she said.

She turned slowly and stepped down into the yard. Overhead the stars were icy diamonds and the lush warmth of the night was like velvet on skin. He stood in the doorway and watched her as she went to the center of the yard. She stopped there and stood looking for a minute at the dark forbidding black outline of the deserted house. Even from the doorway to his room Britt could see her shoulders suddenly gather and square. She turned and looked back at him.

"Britt?"

He came forward now, went to her side, but did not touch her. "Yeah?"

She spoke slowly, deliberately. "I want you to take me up to the Winters place. I'm gonna spend the night there. I can't take this place tonight, not tonight!"

A little wave of relief broke somewhere inside him. It was right she should go there tonight, right now. After the beef in town, no tellin' what might happen before the night was done. Nothin' must happen, not now. "Sure," he agreed readily. "Come on."

They climbed into the old Plymouth and he started the engine and switched on the headlights. She was sitting straight now, her hands folded easily in her lap, her eyes wide and free of fear. Impulsively he reached over and put his arm around her shoulder. She came willingly and their kiss was brief. Britt released her and started the car forward. There was a sudden new feeling of strength and purpose in him. They'd get off the place, go somewheres a long ways from all this and get married and have their lives together! By God, he knew now where he was goin', what he wanted to do, for the first time in his life!

Cora Winters answered the back door in her wrapper with her hair tousled and her eyes heavy with sleep. She stared at the two of them through a narrow crack and then opened the door and let them into the kitchen. Curiosity brought sharp wakefulness to her quickly.

"I'd like to stay here tonight," Marcy said quietly.

Cora fought to wipe the slumber webs from her brain. "Why, sure thing, child." She glanced rapidly from Marcy to Britt and back again. "Somethin' go wrong?" she ventured cautiously.

Marcy shook her head. "Nothin' important. We ran into Rigger in town, that's all."

Cora Winters sucked in a shocked, knowing breath and wet her lips. "Oh, my God!"

Neither Britt nor Marcy seemed to want to tell her anything further and she did not press them. The two of them looked so queer standing there, as if they had secrets or something between them. Cora Winters had a vague feeling of misgiving. She sure hoped she was doin' the right thing, lettin' the girl spend the night here. She sure didn't want to get mixed up in no Kates family fight.

She crossed the floor and pulled the door to the hallway shut. "Fred's dead to the world," she said. "Poor devil's been workin' like a horse all day." She eyed the two of them standing there saying nothing, making no move. "Some coffee?" she suddenly asked.

"Nothin' for me, thanks," Britt said. He turned to Marcy and his tone was lower, softer. "I'll be gettin' on back to the place."

Marcy nodded and kept her eyes impersonal. She said nothing.

Cora Winters went to the back door with him. "Want to take the car, Britt? You can bring it back in the mornin'."

Britt shook his head soberly. "Thanks, Mrs. Winters, I'll hoof it. Ain't so far and the hike'll do me good."

" 'Night, then," Cora said. She watched him go striding off alongside the house to the road until the darkness had swallowed him. She turned her eyes to the sky. Not a cloud, not a breath of air. Tomorrow'd be another blisterer, all right. Tardily she remembered Marcy Kates sitting in her kitchen and she frowned. Almost reluctantly she stepped back and eased the screen shut and went to make some coffee.

Britt stirred restlessly. It was unearthly still and the heat was unbearable. He lay naked, stretched on the flat of his back, staring with wide sleepless eyes into the shadowed ceiling. The sweat beaded on his body and went trickling, dripping to the sheet. The night happenings had kicked up a whirlwind in his brain. He sought sleep avidly, desperately. The frantic striving only underlined his wakefulness. He turned irritably on the bed. He stared toward the planked wall. He saw again Marcy's look of disbelief and hurt when Rigger had slapped her. He saw Rigger's surprised face as he had fallen. The area around his nose where Rigger had hit him had begun to throb. He thrashed on the bed, flipping over on his belly, burying his face deep in the pillow. The fragment pictures kept returning. His hand hurt, too, where he had connected with Rigger's jaw. A vague spray of unrest bathed him as he remembered. He saw Rigger stretched out like that at his feet, just like that guy in Oklahoma had been, like those other guys in Memphis, in San Diego, and all the rest. Minute panic swept over him. He'd gone and done it again, despite all the resolves, all the big fat promises to himself. Only Rigger Kates had been askin' for it—not just this time only, the other times, too. In a moment he had whipped over on his back once more. He jackknifed his legs and locked his fingers under his head. It was not even midnight yet. There was a long snail line of hours yet to come. He forced all the other thinking from his brain and tried to concentrate on Marcy. She'd have to divorce Rigger right off. They'd go away somewheres, somehow, and they'd make a brand-new life, far from all this. Thinking of her did not encourage sleep. It just made the wakefulness more bearable, that's all.

He finally drifted into a kind of suspended consciousness, but not sleep. His eyes were closed and his breathing steady, regular. He had no power or control over his muscles and yet his mind remained active, alert. He lay still but there was in him a readiness, a sandpapered sensitivity. The first sounds touched him and brought his eyes open instantly. He did not change position. He lay very quiet and listened.

In the silence of the place outside he knew instantly what it was that had registered in his consciousness. It had been the simple, almost imperceptible whine of the screen door to the house.

Britt got to his feet and reached for his Levis. He pulled them on, fastened a couple of the buttons, and went barefooted to the door. Standing in the darkness of the room, looking out over the yard, he saw the light come on in the kitchen. In the slanting rays he caught a glimpse of the red pickup truck standing alongside the house. Rigger must have come back! He hesitated. He certainly had no desire to see that little bastard again tonight. Yet something drew him forward. He stepped down into the yard. The night heat was like a cloak over his naked shoulders. His feet padded over the warmth of the dirt and he headed directly for the house. He had no intention of going inside. He edged close to the screen door and peered through. The kitchen was deserted. Rigger must have gone to bed and forgotten to turn off the light. Britt straightened. Before he could turn away Newt Kates suddenly came from his bedroom and hurried to the kitchen table. Britt crouched down and stared. Newt was grinning like an ape. Britt raised himself a little, carefully, trying to see what it was Newt had brought with him from the room. What he had tossed to the tabletop was only a pair of khaki trousers. Newt was already working with his belt. He unfastened the buckle, ripped open the fly with a single downward thrust. Quickly he stepped out of his dirty, smeared pants and put on the clean pair. As Newt worked to button the fresh trousers, Britt found himself staring at the discarded lump of cloth before him on the other side of the screen. He swallowed hard and raised his widening eyes to the older man. The lips were still twisted in that unchanging, almost triumphant grin.

Newt moved toward the door and snatched the trousers from the floor. He took them over to the stove and, working feverishly, he took the lids off the trashburning unit and stuffed the garment down into the empty maw. He reached up and got a match from the wall container. The flame held against the cloth spurted sluggishly and failed to ignite the wadded mass. Newt cursed in a whisper. He thought hard for a moment, then went over to the sink and bent down, opening the little doors behind which Marcy kept her cleaning things. He got a bottle, returned to the stove, and emptied the contents over the pants, soaking them thoroughly. When he touched the saturated material with the second match the flames burst forth hungrily. Newt stood back and watched the stuff burn to a black stiff ash. When the flames had done their work he leaned over and poked the remnants with his hand, breaking down the fragile shelled remains, powdering the ash. As he set the lids back into place Britt slipped off balance and his hand grabbed at the boards of the side of the house. Newt cocked his head and his eyes narrowed. He came quickly to the screen door and stood peering out over the yard. Almost at Newt's feet Britt held his breath and fought to make himself small. After a moment Newt gave up and moved back into the kitchen. Britt ducked away and ran as fast as he could across the yard, making for the sanctuary of the little room.

Once inside Britt stayed by the door and stared out across the inky black moat of the yard. Newt had come back to the doorway opposite and stood there, outlined by the lights behind him. He was standing rigid, legs braced, arms akimbo, head pulled back, listening intently. Britt kept to one side of the doorframe, shielding himself. Newt finally moved from the doorway. After some moments the light in the kitchen was extinguished. Britt remained in his observation post. Newt must have gone to bed. He shifted to leave the door, to get to bed, but further sounds stopped him, brought him back.

Newt Kates had come outside. He let the door close, guiding it shut with his fingers, keeping the noise down. Britt saw him glance toward the barn. Then the older man went quickly, quietly along the back of the house, around the building to the truck. He started the engine and without turning on the headlights he backed the machine around the house to the cleared space out front. Only when the car faced the highway did he turn on the lamps. The truck moved slowly to the road and turned toward town. Britt watched the taillights disappear.

He turned from the door and stared, frowning, at the dim outline of his chair, his table, and the cot. Something was wrong. Long strands of misgiving began to come like giant tendrils, binding themselves quickly about his insides. He sat down on the side of the cot and rubbed his forehead hard. There was in him a growing sense of wrongness about everything. How come Newt Kates was driving the red truck, when it was Rigger who had taken it to town? How come Newt Kates was back again? Where was Rigger? An instant driving urge to put on his clothes, to go after Marcy *now*, to get the hell out of this place prodded him. But he knew that was out. He swiped at his sleek forehead again. It was gettin' hotter and hotter by the minute, seemed like.

He got to his feet and stripped naked. He crossed the open deserted yard to the pump by the back steps. Bending down, he grasped the handle and began to work it vigorously. As soon as the chill icy water came gushing, he crouched and moved in to let the cascade come spilling, flooding over his head and shoulders, dousing him. His breath caught and his teeth chattered but there was something cleansing, settling in the very shock. Still squatting, he reached up blindly and found the handle again, encouraging the flow. Finally he moved out crablike from under the curved spigot and stood erect. His body tingled all over. He brought his hands down over his chest, over his belly, and, bending over, he used his palms as scrapers to slough the water film from his skin. He straightened and stood in the dark, feeling the absorbent warmth of the night. He felt a lot better now, refreshed, renewed. He raised his eyes and scanned the dusty white of the sky. Suddenly it seemed as if there were beauty everywhere in the night about him, in him, and for a brief moment all the ugliness and the unpleasantness of the days past were gone. He wished she were with him now, in this instant, that there were only the two of them left in this kind of world, that they might have each other this way, together from this time forward in open honesty, in fullness and completeness.

CHAPTER FIFTEEN

ORA WINTERS came into the kitchen, carefully shutting the inner back door, mindful always of her sleeping husband in the front part of the house. She straightened and looked across to Marcy Kates. The girl had her elbows on the table and her head bent forward, with her palms on each side of her head, the long fingers buried deep in her hair. "Washed out, honey?" she asked sympathetically as she came forward.

Marcy raised her head, not taking her arms down, bringing her hands together, cupping her chin. "It's been a long night already," she observed thickly.

Cora Winters pulled her wrapper close about her and dragged a chair out and sat down. "Reckon you'll want to be gettin' to bed right off."

Marcy straightened and leaned back in the chair, clasping her hands out on the oilcloth before her. "No, not yet. I don't reckon as how I could sleep, way I'm feelin'."

Cora Winters hesitated, then chanced it. "Just what all happened in town tonight?"

Marcy managed a thin, grim smile. "Well, we got to see the movie, at least," she said ironically. "It was a good one, too." Her eyes shaded suddenly and she looked away from Cora Winters' flat, restrained face. "Afterward we stopped for a beer and ran spang into Rigger and that woman of his."

"Oh, my God!" Cora Winters breathed.

Marcy acted as if she had not heard. She swallowed with difficulty and tossed her head faintly, bringing her chin up a little. "I'm gonna walk out on him, I reckon," she said bluntly.

Cora Winters stared in disbelief. Things must have been pretty rough downtown, at that. She'd thought it was nothin' more'n a beef, but if Marcy was thinkin' of pullin' out—well! "You're gonna leave Rigger?" she echoed dubiously.

"Yeah, that's it," Marcy said. "I reckon as how maybe I got enough of this kind of livin' at last."

Cora Winters' agile mind went flashing. "This here Britt fella—you and him's thinkin' of takin' off together, ain't you?"

She had not made it so much a question as a dull statement. Marcy came forward a little and peered into Cora's rounding eyes. There was a kind of tentative troublesome worry there. Marcy sat back. "Yeah, Cora, that's it," she admitted flatly.

Cora Winters gulped and her burned color faded a little. She clasped her hands tight in her lap, unclasped them in the next moment, and finally got to her feet and went away from the table, over to the sink, and stood for a long time looking up out of the window at the black sky.

Marcy watched her patiently. For some reason she suddenly wanted Cora Winters to get it straight, to understand—and yet there seemed to be nothing more to add to the bald truth already out in the open. "Cora, don't you see—I gotta get out! It's just one damn thing after another. A body can't go on takin' it forever." Marcy's voice steadied. "I reckon as how I tried the best I could to make a go of it. I ain't said nothin' about the woman, I put up with the drinkin' and the fightin' and all the rest of it for a long time—four whole years of it now. There's been other things too, nobody knows about, nobody has to." She faltered. Cora Winters' back was solid against her. For all Marcy could tell, Cora wasn't even paying any heed to what she was trying so desperately to say. "Rigger struck me tonight in town, Cora," Marcy said coldly, clearly. "It—it ain't the first time-only it's gonna be the last."

Cora Winters shut her eyes hard and gritted her teeth. She waited for Marcy to go on, to get the whole thing off her chest. But Marcy Kates had apparently finished. There was nothing more. Slowly Cora Winters forced herself to turn at her place and glanced across the room. Marcy was sitting bolt upright in her place, her hands quiet in her lap, watching her levelly.

"Course, I reckon you know what's best for you, Marcy." Cora stumbled on unfamiliar ground. "I ain't wantin' to be gettin' mixed up in other folks' troubles. Lord knows, I got me plenty of my own." She forced a deep breath. "You ain't tellin' me nothing about them Kates fellas I ain't been knowin' all my life. Their daddy was a hell-raisin' ole sinner and them boys followed right in the old man's footsteps, I reckon. Only them boys is doin' their daddy one better ever'time they turn round." Cora Winters had not left the sink; she leaned against the edge with her hands on each side of her, her thin arms supporting her lank body. "I been wonderin' for a long time how you put up with them two. I know you done all you can. I ain't sayin' as how you're right or you're wrong, doin' what you're gonna do. It's just I ain't much for this here runnin' off with another man, that's all."

"I'm in love with Britt Callum, Cora," Marcy said very softly. "And he loves me like I ain't never been loved in all my life. I ain't sure no more what's right and what's wrong. Seems to me like if somebody's happy and there ain't no more bein' scared and there ain't no more bein' hurt, then it's right more'n it's wrong."

Cora Winters sighed heavily. She turned sideways and dug her blunt uneven fingernail into the soft wood of the drain board. "I ain't up on these here things," she confessed. "I been married for near thirty years to Fred Winters. He ain't no romantic kinda man, but he's been a right good steady man, in his way. I ain't been dancin' in the streets bein' happy, maybe, but I been mostly satisfied, I reckon, takin' all in all." She straightened slowly. "I reckon most times this love stuff's all in them movies down at the Wichita. Folks I know just gets along and sticks, no matter what."

Marcy smiled, faintly derisive. "You reckon as how I'm turning into a right bad woman, don't you, Cora."

The older woman colored in deep confusion. "I ain't sayin' nothin! I ain't judgin' nobody. I got my hands full just takin' care of me and Fred Winters." She shoved herself from the sink, working to keep her eyes away from Marcy Kates, to restore her control, and she went to the cupboard. She took down the large container and spoke without looking back. "I'm fixin' us some coffee. Reckon as how maybe both of us could do with some."

Marcy Kates exhaled slowly. It wasn't no good. Cora Winters was scared to death, she could tell. There just wasn't nobody she could spill over on. Well, this here was one time she'd have to make up her own mind and make it up right.

Cora Winters busied herself with the coffee things. She could feel Marcy all tensed up behind her. The whole talk had made Cora Winters uneasy, nervous, and her hands shook as she tried to measure out the coffee. She had a feeling of doom in her and yet truthfully, as she reasoned now, she tried to know that Marcy Kates was right. She sure couldn't go on like she was, with that Rigger Kates. It was only this other guy, this Callum, her goin' off with him. There was somethin' that stuck in her craw, her doin' a thing like that. She got the coffee on the stove under a high fire and went over to the sink window and peered out. "Looks to be another hot one tomorrow," she observed shakily.

Marcy came slowly back to the moment. "Yeah."

Cora Winters could think of nothing to say. Her gaze drifted around and came to the face of the clock on the sill. "Almost twelve already," she murmured. Her fingers found the switch of the little radio on the shelf at her left. "There's some news at midnight. Might as well see what's doin'." Anything to keep the conversation away from that other business.

The little set took a moment or so to warm its insides and then the room was filled with the coarse scratch of static. She moved the dial marker slowly, keeping the volume down. Some western music was mercifully buried under the ripping interference. "Lots of electricity in the air tonight," she muttered. Finally she found the station she wanted and the reception was all right. The announcer's voice was bored and uninspired, reading a long-winded commercial announcement for some local outfit. She took her hand away and put some slices of bread in the oven to toast.

Marcy turned her head and stared out of the window at her side. The night was inky black, no moon at all. She could see nothing outside; all she saw in the pane was the reflection of herself, and she stared, seeing the lines of fatigue and the worry marks around her eyes. The commercial dragged on to a finish and there was an empty pause as the announcer apparently collected his items.

He took several minutes to report on some hearings in Washington, quoting long and contradictory statements from obscure politicians. "All the time talk, talk, talk!" Cora snorted. Marcy kept looking at the window, paying little attention to any of it. Her mouth still hurt where Rigger had bruised her. She brought her hand up and gently rubbed her lips with her fingertips. The announcer went on down the list of his reports. There had been an auto accident on a farm road near town. Two youngsters killed, local residents, vets. Funeral services pending. Some obscure movie starlet was in town to make personal appearances at the movie house. Wheat was up, hogs were down. "Oughta be gettin' somethin' on the weather soon," Cora Winters said.

As if he had heard her the speaker switched controls to Kell Field and the weather man read his report. There was a cold front building in the northwest, lots of thunderstorms and hail in the western plains. Much damage to buildings. High winds could be expected here late tomorrow. Another big dust storm was stretched from Amarillo in the north to Lubbock in the west, possibly headed east. The dusty heat would continue. High for tomorrow in the upper nineties.

"Well, that's that," Cora Winters grunted. She peered out of the window. "Reckon he's tellin' the truth, from the looks of it." She moved over and switched off the flame under the boiling coffee and pulled the oven tray out, spearing the browned slices on a fork, stacking them on a plate. She came over and set the pile on the table before Marcy with a shallow smile. When everything was ready she went over to the sink to turn off the radio. Her fingers reached up and she touched the control knob. At that instant Cora Winters froze into place.

Her eyes rounded and she stared up at the brocade-covered mouth of the speaker. The announcer's voice had gone on reading his news dispiritedly. Marcy's head snapped around and her lips parted, her eyes darkened instantly, and her hands jerked from the table and gripped the edge, the knuckles going white under the force of her clenching fingers.

The two women were motionless, breathless, caught in the common paralysis, fixed in their places, brought to instant shock by the casual, everyday phrases that came so easily, so routinely from the lips of a man they did not even know:

"Wichita Falls police tonight are investigating the puzzling circumstances surrounding the apparent brutal beating of a young, widely-known local farmer, Rigger Kates, aged twenty-eight, who was found unconscious and seriously injured in a back alley in the downtown district about two hours ago. The identity of his assailant or assailants is unknown at present, though it is known that Kates had been involved in a dispute in an Ohio Street tavern earlier tonight. Kates was rushed to Rose Circle Hospital here, where, at the time we went on the air, he had not regained consciousness. Attending doctors at Rose Circle hold out little hope for his recovery."

CHAPTER SIXTEEN

THERE WAS a tiny click as her fingers automatically shut off the set. After that there was an absolute silence in the room. Cora Winters stared straight ahead out of the sink window and her mind began to work slowly, to pick up momentum, to begin to sort out the thinking into proper piles for action. She tried to catch Marcy's reflection but the girl was out of range. Bringing all her force to bear, Cora Winters made herself turn around and look at Marcy Kates.

Marcy was simply sitting there, her face gone chalk-white, her lips thin and bloodless, staring beyond Cora Winters, her gaze wide and stark on the little white box on the shelf. After a little eternity Marcy's lids flickered and her mouth began to work convulsively. Suddenly she groaned and threw herself forward across the tabletop. She did not weep; there was no other sound from her, just that single groan, as if someone had kicked her in the pit of the stomach. She lay on the table with both arms out-stretched, her cheek on the smooth oilcloth, her eyes open, her breath labored in scraping draughts.

Cora Winters hurried to her and put her hand on the girl's shoulder. "Marcy? Marcy, you all right?" There was no response. Marcy made no attempt to lift her head, to look at her. It was as if her eyes were fastened on some far object. Cora Winters was scared. "Marcy, honey! Are you all right, child?" Still no response. She stood at the girl's side, her hand useless on her shoulder, and tried desperately to think what to do next. She suddenly heard the coffee sounds and, crossing quickly to the stove, she managed to force her trembling fingers to pour a cupful of the steaming black stuff. She came back to Marcy and dragged a chair up beside her. "Here, honey. Try and get some of this down." She struggled with one arm around the girl's trunk to raise her from the table, to get her into position to sip the brew. The girl was a dead weight. Cora Winters worked hard and finally she pulled Marcy erect. The girl slumped hard against her, her face close. Working under difficulty, Cora Winters managed to reach the cup, to bring it to Marcy's lips. "Mind, now," Cora said softly. "Mind, it's plenty hot."

The first contact of the cup with Marcy's lips brought a kind of long shudder through her body. She twisted her head, taking her mouth away, and tried to pull from Cora Winters' clutch, to sit up. But the older woman tightened her hold and kept her in place. "Here, now," Cora ordered brusquely. "You take some of this, Marcy. You need it, child. It'll do a parcel of good for you."

Without further resistance Marcy yielded. She came slumping back against the woman and allowed the cup to come to her lips now and again. She took little sips and Cora Winters waited.

When the coffee was finally down Cora Winters shifted in her place. The color was coming back into the girl's face; her lips looked better now. She gently forced the girl erect in her chair and testingly took her arm from around her. Marcy sat straight, her eyes closed. Cora Winters waited a moment. It was going to be all right now. She took the cup over to the sink and in a second was back in her place at Marcy's side.

Marcy opened her eyes and reached up vaguely, touching her hair with her fingertips. "I'm right sorry," she said slowly. "It come over me all of a sudden."

"That's all right, honey. You'll be O.K. now."

The memory of the broadcast came tardily to Marcy's brain. "Cora! Rigger's been hurt bad!" she cried.

"I know, child, I know."

Marcy's eyes darkened in horror and she doubled swiftly, bringing her two fists up close under her breasts. "Oh, God! What am I gonna do now? What am I gonna do?"

Cora Winters tightened her jaw and frowned at the back of the girl's head. "There's only one thing you can do, Marcy," she pointed out quietly. "You gotta be gettin' in to the hospital pronto."

"Oh, yes, yes!" Marcy looked around wildly. "I gotta go right off!"

Cora Winters' sigh of relief was thin. She got to her feet quickly, efficiently, and stood looking down at her. "I'll be gettin' some clothes on me. Back in a minute."

Marcy nodded, not looking at her. Cora Winters left the room, carefully shutting the door into the hallway.

Marcy Kates sat alone in the kitchen, trying to bring some kind of reason to all this. The man had said Rigger was hurt bad, that he was unconscious still. None of it made any sense to her. He'd been all right only a few hours ago. What had happened? How could Rigger be hurt like that? She tried to think of Britt, but the face of Rigger Kates kept coming between, blocking everything else away. The man had said there wasn't much hope for Rigger. That meant Rigger might die, even! She tried to think what this would mean, what it would be like without him alive and like he was. Even that was too hard to put together; she couldn't work it out. She raised her arm and ran her hand hard through her hair, cupping the back of her skull, squeezing it tight, as if she might press some clarity into place.

Cora Winters had come back into the room. She saw Marcy Kates sitting there, her hand clutching the back of her head, that pained, twisted expression in her eyes. "Got a headache, Marcy? Want somethin' for it?"

Marcy glanced at her in surprise. "I ain't got no headache," she said. "I ain't got no headache at all."

Cora Winters nibbled at her lip and straightened. She'd put on a cotton house dress and a little jacket and was ready. "Let's get goin'," she urged. "I'm drivin' you into town."

Marcy obeyed. She emerged from behind the table and followed Cora Winters through the wash porch out into the back yard. Cora turned suddenly when they reached the car and saw that Marcy had left all the doors open in their wake. She said nothing, simply went back and shut first the inner door, then the outer one quietly, so as not to wake up Fred, if she could help it.

She got behind the wheel of the old Plymouth and leaned over and shoved open the other door for Marcy. The girl got in without a word and sat almost primly, her hands in her lap, her eyes big and wide, her legs drawn up close to the seat, while Cora Winters worked to get the car out to the highway to town.

The only words spoken all the way to town came when Cora Winters attempted to comfort her. "Truth of the matter is Rigger probably ain't so bad off as the radio said. They usually get everything balled up." Marcy made no reply. Cora Winters shot her a quick look, anxious at the way she just sat there, watching the road ahead with those big, dark uncomprehending eyes. The girl seemed all right, seemed under control, just quiet, that was all. She abandoned any effort to force her into further conversation.

Cora Winters let her out in the open space in front of the Rose Circle. Marcy slammed the car door and did not wait for the older woman to park the car and join her. She went immediately across the sidewalk, up the front steps to the wide glass doors. Only here did she hesitate. She paused and drew herself quite straight. She went inside.

The Rose Circle was a fairly new installation. The large reception room was roomy and comfortable and brightly lit. Marcy hesitated, peering around. There were some people sitting around the room, saying nothing, caught in the ill-at-ease vise of fearful waiting. There was a glassed-in office at her left, in which a girl was working a small switchboard. The young woman glanced up and saw Marcy. She reached up and slid a little window to one side, making a small opening between them.

"Do somethin' for you, honey?"

Marcy shifted and swallowed. "Yes, please. It's my husband. He's Rigger Kates."

"He a patient here?"

Marcy took a step nearer the opening. "Yes, he is. You see, there was an accident. They brought him here, they said."

"Oh." The girl eyed her professionally for a moment and then riffled through a card index beside her board. "Rigger Kates. Yeah, that's right. He's here, sure enough." She studied the card for a moment and moistened her lips before bringing her eyes to the pale face again.

Marcy felt suddenly as if she was going to be sick. "He's all right, ain't he?" She asked huskily.

The girl's eyes softened. "Yeah, honey, he's all right. You take it easy, now. You're lookin' kinda pasty. Why'n't you sit over there and I'll see if I can get hold of the doctor who's been takin' care of him."

Cora Winters came through the big doors and glanced around apprehensively as she came to Marcy's side. "Anythin' happen?"

Marcy shook her head. "She's gonna find out for us."

The two women crossed the room and sat down, facing the others. Marcy averted her eyes to avoid their passive curiosity and nervously worked her hands in her lap. Cora Winters sat bolt upright, rocklike and formidable, as if she were defying the austerity of the place. Marcy wanted to talk, to make some sound, any kind of sound that would break the pressing vacuum of the room. Only there wasn't anything to say.

"That girl over there—she's makin' signs at us," Cora Winters said suddenly.

Marcy raised her head. The telephone girl was half on her feet, leaning forward over her barrier, beckoning. Marcy got up and crossed the room alone. Cora Winters made no effort to follow.

"Your husband, honey—he ain't so good right now." She paused, expecting the usual fright to come sweeping over the face. Marcy's eyes widened a trifle. There was no gasp, no fear. The girl frowned faintly. "They just brought him outta Surgery, honey. You can go in for just a minute, that's all. He's not awake."

Marcy said nothing, just nodded. At that moment a tall, blond young man in white appeared from somewhere behind the office block and came up to her.

"Mrs. Kates?"

"Yeah, that's me."

"I'm Dr. Grimes. I'd like to talk to you for a minute and then I'll take you to your husband." He watched her as the girl had watched her, as if they expected her to cry out or to faint. She simply stood there looking at him in a sad, tired way. He reached out and touched her elbow gently. Just before they started down the long corridor away from the reception room she glanced back. Cora Winters was still just sitting there, watching. There was a faint nod of her head now but she made no effort to follow.

"Your husband's been hurt pretty badly, Mrs. Kates, I guess you know." He was talking in a low voice, his fingertips on her elbow, guiding her down the long hall with all its doors and numbers and doctors' names under the numbers. "He hasn't regained consciousness yet. It was necessary for us to operate immediately." He glanced at her quickly. "His brother was here. He gave us permission." She made no comment and the doctor breathed freely.

She suddenly stopped near the end of the corridor and looked up at him with those big, uneasy eyes of hers that made him edgy. "Is Rigger gonna die, Doctor?"

He eyed her sharply for a long moment, then sighed and peered down the reach of corridor. "I don't know," he said slowly.

"You can't tell with something like this. It's too soon to tell." He forced his attention back to her intent face. "You see, Mrs. Kates, he's pretty badly hurt. Somebody must have used a hammer on him, from the looks of things. His skull was fractured and there was some pressure on the brain. We've tried to take care of that tonight. I don't know—it's too soon to tell."

She had closed her eyes and her face had grayed a little. He stepped close suddenly to be where he could catch her. In a moment she opened her eyes, took a long slow deep breath, and wet her lips. "Can I see him now?"

"Yes—yes, of course. He's right in here."

He opened the door and she brushed past him into the little room. There were some pieces of furniture, a chair, a washbasin, a small table on which a little lamp now burned with a soft glow, and the bed. The doctor came inside and eased the door shut behind him and stood watching her curiously.

She crossed the room to the side of the bed and looked down at him. His head was turbaned with bandages and his face was severely beaten. The swelling gave him a queer fatty look. She bent forward and looked at him closely. Under his lids she could see a bit of his glassy pupils. He looked dead to her. There were no signs of breathing, even. She straightened suddenly and wheeled, staring at the doctor. "He's dead," she said flatly.

He came to the bedside and looked down at his patient. "No," he said quietly. "He's bad off, but he's not dead, poor devil."

She turned then and went away, leaving him behind her. She went to the door, pulled it open, and stepped out into the corridor. When the doctor came after her he found her waiting for him. "Thanks for lettin' me see him, for tellin' me how it is," she said quietly.

Her manner unsettled him. She looked numbed, and yet there was no indication that she was bordering on shock or hysteria. "We ought to know in a day or so," he offered lamely.

"Thanks."

He stood watching as she went down the long hallway toward the reception room. He watched until she had made the L turn, had disappeared. Then he shook his head and glanced with troubled eyes at the closed door to Rigger Kates' room. "People!" He suddenly spoke aloud in the vacant corridor. "Goddamn 'em!"

Cora Winters rose quickly as Marcy approached. She scanned the girl's face anxiously. "How's everythin' goin'?"

Marcy nodded, her eyes vague. "He's still out." She hesitated and looked at Cora Winters solidly. "He looks like he's dead," she said. Without another word she pushed past the older woman and went to the wide doors and outside to the top of the steps. A little breeze had come up to stir the tepid night. She stopped for a moment and took a deep breath, cleansing herself of the close clinging smells of the hospital. Cora Winters came up to her side and touched her arm.

"Home now, huh?"

"Yeah, home," Marcy said.

The two women picked their way carefully down the steps and started along the narrow sidewalk toward the old Plymouth. Someone was coming toward them, headed for the hospital, and Cora Winters stiffened and glanced at Marcy.

"It's Newt," she warned.

Marcy's chin lifted a trifle and her eyes lost some of the glaze and began to narrow slightly. He came directly up to them and stopped, blocking their way.

"Was thinkin' you wasn't gonna show up," Newt said.

"I come as soon as I could."

Newt moistened his lips. "Reckoned as how maybe you was off somewheres with him, that boy friend of yours."

"Oh, shut up, Newt! For God's sake, leave her alone!" Cora Winters exploded.

He tilted his head faintly and eyed her coldly. But he said nothing to her.

Cora Winters glanced at Marcy, and there was a grim warning in the drawn line of her lips. "Marcy's been with me," she countered bluntly.

Newt worked his mouth but said nothing for the moment. He took a single step forward and peered closely at his sister-in-law. "Reckon you heard already what happened to him," he probed tentatively.

She nodded dully. "I heard, Newt. I been talkin' to the doc. He told me."

He retreated to his original stand and eyed her glumly. "You don't look so broke up to me." He hesitated. "Rigger ain't doin' so good."

"I know, Newt, I know."

Cora Winters frowned. There was something peculiar about Newt Kates tonight. He was so quiet, so sure. She leaned forward imperceptibly to get a good look at his face in the half-light under the trees. His face was sober and slack-muscled, his eyes dull on the girl. He suddenly became aware of the older woman's attention and his head jerked as his eyes came to her. "It was a terrible thing to happen," he offered.

Cora Winters straightened. "Yeah, Newt, it sure was."

He nodded with elaborate sorrow and looked back to Marcy. He managed something akin to actual grief in his tone. "They had to cut him, too. They asked me, I said O.K. It might save the poor little devil."

"You done what was right, Newt, I reckon."

"You wasn't here to say O.K." He accused her.

"Oh, Newt, please. I don't want to talk no more." She moved off a little to one side and her attention strayed. There was a sudden grinding fatigue in her and there was nothing more to say to him.

Newt watched her closely. She had her back half turned on him and his lips tightened and his little beady eyes hardened and became squinty. Cora Winters shifted uneasily and the sound of her brought Newt's eyes around. "It's been a long hard night," he said vaguely.

"I reckon as how it has," she countered acidly.

His glance was swift and the eyes seemed to sharpen. Immediately he slid a screen into place. "It was a terrible shock," he canted, shaking his head.

Cora Winters felt disgust rise like a great wave in her and her lips thinned with distaste. "Oh, come off it, Newt! You ain't about to go bustin' into tears, and you and I know it! You don't give a rap what happens to Rigger."

He drew himself stonily erect and fixed her with dark reproachful eyes. "He's my bud!" he cried indignantly.

"I reckon as how you had the same ma and pa, if that's what you mean."

He scowled and looked down at his feet, making no attempt to carry the talk further. She watched him closely, wondering. Suddenly he was looking at her again and his face was dark and mottled, his eyes firing. "When I get my hands on the dirty bastard that done this," Newt Kates cried, "I'm gonna kill him, beatin' my poor bud like that!"

The unexpected outburst startled and frightened her. That face of his was murderous. Suddenly she didn't want any more of the Kates boys tonight. She reached out hurriedly and caught Marcy's elbow. "C'mon, honey. Let's be gittin' for home." She crossed directly in front of Newt, propelling Marcy forcefully toward the car.

Newt Kates stood alone on the sidewalk and watched them get into the car. He waited until Cora Winters had managed to extricate the machine from the tight knot of parked cars, until the single taillight had blinked itself out of sight. He drew a long breath and fished in his shirt pocket for his cigarettes. He got one, lit it, and rolled it over to the corner of his mouth. His eyes were on the empty street ahead and the flash of the white heat of the moment previous had cooled in his eyes and the craftiness was in place. Not hurrying, taking his time, he started to walk again down the pavement toward the hospital steps and the vigil.

Cora Winters felt a little better once she got away from the hospital, from him. She sat rigid behind the wheel and gunned the car, driving rapidly down Seventh, heading for the railroad tracks and the start of the open road to home. Seemed like she had never spent such a long night in all her life. The only thing she hoped was Fred hadn't wakened and got himself all worked up when he found her gone this time of night. She glanced at Marcy. She was all right, sitting quietly, absorbed in her thoughts, her eyes on the road ahead.

"That Newt gives me the creeps," Cora blurted.

Marcy said nothing. Cora Winters wanted to ask about that other business, about her leaving Rigger, only she didn't know how to get the thing into words. She drove fast, trying to put her whole concentration into the task. The landmarks slipped by quickly. Cora Winters snatched little side glances at Marcy now and then. She sat now with her head back against the seat, her eyes closed, the color streaked in her face. The poor kid was beat. She slowed the car a little and reached over and touched her tentatively. Marcy raised her head and smiled thinly. "I'm O.K.," she murmured. "Just plumb wore out, I reckon."

Cora Winters knew what she meant. She devoted herself to her driving. As they neared the Kates place Marcy brought herself up straight and eyed the land intently. The house was a dark pile. "Looks so empty, don't it?" she observed loosely.

"Never you mind about the place," Cora Winters said. "You come on back with me and get somethin' to eat and some rest."

"No," Marcy shook her head slowly, her eyes clinging fast to the Kates place. "No," she repeated quietly. "Stop the car, Cora. I'm gettin' out here."

Cora Winters' lips parted and alarm came quickly to her eyes. "That Newt's gonna be comin' back in a little while."

"I don't care if he comes back or if he don't!" Marcy flared. "This here's where I live! This is where I belong!" Cora Winters flushed and brought the car to a sharp, squealing halt.

Marcy leaned over suddenly and put her hand on the older woman's arm. "I didn't mean to be onery. It's just—well, I reckon as how the time's come to face up with things. It ain't gonna do no good runnin' away from what's gonna have to be worked out sooner or later. Things ain't the same's they was a couple of hours back. Bein' off the place now could maybe make things worse still. I'm stayin' here tonight."

Cora Winters worked hard to find the reason in all this. She was so tired now her mind was all fuzzy. All she seemed to be able to remember was Newt Kates and that look on his face a little while back. Suppose he came back later and she wasn't here. Suppose he went after Britt Callum—or, even worse, suppose he came snoopin' up the road and found Marcy at her place. Fred hated the Kates boys. There'd be all kinds of trouble, everybody gettin' mixed up in the lousy mess. "Well, honey, if you think…" She yielded carefully.

Marcy smiled faintly, knowingly. "Thanks, Cora, for takin' me in, for standin' by, like you done."

Cora Winters felt kind of ugly inside, as if she were ducking out on something to save her own skin. "If there's anythin' I can do, Marcy—"

"Yeah, sure."

Cora Winters opened her mouth to say something more but nothing came out. Automobile lights suddenly lit up the countryside behind the machine and she watched the twin bright beams in the rear-view mirror, feeling the cold lick of apprehension. She didn't want to be sitting here like this when Newt Kates came back. The car swept past in a rush of sound and wind. Cora Winters let her trapped breath escape cautiously. "Take it easy, kid," she said almost brusquely, and started the car rolling. In the mirror she saw Marcy turn and start up the dark path to the house. Alone now in her car Cora Winters slumped down behind the wheel, and relief and weariness mixed themselves and flowed over her.

Marcy quickened her pace as she went up to the lonely house. Now she was alone at last, free to think and make her own decisions. She hurried past the front of the house and went down alongside the building until she reached the open flat of the yard. The barn rose before her like a shadowed mountain in the black pitch of the night. Her lips parted and her eyes widened and began to shine as she almost ran toward Britt's room. Suddenly she brought herself to a halt in the middle of the clearing. She was doing the wrong thing! She was losing her head! She didn't dare risk being with him, not tonight, not with the rest that had happened already. Newt might come back any time now, unexpectedly.

She stood swaying slightly, her rounded eyes on the doorway, her every flaming desire and desperate need centered on the little room and the man inside. But slowly she surrendered to reason. Her shoulders sagged and she sighed heavily and turned her back on the barn. Quietly, deliberately, she made her way back to the house and reached for the screen-door handle. Tardily she remembered the door squeaked at times. She must not wake him, bring him to her, not feeling like she did right now. Carefully, cautiously, she retraced her steps around the side of the house and entered by the front door.

The place seemed darker than ever. If she turned on a light he'd see it and maybe come to find out what the trouble was. She felt her way down the hall and went into the kitchen. From the window over the sink she could see no light, no sign of life in his room. Safe now, she turned and crossed to the bedroom and shut and bolted the door behind her.

Marcy lay wakefully on the bed, waiting. The ever present threat that lay behind Newt's possible return keyed her and kept the wanted sleep beyond her. Outside the night was impenetrable and the slowly rising wind guyed her mockingly. She could hear the gentle rub of the few plants along the side of the house. She worked to ignore the baiting breeze. When she paid it no heed it tittered, taunting her with its whispering. She shut her eyes hard and demanded sleep. The memory of Britt Callum, his arms, his lips, came back strong and clear, setting the fires burning in her. Her body thrashed, churning the bedclothes into tight bands that caught and held her. Perspiration broke out over her entire body, soaking her nightdress, dampening the sheets. She lay on her back and stared hot-eyed into the void.

She tried to think about Rigger as she should. It was strange, disturbing. She lipped the name Rigger silently. It did nothing. She worked to mouth it over, and again—nothing. She tried to call up a tiny image of him in her mind, but the picture eluded her and there was no response. She could not even summon the all-familiar outline of his body. She turned slightly and stared at the vacant place at her side, trying to visualize him as she had known him these four long years, but the place was empty, deserted. The frustration depressed her. She should feel *something*, some kind of emotion, some sense of loss, of gain, even. But there was nothing. It was as if Rigger Kates had never been a part of her at all.

Her toes found the footboard. She pressed against the barrier, tensing her body, feeling tall and straight and strong. She wondered if Britt were thinking of her now, if he were lying there so near to her, thinking of her, wanting her. For a moment she could see him before her, standing at the foot of the bed, smiling, his long firm arms held out to her, his teeth white and strong in his smooth dark face. She brought herself quickly on her elbow and her lips parted, the light breaking sharp in her eyes. But there was nothing there, no one, nothing but the darkness. Her face flushed and she hastily peered around the room as if she feared someone might have seen her. She let herself sink back to the twisted, damp pillow. She closed her eyes and tried to keep her thinking on him. There was warmth and security in holding him with her. The coming sun had begun to mix its colors on the window sill. Marcy Kates slept.

CHAPTER SEVENTEEN

S HE HAD NOT long to sleep. At daybreak the knock on her barred door was sharp and insistent. Marcy opened her eyes and stared at the ceiling, waiting. The knock came again, more insistent, undeniable. Wearily she stirred, swinging herself from the bed, and crossed to the barrier. "Yeah?"

"You gettin' up in there?" Newt's voice was hard, demanding. "I'm wantin' my food right off. Got work to do."

Marcy pulled herself straight slowly and rubbed her heavy, burning eyes. "O.K., Newt, O.K.," she said, just loud enough so he would hear. "I'm comin'."

She heard his steps going across the kitchen to the back screen and waited to see if he were going outside. But he had stopped and she knew he was standing there, looking out over the place, speculating. She sighed and turned from the door and went back to the bed and picked up her scattered clothes. She dressed automatically and went to the mirror, pulling the comb through her snarled hair halfheartedly. She laid down the comb and bent forward and surveyed herself. There were fatigue rings under her eyes and she looked downright puny. She pressed her teeth on her lower lip, trying to bring some color.

As she came into the kitchen Newt turned from his place at the door and eyed her sharply. "You sure been takin' your goddamn time," he snarled.

"I was tired—after last night," she murmured limply.

"Reckon you was."

She glanced at him shortly, wondering if there were anything behind the remark, but his face was noncommittal. He came over and dragged out his chair and sat down to wait for his breakfast.

As she worked the whole sequence of the night before began to come clear in her muddled mind. As she slid the skillet over the burner and started the bacon and eggs she glanced down at his rounded back. "How was Rigger when you come back?"

"Same," Newt replied quietly. "Ain't no change."

She said nothing to that. For a moment she could see him again, stretched out like that, all bandages and bruises and no breath in him. She worked over the stove, keeping her attention solely on her duties.

When she brought the plate over to the table and slid it before him Newt looked up at her. "Ain't you eatin'?"

She shook her head dully and ran her hands down her thighs. "I ain't hungry just yet," she said.

He did not start eating immediately. He sat there with his elbows on the table edge, watching her. She puzzled him. Last night she looked like she didn't much give a damn whether Rigger lived or not. This morning she looked kind of washed out, like she might have been in there awake all night, maybe worrying about the little guy. Almost reluctantly he took his eyes from her and went to work on the food.

Marcy moved absently across to the sink. Standing there, she gazed out over the whole sweep of the place. There were a few scattered clouds, but the sun was fiery red and fierce, low in the eastern sky. "It's gonna be another hot one," she observed glumly.

Newt was hunched over his plate, both forearms on the table, shoveling in the food, chewing noisily. "Yeah," he mumbled through a packed mouth. "It's summer."

As she stood there, Britt Callum suddenly came out into the yard from the little room and stood in front of his door for a moment. He was bare to the waist, holding a wadded T shirt in his hand. He peered around the place, up at the sky, and yawned, stretching lazily. She saw him scratch that big chest of his, then start across the yard toward the house. By raising on her toes she could see him stick his head and shoulders under the pump, see him bring the water spilling over him. He straightened and flicked the water from him with his palms and used the T shirt as a towel, wiping himself briefly. He slipped the damp shirt over his head and the sound of him on the back steps came into the room.

Newt hesitated in his eating and glanced up at her. She was aware of him behind her and did not turn to look at the back door. Newt went back to his eating. Britt Callum came inside and stopped, surprise bringing his mouth open, his eyes wide.

"Mornin', Britt," she greeted overcasually.

"Hi," he murmured. "Hi." He questioned her with his eyes as she went past him to the stove but she gave him no open satisfaction. There was only a spark of warning, a tiny twitch of her head in Newt's direction.

Britt frowned and slowly took his place at the table.

"You come back," he said to Newt.

"Yeah, that's right, big fella." Newt looked up from his plate and his jaws went right on working. "Any reason why not?"

Britt flushed and wet his lips. "No. It's just I—"

"I come back," Newt said, his jaws stopping. His eyes went flinty and his lips worked in the unfamiliar task of a half grin. "It's time somebody took aholt round here," he stated loftily.

Britt moved his body so Marcy could put the plate in front of him. For a split second their eyes met and he saw once again the bright spark of warning.

Marcy poured herself a cup of coffee and carried it over to the drainboard. She sipped it slowly, keeping her back on the two of them. She dared not be in a position to attract Britt's eye, to run the risk of giving Newt any ideas. The two men worked on their food in thick silence.

When he had finished Newt shoved his chair back and crossed his legs. He found his toothpick and poked away at his teeth, eyeing Britt curiously, speculatively. Britt kept his head down. He knew Newt was concentrating on him, that Newt had something on his mind. After a few minutes Newt flipped the matchstick into his plate and took out a cigarette. It bobbed nervously in the corner of his mouth as he spoke.

"There's been a couple of changes made round here," Newt said slowly, very distinctly. "Seems like maybe Rigger ain't gonna be with us for a spell. Since he ain't, I'm kinda lookin' out for his side as well as mine."

Britt straightened and stared across the table. Newt did not leave him an opening for questions. "Point is," Newt continued, "there's things I been wantin' done round here, so from now on you'll be doin' like I want, see?"

Britt shifted under the sting of Newt's direct challenge. He pulled his chin up faintly and returned Newt's cold, level gaze. "Such as," Britt said.

"Such as, you can stop foolin' round some of that stuff Rigger's been havin' you do, that damn-fool hoein' and scrapin', and get down and put them muscles of yours to work for a change."

Britt's face was dark and he brought his jaws together hard. "And if I don't?" he said quietly.

Newt took the cigarette from his lips and inspected the long ash on the end. Airily, confidently, he flicked the ash on the kitchen floor and put the thing back in the corner of his mouth. "You can get your ass off the place any goddamn time you want," Newt said pleasantly.

There was an utter stillness in the room for a minute. Britt wanted to tell him to take the whole crumby joint and stick it, but he didn't. He was conscious of Marcy behind him, aware of the strict arrest she was imposing on his actions and his words. He let the whole thing rest.

Newt Kates finished his cigarette leisurely. He came forward and snuffed the butt in the coagulating egg yolk in the plate and sat up straight. "I'm headin' out to have me a look at that there wheat. Then I'm goin' to the barn loft. You be there when I'm there," he instructed grimly. With that he got to his feet and left them.

Britt swung instantly in his place as the screen door shut. His eyes were stretched wide and hot and the thick corded vein in his neck pounded under the thin coat of flesh. "What the hell?"

She shook her head violently and waved him still with an imperious flick of her hand. She was standing sideways to him, raised on her toes a little, looking down along the side of the house, watching her brother-in-law as he went to the red truck. She glanced down at Britt and again shook her head. She said only one word and that very quietly. "Wait." She returned her attention to the window and the outside. In a moment she had lost sight of him out there, was not sure. The sounds of the truck starting came into the room. Newt was racing the engine, warming it, and then the machine spurted across the yard and went rocking along the makeshift trail that led to the distant field.

Instantly she came to Britt and knelt in front of him, her arms hard against his big legs, her fingers tightly gripping his hips. "It's Rigger!" she cried. "He's been hurt awful bad. He's in the hospital, Britt, he ain't even conscious yet!"

He drew his breath in horror and his eyes narrowed. He came forward and his big palms caught the sides of her head and he brought her face up to him. "Rigger?" he said. "How? When?"

Her eyes were fearful. "Sometime last night, they say. Sometime before midnight. They found him in an alley. We went to the hospital. Somebody beat him up bad. They hurt his brain some way."

Britt stared at her, then released her abruptly. He drew back in the chair and peered at her uncomprehendingly. The things she said made no sense to him. Somehow he had missed the quick run of her story, had caught only words here and there as they jerked from her. Last night. Before midnight. Beat him up. His brain some way. Britt ran his fingers through his hair and tried to get his thinking straight. Her grasp on him tightened and he could feel the sharp points of her nails.

"Britt, listen, listen! Don't you go gettin' Newt riled. Don't be lettin' him get your goat none. He's gonna try. This is what he's been wantin' for a long time. He's been waitin' for the chance to take over. Ain't nothin' we can do to stop him. I'm scared of him, Britt. Don't go doin' nothin' to get him sore."

He said nothing. He looked down at her and all he could see was that funny, helpless look on Rigger's face last night when he had slugged him. He reached down and forcefully pulled her hands and arms from him and stepped out of the circle of her hold. He went over to the screen door and stood there, rubbing his bearding face hard with his palm.

She had. turned slowly but had not risen. Crouched like that, she watched him fearfully. She had no idea what was going on in his head, what he was going to do.

In a moment or so he turned and glanced at her, saw her down like that, the look of dread sharp in her eyes on him. He summoned a faint smile and came back to her, reaching down, taking her shoulders, bringing her to her feet. Without a word he gathered her close to him and held her hard. Then his hands came up and he took her hair gently at the nape of the neck and pulled her head back. He kissed her twice. He kissed her briefly the first time, captured and held her with the second. And then he released her and went to the screen door.

"It'll be all right," he said low, and went outside to meet Newt Kates.

Newt was late. Britt climbed the rickety ladder to the unused loft and stood peering around. It was the first time he had ever been up here. There were some bales of hay in the corner and the floor was littered with hunks of rusted, cobwebbed machinery. He figured Newt wanted something done with the stuff, but he'd have to wait until Newt came.

Britt crossed over and sat down on a bale. It was hot and stuffy up here under the peaked, beamed roof. He wiped his brow irritably and leaned back against the piled hay. His mind went back to what she had told him. Again the sharp picture of Rigger's face came into the frame of his conscience. He saw Rigger again on the floor at his feet, out cold, lifeless to the eye. Inside him somewhere there was a sudden chilling, a quickening wave of fear that inched through him. He shivered suddenly despite the heat and sat up straight and stiff on the bale. As if it had become alive of its own accord, his right hand came from his leg and held itself up for inspection before him. He stared at the knuckles, at the faint discoloration, the puffiness that the blow on Rigger's jaw had caused. Britt turned his head suddenly, trying to avoid the sight of the accusing hand. He brought up his left hand and seized the mocking member, pulling it down, crushing it hard against his loin, covering the now throbbing area with the guiltless palm. He worked desperately to recall everything she had said. Rigger was hurt bad. He was unconscious yet. He had something wrong with his brain. Suddenly all the others, Oklahoma, all the rest of the guys came forth to him. He tried to grab hold of the memories of them. None of them had been hurt bad. But they slipped way, eluding him. Only Rigger remained. Rigger Kates and his surprised face and his little hard body so still on the floor of the bar at his feet. The vast overwhelming nausea came down upon him like an avalanche. He pressed the hand still harder against him and turned aside and gave himself to the sickness.

Newt came eventually. He found Britt sitting pale and silent, waiting patiently for him. Pleased, he pointed out the various pieces of equipment he wanted taken from the loft and piled out front. Later he intended to cart them into town and sell them for junk, he confided. That metal ought to bring good dough, especially now. Britt made no comment. Newt finished his instructions and went to the head of the ladder and hesitated.

"Me and Marcy's gonna go on to the hospital later. You want to come?" He made it plain he expected a negative.

Britt moistened his lips and kept his face away from the older man. "No," he murmured. "Not today. I got me plenty to do here. It's better I don't go."

Newt was pleased again. He said nothing and crawled down the ladder. Some time later Britt heard the truck engine start, heard the sounds of the machine fading off. The uncertain, queasy feeling came back. He yanked off the soaked shirt and tossed it over in the corner and went to work. Time dissolved into nothingness. Britt Callum worked like a man possessed, driving himself beyond limitation, keeping his mind blocked, empty, safe.

Marcy and Newt made the trip to town. They got to the hospital, made themselves known at the desk, went to Rigger's room, looked down on him, stretched there as he had been the night before, straight, unmoving, death in life. They did not see the doctor anywhere. They saw the nurse. She said there had been little change. It was still too soon to tell. After that Newt and Marcy drove back home, the way they had gone into town, in utter silence.

Britt lay fully clothed on the cot, unable to sleep, unable to deaden the gnawing conviction that worked to consume his very insides. His body was sore, strained, every muscle taut and drawn after the flaying; driving demands he had made upon it through the long blistering day. It was very late, perhaps midnight or beyond.

She came to him quickly, quietly. He heard the swift light pad of her feet on the earth, and as he came from the bed she slipped inside the room and shut the door behind her. Without a sound she came to him in the darkness. Her arms locked him tight and she pressed herself to him with all the strength she could summon and her hands moved over his body as they had done before, seeking him out, knowing him again. The white heat of their desire came bursting bright and their arms caught the sleekness of their bodies and drew them together in a desperate striving unity.

She left him later, the way she had come. She left him in exhausted sleep, moving from his side cautiously, carefully, and dressed rapidly, slipping outside without a sound. In the yard she paused and let the tiny warm breeze touch her and bring her back to the present. Idly now she went away from the barn, skirting the edge of the house, going alongside to the front. It was very dark and yet the stars seemed so bright that she could make out all the old familiar things about the place. She came to the front steps and climbed them and turned to look out over the flat before the house. The mesquite tree was shadowy, like a blackened spider's web against the blue-black distant horizon. Marcy went over to the wicker chair and sat down.

She sat there thinking of him, of what he had come to mean to her, of his strength and his firmness, of his gentleness and his goodness. And, sitting there, she thought, too, of Rigger Kates in that hospital bed.

She couldn't do anything now, plan anything like she had before he'd been injured. There was nothing she or Britt could do now. She couldn't just up and walk out at a time like this. Later—later on, when Rigger got better, when he came home, she and Britt would go away together then, do like he kept saying, get married, have their own lives somewhere far away from all this mess.

Or—Marcy straightened and peered out over the railing into the darkness, her sight sharpening—suppose Rigger didn't get well at all! Suppose he was to die, now, in the next day or so. The doctor had said he couldn't tell. Rigger *could* die. He looked dead right now, for all she could tell. Nobody could look like that and go on living. People didn't go on living when they was hurt so bad like that.

Quickly the run of thinking took root in her and flourished. When Rigger was dead, she'd be free right off. There wouldn't be no more waiting, no more of this creeping around, stalling. When Rigger was dead, everything would be solved. There wouldn't be nothing more to figure out. There'd just be Britt and her then, and everything would be right. Her breath quickened and instant sweat oiled her palms, between her fingers. She ran her hand through her hair and slid from the chair to her knees before the railing.

"Oh, dear God!" she whispered huskily in the stillness of the porch. "Please, God, let him die, let him go soon, God, please!" She bent forward suddenly and crossed her hands on the rail and pressed her slick forehead against them and the tears came.

CHAPTER EIGHTEEN

I N THE two weeks that followed the pattern of life on the Kates place was virtually unchanged. Newt had assumed the high command and thrived on it. His orders to both Britt and Marcy were delivered with solid authority and strengthened by their knowledge that his position was impregnable, at least for the time being. Britt worked himself desperately, relentlessly, doing whatever Newt bade him do, unquestioning, hurling himself into every task with all the strength he could muster, striving always to keep the reminders of Rigger Kates from his mind. In the nights she came to him when she was able and they lay together planning for the days that would come when the furtive meetings, the deceptions would be done.

It was during the two-week period that Rigger Kates finally stirred and wakened from his coma. Newt and Marcy had made their daily weary trek to the hospital, had been in the room itself when it had happened. There had been a kind of long shudder through the little frame and the eyes had opened.

It had been Marcy who had seen first. She had been looking at him, the same way she had been looking down at him all during the long ten days, when the lids flickered and he was looking up at her. It startled her, frightened her. He simply looked at her. There was no sound from him, no twitch of his face, no more life in him than there had been before. Except the eyes. The eyes had opened and he was looking at her.

"Newt!" she had cried out. "Newt! He's awake!"

Newt had come over to the bedside then, had stood at her side and stared down at his brother. She had waited for Rigger to move, to say something, but nothing had happened. Automatically she had put out her hand vaguely, had touched Newt's sleeve in fear, had glanced up at him. She had taken her hand away and moved then, away from Newt Kates, staring not at Rigger in the bed, but at him, at Newt, at the look that had come into his face. And then, panic-stricken, she had bolted from the room, had sought out the nurse and told her what had happened to Rigger.

It was not until two days later that that same nurse had told them the truth. Rigger was awake but he could not move. He made sounds now, too, awful grunting gasps that meant nothing. Again the hospital could not tell them anything. Maybe, as the days wore on, the condition would resolve itself. There was nothing to do but wait. The daily trips continued. When she got back to the place in the late afternoon now she was often sick at her stomach and very nervous. The ordeal of watching Rigger trying so desperately to say something, to tell her something, exacted a terrible toll.

When Marcy had the midday meal on the table she went to the back door and called to Britt, working on the piled machinery in front of the barn. He nodded and in turn yelled to Newt in the distant field. In a moment both men were on their way to the house.

She was already seated when they came inside. Britt eyed her closely. She was pale, very tired. She managed a thin smile as he took his place. "Awful hot, ain't it?" she said.

Newt looked up from his place. "Too goddamn hot."

Britt began his meal. "That job's a hot one, that's for sure."

"It's gotta be done, heat or no heat," Newt snapped quickly.

Britt glanced up briefly but let it pass.

No one said anything for a long period. It was Marcy, finally, who spoke. "Newt, I ain't goin' in to the hospital today," she announced flatly. "There ain't no need goin' in every day now. I'm just plumb wore out. I'm gonna stick around this afternoon."

He straightened and eyed her sharply. "What's Rigger gonna think?" he demanded.

She shrugged. "I can't help it!" she said. "It's just too damn much!" She turned her head away from him and her gaze found Britt. "Britt—Britt, whyn't you go see Rigger?" she suggested quickly. "You ain't been in to see him at all, not once."

Newt had stopped his eating entirely now. He watched with heightening interest.

Marcy pressed the advantage. "It'd be right nice if you was to go in, Britt. Rigger'd probably like that."

Britt felt the thick flush come creeping up the column of his neck, felt his cheeks going hot. "I—I don't know," he hedged. "I got that there work to get caught up."

Suddenly Newt Kates blinked rapidly. He cleared his throat and Britt glanced at him. Newt's face had lightened and his lips had worked to raise themselves into the softening arc of a smile. "Sure, Callum. Be right nice if you was to go see my bud," he agreed blandly.

Britt swallowed. "But the work—"

Newt Kates waved his hand magnanimously, still smiling. "Work can wait a day," he said. "I got me things to do here today. You go ahead, take the truck, go see my poor bud. Like Marcy says, he'd like that real well."

Britt was still hesitant. Marcy leaned forward and searched his face. "You want to see him, don't you, Britt?"

He was looking at Newt when she said it and there was a faint, almost imperceptible lessening of the smile and the eyes hardened and held steady. Unnerved, Britt turned to her. "Of course. Sure, I'd like to see him."

"Then it's settled," Newt said quietly. "You're goin'."

"Sure," Britt said. "Sure."

Alone in the boiling cab of the truck headed for town, Britt Callum wet his lips and ran his sticky hand hard on his pants leg. There was in him a sense of utter dread, of near horror, at the ordeal to be faced. If he could have just told her why, if he had only told her before this! If he had had some way to make her know that this was all wrong! With her alone it would have been all right, easy. But always there was that sonofabitchin' Newt hanging around, watching, waiting, acting like he knew something more than was good. The thought snagged in the flow and bobbed to the surface. *Did* Newt know? How could he know? Had someone seen the fight, told him? There was no way out. If Newt had an idea, even, and he had refused to see Rigger, then Newt would know for sure. He gripped the wheel and pressed the accelerator hard to the floor boards. The truck spurted forward and flew along the paved strip that shimmered under the weight of the summer's heat. There was no way out. He had to go through with it, go look down on Rigger, no matter what. Britt Callum worked his throat muscles, trying to force down the harsh gorge of apprehension and fear that kept pressing to rise.

Newt Kates came into the house in the middle of the searing afternoon. Marcy was in the bedroom when he came in the back door. He was sitting at the table, his back to her, lighting a cigarette, when she came into the kitchen. She went past him to the sink and got herself a drink of water. "How come you're inside this time of day?" she asked quietly, looking out of the window.

He watched her closely as she began to arrange things on the board. Slowly his eyes shifted and he peered down the length of her figure. "Got too goddamn hot out there," he said briefly. "Felt like talkin' some."

She drew a shallow breath. "It's too hot for talkin', even," she murmured.

"For talkin'?" There was surprise in his voice.

"For doin' anythin'," she grunted. She crossed over to the stove and began to wipe off the surface with long, listless strokes.

"Why work, then?" he said.

She said nothing to that, went on with her chore. She put all her concentration to the task, trying to ignore his presence.

Newt cleared his throat. "You don't have to work so hard," he said quietly.

She shrugged her shoulders. "I got my work, same's you. This here's my job."

She came back to the sink and dampened the rag in a pan of water. He stared at the white skin of her neck. Bent forward like that, her hair parted like curtains, the flesh showed a creamy triangle. "You don't have to be workin' so hard, not with me runnin' the place."

She threw him a glance touched with surprise. "What'd you say?"

He lolled back and his eyes were shaded by the half-lowered lids. "I ain't like Rigger. I got appreciation for a dame. You and me might be workin' out some kind of deal, maybe."

"The heat's got you," she snapped. Suddenly the whole detailed map of his plan unfurled tardily before her and she tightened her lips. "Newt, for God's sake, please! It's too hot to be playin' games! Whyn't you get to work and stop pesterin' me." She went back to the stove, brushing close to him as she passed.

He tried to take the cigarette from his lips but his fingers fumbled and he dropped the thing into his lap. With a muffled curse he sprang to his feet, slapping at the front of his trousers frantically. When he glanced at her she was paying him no attention, busy in her work. "I coulda burned myself bad!" he cried.

"Um." She slipped past him to the sink.

He turned in her wake, staring at her. Suddenly, without warning, he moved up behind her and his arm slipped quickly around her middle. He drew her tight against him and his face found the parting of her hair.

Marcy gasped and began to struggle fiercely. She twisted in his hold, writhing, clawing at his locked hands with her fingers, pulling against the tough flesh of his forearms with all her strength. The room was filled with the scuff of their feet, the grunting efforts of their breathing. Savagely she ripped at the skin on the backs of his hands with her nails. He let her go instantly. She spun swiftly and pursued him, her fingers bent, curved into barbed talons, hooked for his tight, cruel face. He tried to back away, flinging up his arms, trying to ward off the frantic attack.

In mute fury she flayed him now, her arms raining blows on his head, his shoulders, her closing fists battering against the hard case of his chest. She drove him stumbling back against the opposite wall. Only when he had the firm support of the barrier behind him was he able to take a stand.

He caught her upper arms and stopped her. He thrust her back from him and held her at arm's length, his grip brutal, inescapable. Her lips were bloodless, drawn tight against bared teeth. Driven by her terror, she struggled violently to escape, trying to bring her fingers against his flesh, to get her nails into his muscles, to work herself from his viselike hold. Her knee came springing, seeking the vulnerability of his groin, but he held her too far from his body. She was captured. Her fury teetered on the brink of exhaustion. Angry tears fought to blind her. Her entire body trembled. Newt lessened his hold. He brought her hard up against him and his mouth left a snail track burning across her cheek as he sought her lips. She jerked her head aside. He pulled back and stared down at her and his lips warped, his eyes fired with anger.

"I ain't good enough for you, is that it, you tramp?" he shouted. "Maybe it's 'cause I ain't no Britt Callum, huh? Well, sister, we're gonna find out. We're gonna see if Newt Kates ain't as good as the next one!"

He let her arm go and, ducking her swift blow, he caught the neckline of her thin dress with hooked fingers. He jerked with tremendous strength. The summer material fell away from her body easily. The sound of its ripping was a faraway whisper. She fought hysterically with her free arm to wrench herself from the pinning arrest of his right hand but he had her fast. He worked with feverish swiftness. His face was black; his lips close to her were almost translucent. He slashed and tore at her few remaining garments, stripping her. He caught her up to him and buried his flaming face deep between her breasts. His free hand went out over her, pinching, patting, stroking, and his kneading fingers brought the ultimate pain that went spreading until her entire body was racked in one awful agony.

Instantly she sensed her opening. With the last fleeting vestiges of her strength she brought her crooked leg up against him as hard as she could. Dimly she saw his face come rising past her, detached, as if it were some grotesque balloon slipped free, floating off. His eyes had gone wide with shock and surprise; the cords of his face were slack. The cutting bite of him on her arm unlocked and a terrible faintness took her. She drove herself back from him, stumbling, staggering without control across the width of the kitchen, held from utter collapse only by the sudden press of the drainboard edge against the small of her back.

Her eyes were stark on him. He was huddled down against the wall, his hands clutching at his groin, and the room was awful with the sounds of his repeated retching. She held herself rigid, her breath harsh, tearing. Her arms were agonized; her body was hurt; there was a throbbing, constant ache in her. The skin of her breasts was galled where his beard had scraped upon her flesh. Slowly, very slowly, every step a tremendous effort, she made herself move. She went in a wide circle around the room, feeling her way along the wall, going between the stove and the table, past him bent and convulsed on the floor, his moaning dull in her ears. She went into her room and closed and locked the door, shutting him away from her and the animal sounds of him as well.

CHAPTER NINETEEN

MARCY awakened with a rude start. She had been roused by some sound. Yet now, her eyes wide on the ceiling, she could hear nothing. She brought her arm up slowly, wincing with the quick jabbing pain in her muscle. She brushed the hair from her forehead and wondered what time it was, how long she had been like this. The sun still streamed through the windows. It must be late afternoon. Quickly, apprehensively she peered toward the closed door. It was locked, she knew, with the chair still propped under the knob for added security. She lay still, listening intently. There was no sound.

She stirred, bringing her legs over the side of the bed, her feet to the floor. A faint gasp escaped her lips as the massed pain seized her. She stared down over her naked body. She was a mass of welts, scratches, bruises. Awkwardly she shoved herself from the edge of the bed and stumbled to the mirror. Standing there on unsteady, weakened legs, she took her inventory. Only her face seemed to have escaped. Newt had not been concerned with her face. She wondered instantly where he was. The fear came swiftly. She stiffened, almost toppling forward. Her fingers found the edge of the anchoring bureau and she held her body arched. Had she heard steps in the kitchen? She raised her hand and tried to push the matted hair from her eyes, to shove it behind her ear. Frantically she glanced at the windows that looked out on the porch. She could escape that way! The hope died at birth. She remembered Rigger had long since nailed the windows into place. There was only one way out. She had to go out the way she had come in, through that door, past him.

She found another dress and put it on awkwardly. Finally, ready, she took the chair away from the knob. The key turned quietly; there was only a faint click as the lock was sprung. With slipping, trembling fingers she twisted the knob as carefully as she could and drew the door slowly open.

The widening crack revealed nothing. There was no one at the table, no one in the room that she could see. Cautiously, stealthily, she brought the door wide and stood in its frame, peering around. She cocked her head and listened. Silence. She had not put on her shoes, and in her bare feet she moved catlike into the center of the kitchen and retrieved her scattered garments. She went back to the bedroom door and tossed them to the bed. Turning, she listened again. The door to Newt's room was shut. Terror touched her. He was in there, waiting for her.

In panic she went quickly, fleeing across the room to the back door, and the weight of her body was in the butts of her palms as she sent the light door crashing open. She ran down into the yard, feeling the sting of the blistering earth on her feet. She stumbled to a halt. The pain in her side was sharp and she stood swaying, gripping her body with tight fingers. She was standing with her eyes closed, holding her breath, when she heard the step behind her. Her body steeled instantly and she waited for him to seize her. Nothing happened. She opened her eyes and stared at the barn ahead. The step sounded once more, closer. Suddenly she knew she could resist no longer. She was whipped, beaten. Defeat came soaring in her and her strength went flowing invisible, draining down from her across the face of the dusty yard. Automatically, woodenly, she turned, arms limp at her sides, to meet him.

Her eyes rounded with startled surprise. It was not Newt Kates at all! Britt was just coming around the corner of the house.

She stared in disbelief. His face seemed paler than usual and his mouth was tight, drawn. She flashed a quick sharp glance at the back door. She must not let him know anything had happened, not even let him sense it. If he ever found out, if he learned the truth, he'd kill Newt, she knew. She must not by any sign, by any token, make a slip.

She drew a long breath and worked to pull herself straight. He was going on past her, had apparently not even seen her right out in the open like this. His head was down and he was nearing the back screen. "Britt."

He stopped short, wheeled, and stared at her. "Marcy!" His eyes went over her quickly, saw the bare feet on the hot earth as he came to her. "What you doin' out here like that?"

She glanced down and contrived a bright smile. "Just playin' a little kid—goin' barefoot." She masked her eyes carefully. He was standing uncertain before her and she suddenly knew that something had happened, something was on his mind. "Britt, what's the matter? Did you see Rigger? Is he O.K.?" He simply looked at her with eyes that were clouded and disturbed but made no answer. Uneasiness seeded in her. She reached forth and seized his arm. "Britt! What's the matter? Has somethin' gone wrong with Rigger?"

He turned his head away from the intensity of her eyes. "Nothin's any different," he said quietly. "Nothin's gonna be any different."

She let go of him then, stepped back a bit, and peered at him, puzzled. "What do you mean, Britt?"

He glanced at her, reached up, rubbed his forehead dry with the palm of his hand. The east side of the barn had cast a long shadow and he took her arm and led her across the clearing into the shade. The old sawhorse was still where Rigger had left it. He motioned her to it. "Sit down, Marcy. There's somethin' I gotta tell you."

She eased herself down carefully on the narrow strip and with her hands loose in her lap she waited for him to speak. The uneasiness within her sprouted slowly, sending long probing shoots through her.

He stood there for a long time, looking down on her, and yet she had the feeling he was not seeing her. Then he turned and went a little past her and stood, looking out over the simmering pan of the place. "Rigger ain't gettin' no better," he said flatly. "He's stayin' the way he is."

She looked down at her hands. "You mean Rigger's gonna die?" she said. The little spiral of hope began to climb.

He turned quickly and his face was contorted. "He ain't gonna die, Marcy! Don't you see—he ain't gonna die, he's gonna go on livin'—on and on and on!"

She frowned, unable to grasp his meaning. "I don't—"

Britt came back to her and took a deep breath. "I seen him, Marcy, like you wanted. I seen him layin' there like that, not movin', makin' them sounds. Oh, Jesus!" He ran his hand through his hair and brought himself under control. "Marcy, I seen that there doctor fella, too. He give me a message for you and Newt. Marcy, Rigger's comin' home."

"Comin' home!" she echoed incredulously. She half rose and then sank back on the crossbar.

"Yeah. The doc says there ain't nothin' more they can do for Rigger. His head's hurt inside, and that's that. He says—he says Rigger's never gonna be any different than he is now. He ain't gonna walk, he ain't gonna talk, he ain't gonna do nothin' but get taken care of the rest of his life. He's got to be comin' home soon, 'cause they can't do nothin' more for him."

Marcy sat staring up at him in mute horror. His eyes were awful on her, muddied with pain and revulsion. She couldn't bear that look. She turned her head aside and closed her eyes. In her mind's eye she suddenly saw the whole frightful picture of the future. She saw Rigger like that, flat on his back, unmoving, making those fearful sounds, and herself, day after day, year after year, standing by his side, just going on and on, taking care of him, waiting for him to die. She saw all the winters to come, the springs, the summers, the falls. Suddenly she brought her hands to her face and began to weep. The tears flooded from every hurt part of her being and the cries of utter despair forced themselves through her fingers and were harsh in the stillness of the place.

Britt moved to touch her, to take her and comfort her. Something stayed him. Instead he went away from her, went down alongside the barn to the opened doors to the truck stall. He stood there, his big legs apart, hands clenched at his sides, trying desperately to shut away from him the sounds of her. He too saw Rigger, as he had seen him that afternoon, heard again the rasping, strangling efforts at denied speech. The fever of self-damnation brought the sweat to his brow, brought it flushing forth from his pores. He brought his big hands forward and looked down on their hairy backs, at the veins, at the knuckles round and hard and deadly. In that instant he knew what he had to do.

"Marcy!" He crouched before her and fought to draw her hands from her face. "Marcy, darling, listen to me!"

She shook her head, trying to turn away from him, her shoulders rocking under the savage onslaught of her grief.

"Marcy—Marcy, let's get outta here! Let's beat it, you and me! Marcy, listen. It ain't gonna do no good us bein' here now. This here's our chance, Marcy. Don't you see? Rigger's comin' back now—ain't nothin' can be done. Marcy, now's our chance we been waiting for! Let's us get out now—go away, far away like we planned. Get away from all this!"

Her arms were like two steel bars, keeping him from her. He tightened his grasp and forced them down and pulled her to him. "Marcy, Marcy, it's now, honey—it's now or never, don't you see? There ain't no more time left!"

Suddenly her resistance collapsed. She hurled herself at him, seizing him with all her strength. "Oh, yes, yes, yes!" she cried.

"Oh, Britt, for God's sake, take me somewheres away from all this! I'll go with you anywheres, any place you want!"

He held her close until the upheaval within her had begun to subside. When she was still against him he pressed her gently from him and searched her streaked face. "When?"

She stared at him as if she had not understood. "When?"

"When'll it be? Now? Today?"

For a long moment she looked at him closely, saying nothing, as if she were working the thing out in her mind, making sure. Slowly she straightened and drew herself firm. She came from the crossbar and went past him, out into the brilliant sunlight, and stood gazing out over the whole of the place. She took each of the fields in its turn, pivoting slowly, marking the familiar contours. She turned almost completely around until her eyes came to the old house, humped and bent at the top of the little rise. Finally she took her eyes away and moistened her lips. She came back to Britt and drew a deep breath.

"Not yet," she said slowly. "When Rigger's back—then."

CHAPTER TWENTY

WHEN THE evening meal was prepared that night Marcy followed her usual custom; she went to the back screen and called to Britt to come. She turned and glanced at the closed door to Newt's room. Her every impulse was to shun him, to make every effort to avoid any possible contact with him; yet, if she were to make it obvious there had been any trouble between them, Britt might put two and two together. She drew a sharp breath and marched over and pushed open the door.

"Your supper's ready, Newt," she announced icily.

He was stretched out on his bed, the pillow bunched under his neck, his eyes on her coldly. There was a thick, sirupy silence as they surveyed each other. "Took you so goddamn long, reckoned as how there wasn't gonna be any," he snapped.

She simply looked at him with eyes that flamed her hate and turned and walked across the kitchen, leaving his door ajar. Seconds later Britt came inside and took his place at the table. In a moment Newt appeared in his doorway, buttoning his trousers, and came over to his chair. He sat down heavily, glanced at Britt coolly, and reached for the bread. "You seen my bud?" he grunted.

"Yeah, sure."

Marcy set the hot plates out and remained standing behind her chair, her fingers tight on the back, looking down guardedly on her brother-in-law, "Rigger's comin' home, Newt," she said quietly.

He arrested the fork halfway to his lips. "Hah?"

"Rigger's comin' home."

He stared with hooded eyes; then he shifted and found Britt. "That right, what she's sayin'?"

Britt nodded. "Doc says it's time he come home now. Ain't nothin' more they can do."

Newt scowled at his plate. "He can't move or talk or nothin'!"

Britt shot a glance at Marcy. She was standing there solid, cold, beyond the two of them.

"That's the way it's gonna be, Newt," she said slowly. "Rigger's like he's gonna be, from here on out."

Newt made no sound. He was bent forward, looking down, as if he might solve the riddle somewhere in the piled food on his plate. Finally he picked up his fork and resumed his eating.

The remainder of the meal was consumed in hard silence. When they had finished Newt shoved his chair back; he looked first at Britt, then at Marcy, and then got to his feet and went across the kitchen into his room and shut the door.

Britt shrugged. "What's eatin' him?"

Marcy's face flushed faintly and she shook her head. "Reckon as how maybe he's upset about Rigger."

She was lying and he knew it. "Reckon so," he said. He lit a cigarette and brought his attention to her again. Suddenly he leaned forward and touched her hand in her lap. "Why go on waitin'. Marcy? Why not tonight?"

She looked at him for a long second, then withdrew her hand from his touch and shook her head. "Not until Rigger's home," she said. "We gotta wait till then."

The days fled swiftly. Newt issued his orders daily and they were followed to the letter. In the hot afternoons he and Marcy drove off to town on their pilgrimage to the hospital. Marcy had seen the young doctor again. He had told her much the same as he had told Britt, told her professionally, gently, as uncomfortable as he had been before, facing those big, luminous, hurt eyes of Marcy Kates. He led her into Rigger's room and showed her the surprise he had prepared for her, trying desperately to work light into those eyes. She had gasped, standing in the opening, seeing Rigger in the new wheelchair, in front of the window. She had turned instant questioning eyes at the doctor and he had motioned her into the corridor again. When the door had closed on Rigger he had told her that the wheelchair was a good thing, that it gave Rigger a change, that it would help her later, taking care of him. The only thing was Rigger had to be lifted from the bed and set into the chair, and lifted back to the bed afterward. He had thought they might take Rigger home the following Tuesday.

Marcy went again into the bedroom. Time and again that afternoon, ever since Newt had left for the hospital, she had been going into the room working to get everything ready, making sure everything would be in place. She came now and hesitated in the doorway, her eyes on the high-backed wheelchair in the corner. She was as nervous as a cat, tense. She glanced around the room just once more. Everything looked set to rights. She sighed and turned and went back into the kitchen, over to the sink. Mechanically she washed her hands and dried them on the towel hanging from the rack. She turned slowly, peering around the room, looking for something that needed doing, something that might occupy her hands, utilize her thinking. There was nothing.

Slowly, somnambulantly, she moved down the length of the little hall to the front porch, went outside, and sat down in the wicker rocker to wait. It was so hot! She shoved her hair away with her forearm. Newt had been gone nearly three hours now. They ought to be gettin' back before too long. She closed her eyes and tried to relax.

"Everythin' O.K.?"

She started sharply, coming erect quickly. Britt was standing at the foot of the porch steps, eying her with concern. "Yeah— yeah, sure. I just been settin' here waitin' for 'em."

He glanced down at his feet, shuffled nervously, then looked up at her again. "I'll be keepin' an eye peeled," he said. "They might need a hand."

"Yeah, sure, Britt."

He left then. He went around the corner of the house, making his way to the rear of the place. Marcy stayed as she was, sitting up straight, her eyes fast on the point where he had passed from view. She frowned and chewed on the inside of her lip. Britt was acting so queer these days, acting as if he had something on his mind. He'd got hot-tempered, all edgy about something, couldn't sit still, had to be getting up, racing back and forth all the time they talked these nights. She tried to think back to when she had first noticed anything strange in his manner, any change. There was nothing, no specific time. Marcy suddenly stiffened and her brows arched. She brought her hand from her lap and pressed the palm hard against her cheek, sucking her breath sharply. Instantly what could be the truth came crashing down on her. It was all tied up with how Rigger got hurt. But that couldn't be so! Or—could it? Oh, God, no! Marcy covered her face with her hands and walled her conscience with the darkness of rejection. Desperately she worked to thrust away such reasoning. Bit by bit she pressed the danger from her. It was nothing but this awful business over Rigger that had them all coming and going in circles. Thank God, there wouldn't be much more. Once Rigger was home, once she knew he would be all right, that he would be taken care of properly, then she and Britt—no matter what had happened—would light out, go somewhere far off and make their own way, right or wrong, good or bad.

The sounds of the automobiles brought her from the half nap. She came to her feet instantly, went to the railing, and leaned forward intently. The white ambulance was at the start of the twin ruts to the house and now came slowly up the trail. Behind the ambulance Newt was driving the red truck. With painstaking care the two cars felt their way over the uneven ground. She

caught her breath and tried to stem the rise of nervous apprehension. For the instant, as the ambulance swung past the front
steps, she caught a flashing glimpse of Rigger inside through the
window, him there and the young doctor from Rose Circle at
his side.

Newt took the truck around to the back. She came down
the steps and stood to one side, hands gripped together tight,
as the doctor opened the rear doors to the hospital car. Timidly
she edged closer and stood at the doctor's side, looking inside
at Rigger, lying flat, his head a trifle higher than his feet, his
eyes on a level with hers. She cleared her throat. "Hello, Rigger.
You're home," she managed in a tiny, quavering voice. His eyes
did not waver on her face. Panic rose in her and she cast an
anguished look at the doctor and spun away. Hurriedly she
climbed the porch steps and watched them from there, looking
down on them.

Newt came around the corner of the house, followed closely
by Britt. With the doctor supervising their moves, Newt and
Britt and the ambulance driver worked to shift Rigger to the lit-
ter, to bring the stretcher from the back of the machine. They
brought Rigger up the steps. Marcy held the screen open as they
passed into the hallway, struggling to work their burden through
the narrow entrance. Newt was carrying the foot while Britt bore
the head, and as they brushed past her, Marcy glanced up at Britt.
He was staring down at Rigger and the sweat was like glass on
his skin.

The doctor took charge in the bedroom. He helped them
transfer Rigger to the bed. Silently he pointed to the dresser and
Marcy got the new bottle of rubbing alcohol and handed it to
him. As their hands touched the young doctor raised his eyes. He
turned his head quickly; she had the goddamnedest lost look to
her every time! Glancing across the bed at the two men standing
there, he spoke. "One of you men get my bag from the ambulance, please."

It was Britt who moved quickly. He brushed past Marcy and left the room. The doctor worked to free Rigger from the little hospital jacket. He tossed it to the foot of the bed and stepped back, uncapping the bottle. "Weather like this you best give him a rubdown several times a day, at least," he said. There was no answer. Curious, he twisted to see her. She had retreated behind him, close to the door, mute, watching with those eyes. "If you want to come closer, I'll show you the way to do this," he added kindly. Automatically she stirred and came alongside him. Without realizing she gasped and her hand flew to cover her mouth, to stifle the outcry.

Rigger lay stretched naked before her. The once hard, perfect little body was warped and broken and the solid, cultivated muscles had failed to flabbiness and hopeless waste. Instantly, from the lowest depths within her, pity and compassion came sweeping, bringing the quick warm flush of tears. Instinctively, suddenly, she leaned forward and put her fingers on his arm, giving a gentle pressure to her touch. The eyes watched her but Rigger Kates made no sound.

The doctor touched her briefly, bringing her straight at his side. He avoided looking at her and began his job. Marcy watched very carefully. As the man worked on her husband Marcy's eyes lifted and she found Newt on the opposite side of the bed. He was standing solidly, his hands deep in his trousers pockets, staring down at the smashed hulk that was his brother. Marcy could not divorce her eyes from his face. The lips were tight, pinched at the corners, gone bloodless. His face was flushed and the eyes were tiny and bright, gleaming with a peculiar intense fire. As she watched it seemed the lips relaxed a trifle, parted slowly. He edged forward slightly, as if he wanted to get a better look, to see more. Bent like that, his eyes sharp, missing no detail, Newt Kates licked his lips and then straightened and drew a long sure breath. His attention shifted and he met her suspicious eyes across the bed. For the instant she fancied he was smiling. She frowned and forced her attention back to Rigger. It had been her imagination. When she hazarded a later, furtive glance at him, he was absorbed again in the doctor's ministrations, paying her no heed.

Britt came into the room behind her, carrying the little bag. He went over and set it on the dresser and moved up to the foot of the bed and looked down on Rigger Kates. His breath hooked in his throat and his eyes pooled with horror. For an instant he saw Rigger as he had been that first morning in the cheap hotel, standing nude in front of the blotched mirror, probing his sturdy, developed body. The picture dissolved and was the misshapen, helpless thing on the bed before him. Britt ran his hand through his hair and jerked his eyes away. He saw Newt staring down in fascination like that, saw Marcy standing near him, mute, steeped in the agony of pity, and suddenly he could not take any more. A barely audible groan forced itself from his lips, bringing Marcy's frightened, knowing eyes to his blanched face. Blindly he wheeled and stumbled from the room, went fleeing across the kitchen, flinging himself into the yellow heat outside, and there, clinging to the pump support, he fought desperately to down the overwhelming tide of sickness that had come upon him.

Supper that night was an ordeal. The door to the bedroom was left open and occasionally Marcy left her place at the table and crossed to the doorway to look at Rigger. He had slept ever since they had placed him in the bed. Newt said nothing; he ate steadily and when the meal was over he left them and went outside. When she took the dishes over to the sink Marcy could see him far off, standing alone in the failing day, looking out over his wheat field, now coming swiftly to ripe maturity.

Britt remained at the table, watching her. She looked so tired, so pale. When she crossed to get more plates he reached out and took her wrist. She managed a faint smile and carefully took herself from his touch.

Suddenly in the silence between them there was a half-grunt-ing, half-choking sound. Britt's eyes rose wildly, instantly to her face. She was in the center of the kitchen, her eyes big and full of dread, looking past him, staring into the room beyond. The sounds continued, filling the whole of the house. Marcy raised a trembling hand to her temple and brought her fingertips down her cheek. There was a desperate appeal in her eyes on Britt.

"It's him," she whispered. "I gotta go see what he wants."

She forced herself to move, to go around the end of the table, pausing for a split second in the doorway, looking back to him, sitting in open horror. "Later," she said. "Later, Britt."

Britt waited in anxious torment for her that night. He could not relax, could not throw himself on the cot as before, give himself to dreaming, to planning. The haunting spectacle of that shattered piece of man that had been Rigger Kates, the raucous, obscene sounds of him came damningly again and again. He sat hunched on the side of the bed in the darkness, fighting to ignore the picture flaming bright no matter where he might look. In a moment he was on his feet again, going to the doorway, peering toward the house, willing her to him. The house lights had been turned off some time ago. Still there was no sign of her coming.

He crossed to the cot and sat down. He beat the palm of his left hand with the hard right fist. He tried to see the pattern of the days now to come. There was no pathway out to the future. The whole of his existence had ground to a halt, trapped in an inescapable dead end. Trembling, he came to his feet quickly. The yard was naked and open, dimly washed by the light of the rising moon, deserted.

He was perched on the edge of the cot when she came. She was in the room, standing before him, looking down at him silently. His eyes came to focus on her legs, came rising slowly up the length of her body to the face, white and drawn.

"Oh, Marcy, my God!"

He was on his feet, seizing her roughly, crushing her brutally against him. "Marcy, oh, Marcy—you been so long in comin'!"

She worked to free herself gently and raised her arm, putting her long fingers through the tangle of his hair. "There's been lots to do," she said simply.

He knew what she meant. Instantly he flushed and released her and went off to the far side of the little room. She turned slowly, surprise high in her eyes, and found him, his back on her, his head bent forward. Quietly she crossed to him and coming up behind him she put her arms around him, locking her fingers on his chest. She nuzzled her cheek against the solid breadth of his back. "I couldn't get away sooner, Britt," she said. "There was so many things needed doin'." She felt him stiffen and the quick swell of his chest forced her fingers apart. He spun swiftly and his hands gripped her shoulders.

"Marcy!" he cried hoarsely. "We gotta beat it! Tonight! It ain't no good, this stickin' 'round here no more! I got a bellyful of this stuff! I ain't takin' no more!"

She stared at him for a long moment, then turned from him and went to the cot to stand at its side, her head drawn back, her eyes wide on the angle of the wall and ceiling. He came behind her and held her within the circle of his arms, putting his face into the soft brush of her hair, and his voice was quiet now, sure.

"Marcy, honey, let's us clear out tonight. Let's not go on torturin' ourselves for nothin'. What's happened's happened. It ain't for us to go on just beatin' ourselves to death!"

There was a long, long moment of silence. She blinked once or twice and looked down at the big familiar hands clasped on the front of her. Curiously, probingly, she touched the thick fingers, toyed with them, as if she were seeking the combination that might unlock their hold. Finally she drew a deep steadying breath and gently, with both her hands, she drew his hands apart. She went from him, leaving him shocked and surprised behind her. She crossed to the doorway and stood in the frame, looking out into the silvered yard.

"Britt," she said huskily, "it ain't gonna work. It ain't gonna work, us leavin' together like we been plannin'."

He stared in disbelief at her outlined in the doorway and touched his lips with the tip of his tongue. He followed and his voice was sharp. "What're you tryin' to say?"

She squared her shoulders and he saw how she was looking at the dumpy frame of the old house. "I'm sayin' it ain't no good what we been plannin'. Reason I was late comin', I been settin' there in the kitchen all by myself in the dark thinkin' things out. I been settin' thinkin'—listenin' to him tryin' to breathe in the other room, listenin' to him makin' them noises of his, all the time rememberin' him like he was." She faltered, turned slowly, and looked up into his eyes. "I can't be runnin' off leavin' him like that, Britt. That's all there is to it."

He backed away from her and his eyes left her face and darted fearfully to the monitor house. In horror he found her face. "You mean—you're wantin' to stick around, spendin' your life seein' what he's like, day after day, year after year? Your whole life, maybe?"

Her chin lifted faintly, defensively. "Britt, Britt—" She failed before his swiftly darkening eyes and set her concentration on the doorframe, digging her nails into the soft wood again and again. "Britt, I been settin' there thinkin' what we been plannin's all wrong, somehow. I ain't able to see it bein' right, runnin' off and leavin' him sufferin' and not bein' cared for proper. It don't seem like nobody could find no happiness startin' out like that."

He took another step back, away from her, and she glanced up quickly. His eyes were round on her and there was the slow unmistakable beginning of a flame. She put forth her hand to touch him but he moved once more, taking himself beyond her reach. "You ain't never been plannin' to go with me!" he cried harshly. "You ain't never once been on the level about us goin' off together."

"Oh, Britt—no!"

His lips curled scornfully and somehow he seemed to grow even larger until he towered over her. "You ain't never been honest, have you? You been havin' yourself a good time, is all! You figured maybe you'd have your cake and eat it, too!"

"Oh, Britt—no, no!" she cried. She took a step toward him. "That ain't so! You're gettin' it all wrong!" She reached out now and her fingers caught him, locking on his forearm. "Britt! Can't you see what I mean? Can't you see I'm married to Rigger Kates legal and all? If somethin's wrong with him, if he's like he is now, then I reckon as how it's up to me, his wife, to stand by, to do what I can, no matter what."

He whipped his arm and flung her touch from him. "Sure, I get it all now!" he lashed wildly. "Sure, you been married all along. You just been havin' a little party on the side. You ain't never planned it would be us, ever. You was safe all the time and you knew it. You just been usin' me like you want from the start."

Her hands clapped over her ears and she shook her head, her eyes shut tight. "Oh, Britt! Britt, for God's sake, don't keep on sayin' things like that! You ain't right, you ain't right! I—I just can't go on takin' no more!"

His eyes on her were flame. "Maybe you don't like hearin' what's the honest truth. Kinda hurts, hearin' what's maybe true comin' right out in the open!" He came forward and wrenched her arms down so she would have to hear him. She had begun to cry now, the tears streaking silver in the half-light on her cheeks. "You can't go on takin' no more!" he railed. "It's me can't take no more, that's who! I'm gonna get the hell outta here! I'm gonna hit the road tonight! Ain't no good hangin' round here no more, punishin' ourselves, sufferin' and doin' nothin' to stop it!"

"Oh, Britt, you can't be goin' off! You can't go leavin' me now! I don't care what's been done, who's to blame!" She raced on hysterically, not hearing the sudden sharp chop of his breath, not seeing the wide quick look of startled fear that peaked in his eyes on her. "Oh, Britt, please—stay a little longer. Maybe a little later on, when things is better, then we—"

The walls moved in on him. For the instant he was trapped with no hope of escape now. "Save it." He shoved her away from him rudely. "Don't go on talkin' 'bout no later ons. You know like I know there ain't gonna be no later ons. We're washed up, done for!"

She staggered back from his thrust until the blade of the doorframe came cutting into her back, holding her rigid from utter collapse. She was bowed forward, her face buried in her hands, and he could hear the quiet weeping across the room as he worked feverishly to drag the old suitcase from under the cot. One tour around the room and everything was in the bag.

Hurriedly, almost eagerly, now that his freedom goal was at last in sight, he shut the case, seized the handle, and came to the door in front of her. She was still like that, bent, her face covered. He stopped in front of her, straight, tall above her, looking down on her, and his face contorted sharply. In the instant everything he felt for her, all the hungering love and desire he had known from the very beginning, knew too well now, came spilling through him, blinding, flooding, closing the too few avenues of escape. Despite his reason he reached out and touched her hair with his free hand. She brought her head up slowly at the contact, took her hands from her glistening face, and her eyes on him were pleading. For a long moment he gazed at her and then he turned his head and glanced out over the clean-swept flat of the yard. He brought his flaming eyes back to her and he cupped her chin and bent and kissed her full on the mouth.

"Oh, Jesus, sweet Jesus, I can't do it, I can't do it!" he choked.

The bag struck the floor with a dull thud as his arms found her and swept her into the closeness of his embrace.

CHAPTER TWENTY-ONE

BRITT went into town to pick up some supplies for her early the next morning, before Newt had come to the breakfast table.

"Where the hell's your boy friend?"

She told him simply and directly that Britt had some chores in town, that he'd gone early to get ahead of the heat. Newt scowled and fed himself noisily.

"Sonofabitch has to pick a time like this to go joy-ridin' right when there's work to do," he complained. "Wheat's 'bout comin' due, too."

She had told him and now she paid no heed as she worked at the sink. Her eyes occasionally lifted, straying truantly to the door of the little barn room, her mind full of last night. For a fleeting instant the hard core of terror twisted a little, scoring the walls of her insides. Supposing—supposing Britt meant what he said last night! Supposing the trip to town was only an excuse, that he wasn't coming back! Hastily she turned from the window and wiped her hands on her apron nervously. She crossed to the bedroom door and looked in to see how Rigger was doing. He was awake, and each time she came to the door his eyes would shift to find her, to remain on her steadily.

Newt lingered at the table longer that morning. He kept watching her closely, his eyes shrunken and hollow, his thinking cloaked behind his scrutiny. Finally he stirred and shoved back his chair, flipping the broken match into his plate. "I gotta get goin'," he grunted. "Now your fancy boy's taken himself the day off, reckon as how I gotta do everythin' myself."

She wheeled at the sink and caught him before he had got through the back door. "Newt!"

He stopped and eyed her suspiciously, his guard up immediately. "Yeah?"

"Newt, you're gonna have to get Rigger in that chair of his. I can't do it."

He scowled and glanced into the room. "Can't the little bastard stay like he is?"

She flushed angrily. "It ain't right leavin' him flat like that!"

Newt shrugged and mumbled something.

Marcy came to the bedroom opening and watched. Newt rolled the chair close to the bed and then reached down and got his hold on the little body. He lifted Rigger easily, as if he were a baby, and set him roughly in the chair. Rigger made no sound. He was watching Newt with those eyes and Marcy felt a kind of slow chill come creeping along the reach of her spine. For a brief, sparking instant she had caught the faint change of expression in the little guy's eyes. He was watching Newt and there was a venomous hatred deep-rooted and bright in the look.

Newt stood straight and glanced across the disordered bed to her. "That what you want?" She nodded. He glanced down at Rigger, stark naked in the chair. "You fixin' to get some clothes on him?"

She nodded again. "I'll take care of that, Newt."

He stood for a moment, looking down on his brother, and there was a peculiar suggestion of a momentary smile that seemed to pull at his lips. "O.K., Brother." Newt smirked and came past her and went to do his chores.

When Newt had gone she went to Rigger and worked to dress him. She had picked up some light sport shirts in town, the kind that button down the front, and she managed to get his arms into the short sleeves, to fasten the garment. She took his Levis and, by circling his torso with her arm, she struggled to raise him enough to slide the pants over his buttocks, to work them to his waist, to button the fly. Finally she had him ready. As she straightened, breathing hard, she reached out tentatively and touched his head. The crew cut had grown long and she smoothed the sandy hair into place. He watched her steadily, his eyes funny, almost as if he were half-smiling.

"It was right nice, Newt helpin' out," she murmured.

At that he rolled his eyes and for the first time that day those dreadful sounds began. She stared down at him, trying to shove the instant fear and uneasiness from her, striving to know what the sounds could mean. A kind of frantic desperation came into Rigger's eyes and he kept on making the noises. Twisting agony caught her and she went to her knees at his side.

"What is it, Rigger? What you tryin' to say? Is it Newt?"

She knew suddenly by the look that came into his eyes that it was Newt. Yet there was no way of knowing, no way of translating the gibberish into meaning. Wearily she came to her feet and touched his shoulder lightly, reassuringly.

"Don't you go worryin' none about him now," she said quietly. "He ain't gonna be pesterin' none."

She went around to the back of the chair and worked the clumsy chair around the end of the bed, easing it through the doorway into the kitchen, up close to the table. Leaving him, she went to the sink. "We'll get some food in you right off," she promised, her eyes suddenly on the opening to the little room in the barn.

After the midday meal, while she was busy in the bedroom giving Rigger his rubdown, Newt Kates stood in the frame of the back door, looking out over the fields, picking at his teeth. The silence was soft over everything, like a velvet rug drawn over the place sleeping in the thick heat. The wind that had threatened to rise that morning had come to nothing. Off in the distance the wheat field, close to fulfillment, was gold and rich in the brightness.

He stood leaning forward, his arms raised, the palms of his hands on the frame, as his gaze shifted slowly, intently over the farm. Everything was in order. Newt took a deep healing breath, and as he exhaled the unaccustomed smile spread. It was a good feeling, this being alone on the place, after all these long years of waiting, this being able to do just what he wanted, when he wanted, without somebody nagging orders, without some god-damn stranger getting the nod every time. He had never dreamed it would feel so good. He took his hands down and pushed the door open with his body.

He went across the yard to the open door of the room in the barn. On the threshold he stood and peered around cautiously. So the big fella had gone sulkin' off to town for the day. Probably gone to have a bit of fun. He grinned. Him and her must've had a fight. Big guy was gettin' too goddamn big for his britches, any-how. Well, once the wheat crop was in he'd bust that up—kick that big rear of his off this place pronto. He straightened and went down alongside the barn, pulling his old yellow straw hat down as he stepped beyond the shade of the building.

He marched through the blinding heat of the day, going out along the narrow rutted trail between the fields until at last he came to the block of rich golden grain that stood firm and heavy-headed, riffling lazily in the wash of the humid, weighted breeze. Newt shoved his hat back on his head and brought his hands up loosely to his hips, and, with his legs apart, he brought up his chin and embraced the plot with the little pinched eyes gone warm and covetous.

This here was the best goddamn crop ever! Just went to show what happened when the right guy took over. The brokers were sure gonna be glad-handin' him over this spread. Few more days now and the combines would be comin' thrashin' and sackin' and rollin' off to tell everybody how they just been out to Newt Kates's, harvestin' the best goddamn field they ever did see.

He turned and eyed the distant house and the lights went from his eyes and his face muscles hardened slowly. He grunted and jerked the hat low and turned and started plodding back. She'd be done with that waste-of-good-time rubdown stuff by now. It was time to put that goddamn Rigger back in his chair again.

It was midafternoon several days later. Rigger was asleep in the bedroom and Marcy sat alone in the kitchen, her hands flat on the table, letting the weariness take her in all-encompassing arms. The past days had not been easy. Rigger could do nothing for himself and the burden was hers alone. She bathed him, fed him, dressed and undressed him, helped him with his toilet needs, everything. She sat now, staring at the backs of her hands, simply waiting for the next round. Idly her mind toyed with the events of the past week. It was almost impossible to remember what it had been like before Rigger got hurt, before he had come back from the hospital.

Laggardly her thinking turned to Britt. Ever since that one night, the night he had almost left her, he had been quiet, reserved, yet troubled still. He avoided the house with its constant reminder of Rigger Kates. She could understand that. She knew how he must feel. He worked hard outside, coming in only for his food. He said little at the meals, putting himself to the feeding task. There were little fleeting moments when she knew he was only waiting, letting the time go by, waiting for her to say the time was now. And yet, how could she know when that time was here? Her eyes swung now to the doorway to the bedroom and her ears picked up the gentle labor of Rigger's sleeping breath. How much longer could this go on? In the instant she cracked. There was an overwhelming need in her for Britt Callum at this moment, for the strength he could give her, for his firmness in this hour. And now came the sudden grinding conviction that the time would never come for them. He would go sooner or later, he would go from her. The knowledge stood within her sure, positive, unchallengeable. The time would run out before she was ready and he would go because he was sick at heart, because there was no way to ignore what was here, no escape, even within the warmth of their embrace.

She summoned the image of him within her now, fought to hold the picture of him, to have just that much at this moment. She saw again the unruly curls, the darkness of his face, the rounded neck, the great shoulders, the chest, felt again the smoothness of his skin, the insistence of his thighs on her. Then it was gone. The ephemeral vision went skittering off behind the blocking shadows of the present, eluding her. Marcy Kates sighed and turned her hands over and looked at the callousing palms. The noise from outside brought her sharply alert.

Next Kates slammed the back screen and glanced at her with an ugly smirk. "What you doin' now? Sittin' round moonin' over your big bastard boy friend some more?"

She had not looked up but she knew he had come close to her. "Be quiet," she murmured, nodding at the bedroom door. "He's sleepin'."

"To hell with him!" Newt snorted. "Where the hell's them keys to the storage bin?"

Marcy came to her feet. "Inside. Wait. I'll get 'em."

She was gone only for a second, easing the door shut softly as she returned. She handed him the ring of keys. "Here."

Newt made no effort to leave. He ran his sharpening eyes over her curiously and wet his thin lips. "You and the big guy still havin' fun?"

She flushed faintly but made no reply, turning her head a little to avoid the hard little derisive eyes.

"You and him have some pretty hot times together," Newt taunted keenly. Still she was denying him the satisfaction of a rise. "Sure remember how one night I seen you two lolly-gaggin' round. Sure was havin' yourselves a time!"

At that she brought her flaming eyes to his face and the contempt was deep in the cuts of her mouth. "Leave me alone, Newt. You leave me be." She pushed past him and went to the sink, setting her palms on the cool edge, waiting for him to go.

He did not go. He came slowly across the little space between them and reached out and touched her upper arm. Carefully, pointedly, he ran his rough finger pads down along the sensitive flesh to her wrist. His thumb and forefinger circled it and he moved instantly, trying to spin her around to face him.

But Marcy was too quick. She snapped her arm from the ring lock and stepped aside swiftly. "Newt, for God's sake, please! Go 'way, please!" Her back was set on him.

His smile was an ugly shadow. He hesitated, then stepped back slowly. "He ain't gonna be round here so much longer, sister. Best be gettin' that in your purty head. He's gonna hightail it soon. When he's gone, that Rigger ain't gonna be doin' you no good, neither. One of these here days you're gonna be wantin' some. Reckon as how I can wait my turn."

"For what?" She wheeled swiftly, her cheeks burning, and eyed him scornfully. "You dirty-minded thing! Why, you ain't even got what it takes!" she lashed.

The anger was instant in him. His fist flew high and he moved on her. Instinctively she cringed before the expected blow. It never came. There was a sudden raw scraping cry from behind the bedroom door that froze them both. Newt's head jerked and his eyes went wide with horror. "Holy Christ!" he whispered hoarsely. He glanced wildly, fearfully at her, and she saw he had gone pale.

With a thin bitter smile she straightened slowly and went past him, over to the door. She put her fingers lightly on the knob, and before she opened the door she looked back at him.

"You best be gettin' used to Rigger's talkin', Newt," she said coolly. "Seems like he's got lots to say since he come home."

She knew that what she had felt that afternoon had already come to pass when he moved from her side that night, when he took himself from her and went across the room to stand close to the open door, staring out over the moon-drenched yard. In the milky shadows she could see only the pale outline of his nakedness and she knew before he spoke that the time had come.

"I can't be stayin' no more time," he said slowly, not looking back to her. "It ain't no more good, Marcy, my hangin' on here, takin' that Newt's crap, hearin' and seein' what Rigger's like, stealin' little bits and pieces of livin' and lovin' with you." He turned wearily and came back and stood beside the bed looking down on her. "It ain't no good this way, you know that as well as me. I figured after the other night maybe I'd hang on, make a stab at waitin', but it ain't gonna work." She saw him draw himself straight slowly, as if it were a terrible effort, and she knew he had taken his eyes from her body. "I'm askin' you to clear out with me in the mornin'. There ain't nothin' I want more in the world than you. You know that already now. Somewheres we can find what's for us, Marcy, you and me. Only"—he was looking down on her now—"it ain't here. It ain't here now, it ain't never gonna be here." There was a tiny pause and she held her breath. "I'm askin' you now, Marcy, come with me—come with me tomorrow, or—" His voice broke and she heard his knuckles crack as he gripped his hands together. "Or I'm gonna have to go it alone."

She stayed as she was on the bed for a long time. He waited some moments, then crossed the room to the door and stood with his back to her and she knew he was waiting. Finally she got up and dressed slowly. When she came up behind him he turned and in the half-light she looked into his eyes, steeped in anxiety and conflict.

"You ain't comin'," he said quietly. "It's gonna be me on my own again."

Marcy swallowed hard. "I can't," she whispered. "Oh, my dearest, don't you see that yet? I can't, I can't run out on him like that. It ain't what I'm wantin' to do down inside that counts—it's what I gotta do that's important. I can't be runnin' out on him, I just can't."

He made a funny little half motion with his hands. "I figured you'd stick," he said. "That's the way I figured."

They stood close, each looking across the silvered clearing to the black pile of the old house. Within that house was the man who had been Rigger Kates.

She did not take her eyes from the place. "When?" she asked quietly. "When's it you're goin', Britt?"

"Tomorrow. Noon, I guess."

She brought her chin up and locked her jaw to try to stop the foolish tremble. "You best be havin' dinner before you go," she said. "Somethin' special you like."

He watched her go from him, go straight and sure across the clearing, her head held high, shoulders squared. Even though the darkness was a cloak for her he knew suddenly that she was walking and crying and then, for the first time in as long as he could remember, the tears came quick in his eyes and stole the sight of her from him.

CHAPTER TWENTY-TWO

MARCY'S ears picked up the faint tapping while she was working to dress Rigger in his chair that morning. She hesitated, then went on with her efforts. The tapping came again, a little louder, more insistent. She finished her chore and, frowning, struggled to her feet. She patted Rigger's shoulder lightly. "Somebody's rappin'," she told him. "I'm comin' back." She left him, went out into the kitchen, and paused to listen. Once again the knock sounded. She glanced down the reach of the little hall and her brows lifted in slight surprise. She could see the woman standing on the porch, her full skirt caught in the eddying little breeze that had come since dawn. Running her hands down over her hips, smoothing out the wrinkled dress, Marcy went to answer the call. Probably some stranger askin' the way to town or somethin', she reckoned.

As she came to the screen the woman reached up and tapped again, little impatient staccato drummings of her fingertips on the frame of the door. Marcy stopped short and her breathing snagged. The woman had turned at the sound of her approach and now the two of them stood with only the meshed screen between them, staring openly, each defensive instantly, defiant.

"You're Miz Kates, ain'tcha?" Ruby said tentatively.

"Yeah, I'm wife to Rigger Kates," Marcy responded coolly. She made no effort to extend a welcome to this woman, to open the door to her, to ask her inside the house.

Ruby glanced nervously down at the big shiny black leather bag she clutched up close to her and she shifted slightly. "Miz

Kates, I know you reckon as how I got a helluva nerve traipsin' out here to your place like this." She raised her head now and a little of the sure hardness came back into her eyes. "Only I'm clearing out tonight, and I—well, I reckoned as how it wouldn't be right, me takin' off to California to stay and all, without maybe—well, without seein' Rigger once before I go."

Marcy ran her eyes over the ripe lush figure. This Ruby was like they said, a big one, with flash and the kind of full-breasted fleshiness Rigger always went for. She knew him well enough to know this one had been too good to pass. Uncertainly she poked at the screen and opened it a trifle. "I just been dressin' him," Marcy said dully. "You can come see him if it's what you're wantin'."

She turned away and the door banged shut behind Ruby as she followed Marcy down the hall. At the table Marcy stopped. She made no effort to turn, to look at the woman; she simply stood staring at the sink, until the footstep sounds told her Rigger's woman had come into the kitchen. "He's inside there." She waved her hand, indicating the opened door. When she heard the sharp incisive gasp, heard the single little startled cry behind her, Marcy wet her lips and closed her eyes. She opened them an instant later. Very quietly, without looking up to see into the bedroom, she went over and drew the door shut, separating them from her. She went hurriedly from the murmuring sound of the voice behind the wall and got a glass of water. Instantly her eyes were on the door to the little barn room. She knew he was there, was inside this very moment getting his stuff ready, so he could take off after dinner. For one mad little second she wondered if she could go there, be with him while the woman was with Rigger. It was too late. It was too risky. She crossed over and sat down at the table to wait.

Marcy turned her head slightly to watch Newt fumble with the back screen. He finally pulled it open and came inside. His little eyes found her instantly and he came close and stared down at her. She tried to ignore him, devoting her full attention to her fingers, splaying them wide over the table.

"See you got yourself the next boy friend already lined up," he jibed. "Sure as hell don't take you so long." There was a hard little chuckle. "No use lettin' the sheet get cold, hey?"

Her eyes narrowed and she brought her fingers together. "What're you talkin' about, Newt?"

He moved then, came into the line of her vision. "I just seen him out there," he crowed. "I ain't no goddamn blind man."

She tightened her lips and eyed him irritably. "Newt, for God's sake, you're talkin' all crazy! What kind of thinkin's goin' on in you now?"

He flicked his grimy fingers toward the mouth of the hallway and sneered. "Don't be handin' me no crap you don't know what I'm talkin' 'bout. I seen him—settin' out front right now in that there big fancy car on the road. Best be shaggin' yourself out to him. When they're ready, guys don't like waitin' too long!"

There was utter disgust in her face and she fought down the impulse to scream at him. She cleared her throat and kept her voice very low. "It ain't none of your business, but if there's some guy in a car out front, he's waitin' on somebody else. There's somebody visitin' with Rigger and I reckon he's waitin' on her." She searched her hands and her lips tightened. "Seems like if you was tendin' your work there wouldn't he no time to go snoopin'."

Her taunt was lost in the quick rise of his surprise. He glanced at the closed door to the bedroom and crossed over close to the panel and, bending his head low, listened intently. Marcy watched him and bitterness rimmed her eyes. Newt scowled and glanced at her. "Who's the dame?"

Marcy had no opportunity to snap her answer. The door behind Newt opened without warning. Ruby burst into the room. She had her big bag shoved hard under her left arm and there was a crumpled handkerchief wadded in her right hand. Her face was flushed and there was a bright glittering sheen in her eyes. She stopped short as she came into the midst of them, her glance darting first to Marcy, then to Newt Kates. Instantly her breath failed, trapped, and she recoiled, stepping back. The closing door clicked shut as she came against it.

Newt's eyes bugged. He turned slowly to face her and stood solidly, running his tongue along his lips, eying her with frank curiosity. "So," he breathed. "Now it's Rigger's fancy woman come to take a look-see too!"

Marcy flushed deeply and dropped her gaze to the table, keeping her eyes from that confused fearful look in the other woman's face.

"Reckon as how he ain't much good for sleepin' round these here nights, hey?"

Ruby tore her eyes from his evil face, from the leering grin, and moved a further step sideways from him. She shot a quick, frantic look of appeal at Rigger's wife, but she had her head down, not watching.

Newt Kates kept grinning. "Never could reckon what a big strappin' dame like you ever seen in him nohow. Seems like a piece like you'd get a helluva lot more playin' with a man 'stead of somethin' no bigger than a kid." He treated himself to a long searching last look, stepping up close to her, peering intently down into the cleft at the neckline of her blouse. "Them's sure a nice pair of cans you got there, Ruby. Reckon as how there was a time Rigger kinda forgot his mammy done weaned him a long time back."

He gave her a pointed smirk and turned and strode across the kitchen. At the screen door he peered back at them. Marcy had brought her flaming face up, was lumped at the table, her eyes pooling with sympathy on the stricken woman. Ruby was white, her lower lip caught in the clamp of her teeth, her breath coming and going in little ragged flutters. Newt grinned sardonically. Then the grotesque grimace died and the old harsh ugliness came sweeping into place. His hand moved forward and found the frame and he pushed the door open, holding it. "Nothin' but a couple of no-good whorin' bitches, the two of you!" he snarled. with that he spat on the floor and went storming out into the steaming day.

Marcy came to her feet wearily. The heat was turning muggy. Without a word she went to the sink and took the soiled mopping rag from its nail. She crossed to where he had dirtied the floor and stooped down and wiped the boards clean. As she straightened her eyes met Ruby's.

"I'm right sorry," Marcy offered huskily. "You get so most times you don't pay much mind to him, to what he's sayin', to what he's doin'. It ain't so healthy if you start lettin' it get you down."

Ruby said nothing. She watched silently as Marcy returned to the sink and rinsed the rag in the water pan. She waited until Marcy had got rid of the rag, until she stood wiping her hands on her dress absently. Then Ruby came forward and touched her lightly, cautiously.

"Miz Kates, ain't there somethin' I could do, maybe, to kinda help out? Ain't there somethin'?"

Marcy stared at the worn features, at the clumsily beaded lashes, at the thick-shelled lipstick sleek on the full, heavy mouth. She shook her head slowly. "There ain't nothin'," she said slowly. "It's all part of the job, I reckon."

Ruby floundered, trapped in her own action. She wet her lips gingerly and pulled the big shiny purse from under her arm. "You mind me havin' a smoke before I leave?"

Marcy shrugged and nodded toward the table. "I don't mind. Whyn't you set?" She raised her eyes again. "Reckon as how you must be a little shaky after that."

The two of them sat opposite each other. Ruby opened her bag and poked inside. She found the cigarette pack and took one with shaking fingers. She struck the match and steadied one hand with the other until the cigarette was lit. As she brought the thing from her lips she tardily remembered Marcy. "Like one, honey?"

"No, thanks." Marcy felt uneasy sitting here across from this woman after all this time. She sent little furtive glances across the table, taking her measure. Suddenly, with a quick start, she realized Ruby was watching her through the veil of smoke, had caught her fleeting look. Marcy colored and moistened her lips. "You—you shouldn't pay no mind to what Newt says," she said hastily. "He's kinda funny."

The muscles of Ruby's mouth tightened; her eyes shelled as she looked past Marcy to the glaring rectangle of the door through which he had gone. "Yeah—funnier'n hell!" she rasped. There was a harsh break and she brought her gaze slowly down to Marcy. The girl's eyes had gone wide, her lips had parted at the explosive comment. Ruby's lids flickered and she took a long drag on the cigarette, absently dropping the ash to the floor at her side. Marcy saw, but the effort to rise, to go get the saucer was too much.

"He ain't so damned funny," Ruby added shortly. She examined the tip of the cigarette and then she got up and went to the door. Pushing it open, she flicked the butt far out into the yard. She pivoted slowly and glanced pityingly at the back of Marcy's head. "There ain't nothin' so damn funny about that Newt Kates," she repeated as she came back to her place. Marcy was eying her dully. Ruby hesitated, then reached for her bag, opened it, and took out a lipstick and a mirror. Carefully, methodically, she added a thickening layer to her lips, working slowly, studying Marcy over the rim of the glass. When she was done she replaced the tools, snapped the bag shut decisively, and came forward on her elbows.

"Honey, I was there—in the Indian Head—that same night you and the big fella was there—the night the big guy took a poke at Rigger." She faltered. "The night it happened."

Marcy went rigid. She set her palms on the edge of the table and made herself alert, defensive.

"Rigger and me was together that night, only maybe you didn't see me. I steer clear when there's trouble brewin'. Well, anyway, after the big fella you was with—that Britt guy—slapped Rigger down, it was me worked on him, got him on his feet again."

There was a sudden tiny hissing breath from Marcy Kates. Ruby raised her brows and slowly her eyes sparked. She came an inch or so farther across the table. "You been thinkin' it was him, the big fella, done it to the little guy." She straightened stiffly and her eyes went grim. "Well, you can get shut of such thinkin' right off. It wasn't the big guy, kid. Sure, Rigger wasn't doin' so good when we left that joint, but he was O.K. enough."

Marcy slumped a little and she brought her hands together on the table, locking her fingers tight, pinning her concentration on them, listening now as the voice went on.

"Soon as I knowed he was O.K., him and me lit out for my place." She caught herself, avoiding Marcy's sharp glance. "I reckon as how it ain't no secret no more about me and him. Well, Rigger and me goes to my room for a little while, maybe an hour or so, I don't know. Then we run outta liquor, so naturally we reckoned as how we best head downtown and get some more. God's truth is we got out in front of my joint and me and Rigger started a big beef about some damn-fool thing. I don't even remember what it was now. You know what Rigger's like when he's carryin' a load. He slaps me like he done you that night— only me, he knocks me on my fanny. By the time I pick myself off the cement, the little bastard's headin' off down the street like a greased pig."

She hesitated to make sure Marcy was listening, following her. There came now the faint suggestion of a grim, rueful smile on Ruby's face.

"Sure, I was sore as hell. I takes out after that Rigger. I reckoned as how I'd bat him one myself. I was good and sore at that little guy, Miz Kates. You know how it is. He's been slappin' me around a long time now." She paused and examined her fingers. "You knowed all about us—Rigger told me." There was no guilt, no apology, only the flat statement for the record. Marcy colored and gave a tiny nod. "Sure, kid, reckon as how the whole god-damn town's been on to us two." She began to work open the bag, took out another cigarette, and lit it. She exhaled the first draught in a thick pluming cloud, and as it drifted lazily her eyes on Marcy were dark and sympathetic.

"He wasn't your kind, honey," she said simply. "Rigger and me, we been two peas from the same pod. He's a tramp, like me. Drinkin' or in bed, it never made no difference with us. We was a pair. We was never nothin' but a couple of lousy tramps, him and me, I reckon." For a moment it looked as if she were going to reach out and touch Marcy. "He ain't never been the guy for you, kid. I reckon there's been plenty times you been knowin' that. There's times he's a lousy no-good little punk, God help him."

Her voice shattered and she blinked rapidly and turned her face aside. When she looked back at Marcy there was a bright splash in her eyes and she was working to hold her lips steady. "Get me!" she shrilled brassily. "I'm sure pullin' out the stops today! Must of got me a dose of the willies or somethin'."

With a swift rush of pity Marcy suddenly saw the whole truth. Sympathy waved upon her. She wanted to reach across the little space, to touch the woman, to tell her by mere gesture; but she made no move, said nothing.

Ruby was silent. She took a couple of nervous drags on the smoke and brought her control tight. Her words when they came again were slow, clear, free of the threat of emotion. "I reckon as how Rigger was maybe a hundred yards up front of me when I got off'n that sidewalk. I started runnin' after him when all of a sud-den I can see he catches on. Instead of goin' on down the street, he cuts up that damn alley. He reckoned as how maybe he'd throw me off." Her voice thickened. She got up again, crossed to the door, and flicked the butt out to join its twin. For a moment she stared at the strand of smoke that wisped from the tip in the dirt and then she drew herself straight and returned to her place.

"I heard 'em before I seen 'em, I got to where that alley starts and I seen the two of 'em already fightin'. That sonofabitchin' Newt was layin' for him all the time." She snared a quick breath. "Drunk as he was, that Rigger sure put up one helluva scrap. Only it wasn't no use, right from the start. Newt—I seen him plain as day under that street light—that Newt went all crazy-like. He got Rigger down. And when the poor little devil was there on the ground, Newt kept right on kickin' him over and over with them goddamn boots of his. He kicked him right up against the side of that building and he went on kickin' and kickin' and kickin'!" She brought her hands up swiftly and covered her face as the old horror flashed through her. In a moment she had taken her fingers away and her eyes were glazed, set. "He never did see me watchin', I reckon. I was there at the start of the alley, and all—all I could do was watch!" She looked at Marcy and her eyes were deep with a plea for understanding. "I couldn't move at all!" she cried hollowly. "Don't you see, kid? Somehow I just went all water in my legs and sick to my stomach. All the time I knew what was gonna happen, only nothin' in me would move!"

"I know. I know." Marcy's hands went back to grip the table edge.

Ruby searched her face desperately. "Yeah," she murmured. Her voice quieted, took on renewed strength. "He went on like that, kickin' at Rigger until he just plumb wore out, I reckon. Finally he quits and he reaches out and grabs the side of the building. He sort of stands over his own brother like that and he's lookin' down and grinnin'—and then he comes away." She stopped for breath. "When he comes down that alley I ducked in a doorway. He went by me so close I coulda touched him. He was all wet with sweat and there was blood all over his pants. He was breathin' like there was somethin' wrong with him inside. His eyes—" She closed her own and shuddered. "I ain't never seen eyes like them eyes of his nowheres, never! All crazy-like they was, so bright like fire was comin' from 'em!" She dropped her head and picked nervously at her cuticle. "I didn't go look at the little guy" she confessed in a low whisper. "I just couldn't go look, not then. I thought—I reckoned he was dead for sure. I just went home to that stinkin' room." Her eyes were dark with anguish. "I reckon as how I run out on him right when he needed me most."

Newt Kates was no longer breathing. He was crouched low beside the back steps, his face gone black, his little snake eyes steady on the mesh of the screen as if the words that came to him were being relayed to him through the network of fine wires. The sun was almost directly overhead, boring into the back of his skull unmercifully. When the woman Ruby stopped her story he stirred and began to uncoil. When he was erect he ran his tongue along his parched pale lips and glanced quickly, furtively around the blazing yard. There was no sign of anyone. His lips worked nervously as he turned and went from the house. He moved quickly across the yard, careful to skirt the half-opened door to the barn room, where the big guy was getting ready to leave. There was no time to lose. He hurried down alongside the barn until he came to the opened door to the truck stall. Quickly, unerringly, he pushed between the truck and the workbench along the wall and found what he wanted. He'd get that loud-mouthed bitch now, right where she sat, before she went shootin' her mouth all over the place, sayin' things like that about him. With the stock of the claw hammer gripped tight in his sweaty fingers, Newt Kates moved quietly across the yard.

Marcy was straight, her fingers tight-gripped on the table edge and her eyes were shut tight. Her face was drawn and pale. She felt the sudden touch cold and damp on her wrist.

Ruby had come forward and her fingers were light on Marcy. "I ain't never said nothin' to nobody 'bout what I seen that night. I reckoned as how it wasn't no business of mine, gettin' mixed up in it. There's plenty reasons I can't afford to be gettin' into other folks' troubles. Only"—she stumbled and her voice came low—"I seen you with that there big guy in town a couple of times." She glanced up and saw Marcy's suddenly paling face. "And when I seen what that Newt's like today, I reckoned as how maybe you better know what's what." Her face softened. Marcy Kates was just sitting there, her eyes closed, and, Ruby saw the lips tremble faintly. "That Britt Callum guy—you're in love with him, Miz Kates, ain't you?"

Marcy opened her eyes and wet her lips, taking Ruby's measure carefully. She looked into the tired, bloodshot eyes, so soft on her now. "Yeah," she said quietly. "I reckon as how maybe I am."

Ruby's fingers tightened a little on Marcy's wrist and there was an inestimable sadness in the deep-cut lines of her face. "It's sure one helluva mess, ain't it, kid?" She took her fingers away and pushed herself to her feet and scooped up the big purse, clutching the sides with sticky fingers. "Christ!" she exploded. "You'd think somebody'd get somethin' decent outta all this once in a while!"

Marcy sat, her eyes shut, working to refuse the sudden pressing insistence of Britt Callum that Ruby had stirred to life. There was a faint rustle and she opened her eyes. Ruby had gone to the head of the hallway and she had stopped, looking back.

"I reckon as how I gotta be gettin' on my horse, kid," she said brusquely. "Gent friend of mine out front ain't gonna be feelin' so happy sittin' on his can waitin' so long."

Marcy came to her feet and followed the older woman to the front porch. At the head of the steps she shaded her eyes and saw the car parked on the shoulder of the road close to the start of the twin ruts. She raised her eyes automatically and scanned the horizon. Clouds had come, piling themselves in an ugly blueblack bank against the northern sky. There was a storm kickin' up. She glanced at Ruby. She had half turned, was looking at the bedroom windows, and there was a sudden contraction of her throat muscles as if she were having difficulty swallowing. Impulsively Marcy touched the other woman.

"Thanks—thanks for tellin' me what you did," she said quietly.

Ruby brought her eyes to Marcy's face. "Yeah, sure, kid. Don't think nothin' of it."

Marcy hesitated. She found Ruby's hand. Holding it flat on her hardening palm, she stared down at the grossness, at the fat stubby fingers and the nails, the bright carmine polish white-chipped and uneven. "I'm really sorry—about Rigger. For you, I mean," she said slowly.

Ruby stared. She peered into Marcy's tired, pale face incredulously, saw the ember of honesty and compassion bright in the eyes that came to meet her own. Suddenly she grasped Marcy's hand between hers and held it tightly. "You'll take right good care of him, won't you, kid? You won't let that Newt do nothin' more to him?"

"Everythin'll be all right."

Ruby released her and crossed quickly to the head of the steps. Standing in the thickening noonday heat, she drew a razor-edged breath. "Yeah," she choked. "Little sonofabitch ain't never been worth shootin', I reckon, only—" Her shoulders lifted slightly and, as they fell, they brought age sudden and deep to her face. "I reckon as how I kinda went for the little crumb."

CHAPTER TWENTY-THREE

Newt Kates let himself in the back door very quietly. One look told him he was too late. The chairs were pushed back from the table, the room still retained the long bluish wisps from Ruby's cigarettes. The only sound for the moment was the harsh rasp of Newt's breath as it was pushed and drawn through a tight throat. He stood very attentively in the center of the room and listened. In a moment he had traced the murmuring sounds of them. Moving to the head of the hallway, he saw them. They were standing outside on the porch, still talking. He saw Ruby glance past the front screen, look toward the bedroom windows. His fingers tightened on the hammer and he took a single step forward.

At that moment the other sounds began. From behind the closed door at his side the strangled guttural chokings of Rigger's voice came cutting across his path, insistent, demanding. Newt backed into the room, his eyes wide and fearful on the bedroom door, his ears magnifying those terrible meaningless splutterings, holding them in jealous closeness, refusing to reject or ignore. He tore his eyes from the door and peered to the front of the house. The women had moved off, away from the screen frame, out of sight. The sounds from the bedroom had stopped as quickly as they had begun. Newt Kates moved forward. He went only two steps this time down the hall. Instantly Rigger began his talk again.

Newt's breath sank to raw whimpering. He brought his free hand up quickly and dug his nails harshly, brutally into his scalp. Why didn't the little sonofabitch let him alone? Why wouldn't he

let him do what had to be done, goddamnit? The bitch was gettin'
away scot-free to go shootin' off her mouth all over town, tellin'
them things about him. He fought to move forward, to take the
step beyond the ring of Rigger's gibbering arrest. Nothing in
him would respond, his legs, his body, his mind. Those awful
demanding noises from inside wound themselves around him
like gripping tentacles, binding him, trapping, holding him.

Instant uncontrollable anger came sweeping from the depths,
blotting away the purpose and the sight of the hallway. There was no
one in the house now, just the two of them, just him and Rigger, no
sounds in all the place now but the damnable continuous blabber
from those accursed little lips. In all the years of his life he'd never
been free of him, always jabbering, yammering, telling him what
to do, what not to do, even now! Newt's fist steeled and he turned
slowly, coming back into the kitchen, finding the closed door that
failed to keep the sounds inside. Quietly he opened the door, letting
it swing wide, opening the whole of the room to his sight. There, on
the other side of the bed, sitting up in his chair, looking like some
innocent little kid instead of what he was, sat his brother.

Newt hesitated only a moment. He stepped inside the room
and kicked the door shut behind him. When the click of the lock
sounded he smiled very faintly, sure, and moved around the end
of the bed. He came up beside the wheelchair and stood looking
down at the little body, at the lips that went on moving loosely,
letting the sounds come bubbling, grunting into the room.

Rigger's eyes were on him and there were hate and knowledge and accusation burning in them. Newt stirred. He crossed
quickly to the windows to the porch and made sure. Marcy was
standing at the top of the steps and the woman Ruby was halfway
to the road and the waiting car. Newt pulled himself straight. He
turned and came up behind the chair so that he would not see
those eyes again. The babbling stopped abruptly with the first
blow. The little sandy bullet head fell back loosely to one side
against the chair.

Standing in the thick heat of the airless bedroom, Newt Kates began to fight for his breath. His ears were closed to the sounds of the house. The clockworks of his mind had jammed and frozen. The victory in him beaded and fell, a tiny drop on the white-hot pan of his expectancy. There was the single puff, the hissing second of ephemeral steam, the instant transition.

The moment warped. There was a dull penetrating pain somewhere in the back of Newt's skull. His eyes bulged, threatening to burst from their pits. His parts felt unhinged from him, falling away, and there was a drunken lightness in him and no sensation. He stared down in horror, trying to force his throat muscles open. He licked his lips and there was a trembling in him.

There was a trace of life before him still. Was that the arm, the leg that moved just then? Was there still a faint pulsing, a hinted rise and fall to the small hard chest? His hand flew up and the back of his forearm smashed against the thin bridge of his nose. The thing before him had shifted convulsively, as if it were hitching itself up in the chair. Hysteria came cycloning. The strangled hoarse cry burst from Newt's clutching throat and he brought the claw hammer high. Frantically he worked the weapon again and again. There was no sound save the mushing metronome beat in the room.

The silence came hedging back, taking its place around him. Stupidly, spastically Newt Kates dropped his arm from his eyes. The thing in the chair did not move again. He pried his sight from the corpse and tottered woodenly, turning away, staggering past the bed, working his way drunkenly through the kitchen to the back screen and the desperate sanctuary of the open yard.

CHAPTER TWENTY-FOUR

Marcy stood alone on the porch steps. She saw the woman Ruby pick her way along the hard-packed shoulder of the road, climb into the big sedan. In a moment the car spurted forward, swung in a careening. U turn, and went speeding off to town. Marcy watched until the machine had gone from sight. Curious, she peered out over the boiling crust of the countryside. The massing clouds had spawned swiftly, mounding a gigantic splotching backdrop in the north. It was unearthly still and the heat had become unbearable. She stirred and wiped the trickling sweat from her forehead. There was one brief weary glance toward the bedroom windows. She had to look in shortly and see if Rigger was O.K. Only not right now. Somehow the recent talk with Ruby had left her all unsettled, all confused; she wanted a chance to think things out. She had an hour before dinnertime. Slowly she moved down off the steps and went along the ruts, idling toward the shimmering pavement. She'd walk for a few minutes, by herself, and then she'd know what was best to do.

Newt Kates came to a staggering halt in the center of the yard. His breathing was harsh and uneven, his energies sapped by the efforts of his labor. He licked his lips and his fingernails made scraping noises as he scratched his cheek. The corners of his mouth were tacked into place, pulling his bloodless lips into a set mirthless grin. He raised his hand and looked at the hammer, at the oily crimson that had sleeked the stock, had greased his hand and fingers. Suddenly his little pig eyes began to brighten and the hurried tempo of his breathing quickened even more. He moved swiftly, going to the open door to the room in the barn. On the threshold he stood and peered in curiously. The big fella had already taken off! Him and Marcy must've had a hulluva bust-up. Big bastard sure made quick tracks. Newt Kates snorted. Sonofabitch wouldn't get so far. When they found Rigger like that, when they found the hammer—that Callum bastard—yeah, and her, too—he'd show 'em! He entered the room boldly and went to the side of the unmade cot. Suddenly he remembered that night he had seen them together, her and him, right here, doin' them things. The craftiness stirred in his brain. He bent down and raised the pillow and shoved the claw hammer across the sheet, dropping the pillow into place. He straightened jerkily, his eyes narrow and hard on the streaked splotches the thing had trailed across the bed covering. Let the smart sonofabitch big-talk himself outta this! Newt laughed once, loud, a tinny clattering noise that spanked the walls.

As he turned to leave he suddenly caught sight of himself in the mirror nailed to the wall. He licked his lips and stared at the strange face that regarded him gravely. He wheeled abruptly, frightened, swamped in sudden hysteria. His fingers brushed along the top of the old chair back. Frantically he seized the thing and brought it high above his head. There was a smashing crash followed by the sounds of little faraway bells as the bits of glass went sprinkling out over the floor boards. Newt heaved the shattered furniture into the far corner. He glanced around cautiously, warily, then moved. When Newt Kates stepped forth into the fierce yellow light of the broiling day, his face wore the harsh mask of cunning satisfaction.

She walked very slowly. The fatigue was deep in her and her mind kept refusing to grasp the problems. The heat hung waist-high above the earth and somewhere far off there was the intermittent roll of thunder. The sweat pearled on her, went trickling down her spine. Ruby's visit and its attendant events had kicked up a whirlwind in her brain. When she had reached the pavement road she hesitated. The purple-black cloud bank towered from the horizon high overhead and the wind was puffing into steadiness. She stood uncertain, working her hands together to try to rid them of that sticky, gummy feeling. As she turned to make her way back, the thought of Britt's leaving came forcing itself upon her. The tiny feathery sadness of complete defeat brushed her. It all seemed so long ago now, even though he had not left the place yet. It all seemed a part of some almost forgotten world through which she might have passed untouched and unseen. Marcy sighed and rubbed her forehead. She dragged on listlessly toward the porch steps.

Suddenly she stumbled to a halt, bringing herself very straight, her eyes wide. She had forgotten to tell Britt that Ruby had been here, the things Ruby had told, that it was Newt! Quick self-irritation stung her. She had to tell him now, right away. Maybe if he knew the truth, maybe once he knew it was Newt, not him, he'd stay on just a little longer, stay just for her sake; She began to run now, ran swiftly down alongside the house to the open clearing beyond. She tripped and almost fell on the threshold of the barn room, grabbing for the door frame to hold herself.

In a moment her sight had cleared and come to focus. The little lines bit deep between her eyes and she wet his lips gingerly. The mirror was smashed, scattered over the floor; the tilted old table was upset, and over in the far corner of the room there was the old chair, kindling now. Dazed, she took her sight from the ruin and turned. Her sharpening eyes scanned the yard. There was no one around, no sign of life. The dull knowledge that he had already gone from her came to her. She forced herself to movement. She crossed the open plot to the house and reached for the handle of the back screen. The door was stuck; it refused her pressuring hand. Irritably she jerked hard on the thing, but it would not yield. Rising on her toes, she saw that someone had fastened the hook inside. She let go of the knob and rapped sharply. There was no answer. Anger goaded her and she kicked against the lower boards. No answer. The irritation suddenly began to sink into the rising tide of a kind of nameless fear, a hinting dread. She stood for a moment.

As she turned away she brushed her hair back from her eyes and looked upward. The swollen heavy clouds had filled the cavern of the sky and the wind had come up fast. The heat hung on, a stifling, suffocating blanket. She moved now, picking her way against the drumming wind, going to the path that led around the house to the front. The gnarled, dried stalks of the springtime iris stood rigid in death, buffeted by the rushing wind, slapping fitfully against the boards of the house. At the front steps she came to a halt. The mesquite arms flayed and whipped, frantically striving to beat back the ruthless gale attack. Off in the distance the first darting stab of lightning brought the fright knotting in her throat. It was only a matter of seconds before the onslaught would be here. A second bolt rent the thick black curtain of cloud, brilliant, rooted high in the muddy heavens for one blazing second, bringing the thunderheads to sharp outline, before it blacked away. The thunder came tardily, pounding down against the earth, rolling, echoing, re-echoing, dissipating into the awful silence of brief respite.

Marcy shivered. The wind was harsh and violent. There was the repeated flick of the whip of strange fear in her and she ran up the steps and seized the screen latch. The door was still open and she hurled herself into the hallway, slipping the bolt of the door in place. She waited a moment to get her breath and then hurried to the kitchen, crossing to the sink to get a cooling drink of water. The glass only barely touched her lips. In the next instant it lay shattered in the sink. Marcy was rigid in horror, her eyes stretched, head pulled back, her breath sealed. The hand that had held the glass was hard against her mouth. Her sight was riveted, frozen on the claw hammer on the drainboard, on the telltale smears on the head and handle, on the now dried blackish trail that twisted down the slant of the drainboard, on the few little sandy hairs that curled between the claws.

The wind howled in the eaves of the house and a door had come unlatched somewhere, slapping out a broken rhythm. The flash of lightning burst in the room with instant brightness. The ear-splitting clap brought the hard drive of the rain. Marcy Kates turned slowly and stared at the door to the bedroom. It was closed, yet she knew already what must lie behind the barrier. She began to move slowly, deliberately. In front of the door she made herself firm and reached for the knob.

At that instant the door opened and Britt Callum seemed to come rising from the floor before her. His massive body filled the frame, blocking away the sight beyond. There was a smear of blood dark against the white of his T shirt, and as her horrified eyes went slipping down the length of him she saw those stains on his Levis, dried already now upon his hands.

Her single cry came ripping from deep within her. "Rigger!" Wildly, hysterically she tore at his blocking body, fighting to push him away from the opening, to get into the room, to her husband.

Britt tried to trap the flailing arms, to capture and hold her, to keep her from seeing beyond him. "Marcy, for God's sake, baby, don't, don't! It ain't no good! It's too late!"

Her struggling failed almost instantly. She stepped back and searched his face desperately. "Rigger's dead in there," she whispered. He said nothing, only nodded, his face twisted in the sick horror. "Rigger's dead," she whispered again. "Rigger's dead in there." Slowly she drew herself from his hold and turned away, covering her face with her hands, fighting to repel the rising rush of tears. She went from him to the sink that way. Standing with her back to him, she took her hands from her face and her sight came once again to the bloodied weapon. Instantly her mind flashed the picture of him behind her, the stains on him. She spun abruptly and her eyes were dark with terror and accusation.

"What have you done, Britt?" she said hoarsely. "Oh, my God, Britt, what've you done to him?"

For an instant there was no change in Britt Callum. He simply stood there in the doorway and stared at her. Incredulously he glanced down over himself, raised his palms and saw the smears and knew what she was thinking, what she meant. "Marcy! Good God, Marcy, honey!" He crossed quickly to her and seized her shoulders hard, shaking her. "You don't think I—You can't be thinkin' it was me!"

Her mouth was half open and from somewhere in her throat there was a faint, odd clicking as she tried to make her answer.

"It was Newt, Marcy. It's been Newt all along and we ain't had God's sense to see it." He begged her understanding. "Marcy, it was him. I seen him duck out of my room when I come up from the truck stall. I found the hammer and I come here. It was too late. I was afraid you'd see. I locked the door. It wouldn't do no good your seein', honey, it wouldn't do nobody no good." He turned his head, taking his eyes from the raw pain in her face. "Poor little guy—poor little bastard—I guess he's better off now."

The burning day had failed to darkness and the old place trembled under the merciless shocks of the storm. Suddenly, held tight in the grip of his big hands on her, she began to weep, crying loudly, desperately, sobbing in utter fear and terror. "Rigger, Rigger, Rigger!" she shrieked. Britt stared at her, trapped in the rush of her collapse. A blue-white flash burst around them with blinding intensity. His hands left her and the slap of his open palm across her cheek was a brittle crack, paired with the cataclysmic blow of the thunderclap above them. The hysteria strangled immediately in her shocked, severed breath.

When her eyes came to focus she saw he had gone from her and was drawing the door to Rigger's room shut. When the door had clicked he turned and looked at her.

"Where's Newt, Marcy? You any idea?"

She shook her head vaguely. "I don't know. I ain't seen him," she responded dully.

He came quickly to her and took her in his arms, holding her close and firm, until her breathing against his chest was easier, until he knew she had weathered the shock. Then he released her and forced her gently from him. "Marcy, honey, listen. It's Newt. We gotta find him somehow. Trucks still here—he ain't off the place yet. We gotta get him somehow, before he does somethin' more." Her eyes were big on him and she nodded slowly, as if she were trying to follow his reasoning. "He ain't past killin' some more," Britt muttered grimly.

His words flowed evenly, and, while he spoke quietly, almost in a lower tone than usual, they somehow filled the house, went ringing through the place, displacing the tumultuous racket of the storm outside.

Marcy's eyes widened in horror as the realization came. Her eyes shifted wildly to snag on the bedroom door. In a burst of fear she seized Britt's arm. "Britt, you won't leave me! You won't go off and leave me, not here with him!"

His face softened and there was a tiny gentle smile in his eyes. He cupped her chin and found her eyes. "I ain't gonna be leavin' you—not now, not ever."

He went to the back screen and flipped the latch hook. Lightning jagged over the house and he blinked.

"Britt! Where you goin'?"

She had come up close at his side and they stood staring out over the storm-swept clearing. The rain drove hard against the earth and the long fingers of water splayed out across the muddy yard.

"I'm gonna have me a look round the barn," he said slowly. "I got me a hunch he's out there somewheres."

Her voice was thin and quavery. "What'll you do, Britt?"

He knew what she meant. He shrugged. "I don't know. Somethin'." He hesitated. "Somethin'."

Her fingers plucked at his side. "I'm comin' with you."

"No, no!" He touched her briefly, but as he did so his sight went beyond her to the door that sealed the bedroom. "Well, maybe so. Maybe it's best that way."

As they stood together, uncertain as to what to do next, the storm sounds began to diminish. Suddenly a tiny pattering tocsin on the roof boards above them came to their ears. She brought her head up instantly and her eyes widened on the ceiling. The rattling noise increased and in seconds had become a pounding tattoo above them, around them. She had caught her breath, holding it trapped in her throat. The hail had come.

It came driving from the angry skies, peppering, hammering unmercifully. Overhead the large stones beat noisily. They went rolling like handfuls of marbles across the roof, the pellets pattering on the hard cushion of the yard.

Suddenly they heard a single strangled cry that came cutting through the clashing racket of the storm, knifing from across the stretch of the place. Britt's fingers closed tight on her arm as he heard her sharp gasp. Newt Kates had come out into the open yard from somewhere in the barn, and he was running as fast as he could, not for cover but away from them, his feet churning in the mud, his body stung and riddled by the bullet hail. Newt Kates was racing across the place, out in the driving storm, and they knew instantly he was desperately trying to reach the stricken fields.

Marcy's face contorted and she moved closer to the screen as if she must see more. The hail battered at the doorframe, went bouncing down the steps, scattering aimlessly like giant frozen peas, whitening the spread of the clearing. Through the streaking, slanting lines they could see Newt Kates still running blindly, heedlessly, too late.

They watched for what seemed a very long time. The hail stopped as abruptly as it had begun. Only the light patter of the epilogue rain lingered. The rain too tapered away. In the lifting of the storm, as the afternoon sun came poking back, its rays piercing the dullness, streaking over the already drying lands, they watched the faraway figure of Newt Kates.

He was wandering alone out there, moving aimlessly, without purpose or direction. The wheat crop was gone, wiped out in a mass, beaten down into a soggy crumpled waste at the very hour of the harvest. For a little moment they had both forgotten all the other things, the tortures and the pain, the cruelties and the killing; they remembered only the frantic covetous labor Newt Kates had spent upon his beloved fields. The wheat crop had been Newt's only tangible possession, the living lie to his total impotency.

"The poor, poor, poor sonofabitch!" Britt murmured. He straightened slowly and took his fingers from her arm and drew a long wobbling breath. "Guess I best go get him now," he said, and stepped out into the reborn sunlight.

CHAPTER TWENTY-FIVE

N EWT KATES stared around the jungled field. He worked to draw himself straight. He looked bleakly over the pathless sea of the crumpled grain stalks to where the old house sprawled and hunched on the crest of the little rise. His eyes rounded and he blinked, trying to identify, to remember. Someone had just come from the house now, a man, a man in a T shirt and Levis. The swift hungering need came rousing sharply in him. *He* would understand when he told him!

Newt Kates began to move toward the house, toward the man approaching. His eyes never left the oncoming figure. His mind churned, seething with anxiety. It had all been an accident. He hadn't meant to hit Rigger like that. Only Rigger had been makin' fun again. He hadn't meant to hit his brother like that. Mother would cry now because Rigger had always been her favorite, the baby. But his daddy was comin' for him now and he would understand. His daddy was a good man. These things happen sometimes, son, his daddy would say. They would forgive him. No one could blame a boy for an accident. His eyes were stretched wide, filled with desperate hope, set unwaveringly on the oncoming figure. He began to run across the muddy, trampled field, stumbling awkwardly, hurrying heedlessly, blindly, slopping his way hysterically through the bent and broken stalks of the murdered wheat, running to the man who came to meet him, to the now remembered frame of the old farmhouse, to his mother's waiting arms and the soft, gentle forgiveness that would come cleansing, comforting him within the circle of her clasp.

In the wake of the storm there was a complete healing silence. The sun had burst forth, burning away the frayed tag ends of the fury, drying the land in minutes. Summer returned, muggy and close, wrapped in the cloak of steam that came fogging from the griddle of the earth. The night was warm and furry and soft.

Marcy stood alone in the center of the kitchen and gazed around the room. All was in order, at peace. They had come and taken Rigger away finally, and had taken Newt, too. And now the old place was still and quiet and there was a kind of peace.

She stood there, not resisting, working again through the remembered afternoon. So long as she lived she knew she would never forget those few brief moments when the men from town had come to get Newt. Burned for all time into her brain was that funny look that had been in his eyes, that empty, bewildered child's look in him as he had sat in the chair in the center of the kitchen, with all of them ringed around him. His clothing was soaked, bloodied, his face streaked and drawn. She had moved toward him, had gone up to him, had knelt before him, had spoken to him, had touched him even. There had been no recognition. He had just looked at her that way as he looked at the others, saying over and over what he had been saying ever since he had met Britt in the field, had taken his hand, had come back to the house like a little boy at Britt Callum's side. His lips worked constantly and the words that came forth were the same again and again. He had looked down at her crouched before him and his eyes were empty. "Mamma?" he had said. "Mamma, I didn't mean to do nothin'. Honest, Mamma, it was an accident!" That was when she had touched him, had reached out and put her hand on his knees, her eyes flooded dark with hopeless pity. "It's O.K., Newt," she had heard herself say. He had begun to weep then and his arms had come reaching for her but she had turned away and gone off down the hallway to the porch alone, waiting until she heard them leave through the back, saw the car taking him away at last.

Marcy drew a long steadying breath. That part was all over now, over and done with. No good would come from remembering. She raised her hand and smoothed her hair from her brow and a little smile came touching her lips as she started down the hallway.

Britt Callum was sitting in the old wicker chair on the porch, his long legs splayed out before him, his head back, his eyes closed, his face tired and drawn. She shoved open the screen door and stood for a moment, just looking down on him, and her eyes were warm and soft. In a moment she let the door drift shut behind her and crossed to the back of his chair. She put her hand down and touched the thick gloss of his hair. His eyes opened and he reached up with a little smile and took her wrist, bringing her hand hard against his breast until she could feel the steady unbroken beat of his heart caught in her palm.

"Everythin' O.K. now?" Britt asked gently, his eyes on her face.

"Everythin's O.K. now," she echoed. In a moment she had taken her hand away and she crossed to the rail. The sky was clear and the stars were very bright, strewn out across the heavens by an extravagant hand. "I reckon," she said very quietly, "the time's come at last for us to be gettin' on our way, Britt."

THE END